STIRRING UP MURDER

STIRRING UP MURDER

AUNTIE CLEM'S BAKERY #4

P.D. WORKMAN

ISBN: 9781989080290 (IS Hardcover)

ISBN: 9781989080283 (IS Paperback)

ISBN: 9781989080252 (KDP Paperback)

ISBN: 9781989080269 (Kindle)

ISBN: 9781989080276 (ePub)

pdworkman

Telepathy of Gardens

Delusions of the Past

Fairy Blade Unmade

Web of Nightmares

A Whisker's Breadth

Skunk Man Swamp (Coming Soon)

Magic Ain't A Game (Coming Soon)

Without Foresight (Coming Soon)

Zachary Goldman Mysteries

She Wore Mourning

His Hands Were Quiet

She Was Dying Anyway

He Was Walking Alone

They Thought He was Safe

He Was Not There

Her Work Was Everything

She Told a Lie

He Never Forgot

She Was At Risk

Kenzie Kirsch Medical Thrillers

Unlawful Harvest

Doctored Death (Coming soon)

Dosed to Death (Coming soon)

AND MORE AT PDWORKMAN.COM

*For sisters, half-sisters, step-sisters, adopted sisters, foster sisters,
and chosen sisters everywhere.*

CHAPTER 1

*E*rin managed to block Orange Blossom from getting out the door as she took out the garbage. She drew in a deep breath of fresh air and enjoyed the stillness of the early morning. There would be plenty of action at Auntie Clem's Bakery. It was good to cherish the quiet for a moment at the beginning of her day. Adele told her that she needed to take more time for herself and be at one with nature and the universe. It probably wouldn't hurt, but Erin's mind was always racing ahead, already working on the next thing.

She held her breath when she opened the garbage bin and threw her bag in. Even though she washed it out regularly, it still made her gag if she caught a whiff of it from a few feet away. Erin glanced up and down the street for any sign of activity and then went around to the back of the house.

There was a light on in Vic's loft over the garage, so Erin knew she was up and around and would be joining Erin before long to start their day at the bakery.

As soon as she was in the door, Orange Blossom was winding around her legs, *mrrowing* for food and attention. Erin bent down to pat him and then to pick him up and give his ears and chin a good scratch.

"Hey, Blossom. How was your night?"

The orange and white cat yowled and yipped chattily, telling her all about it. Even after having had him for a few months, it still made Erin laugh at how vocal he was. She'd never known any cat to be so noisy and interested in carrying on a conversation with his two-legged companions.

"I see. Well, that all sounds very interesting," Erin told him. She put him down on the floor and washed up, then went about getting his breakfast ready while her coffee brewed. Blossom stood up on hind legs and batted at her with soft paws while she opened a smelly can of cat food and scooped it into a dish for him. When she put it down on the floor, he immediately pushed his nose into the bowl and began to chow down, his loud purr rumbling through the kitchen.

The coffee finished brewing just as Vic tapped at the back door and entered. Erin wasn't sure how she managed to look fresh and polished so effortlessly first thing. Erin always felt so awkward and plain beside her young bakery assistant. Vic's height was the only aspect of her appearance that hinted at her transgender identity, and her height only increased her poised, willowy air.

"Morning," Vic drawled. "If it isn't just as crisp as a new dollar bill out there this morning. I do love this time of the year!"

Erin smiled at her Tennessee twang. "It really is lovely," she agreed. "If it could only stay like this all year instead of getting so blasted hot."

"We had such a mild summer, you don't know hot."

Erin shook her head. "Ugh. Don't tell me that."

Erin poured them each a cup of coffee.

"Now that the holidays are over, we need to be thinking about what else we can do to draw customers." Erin studied her coffee as if the answer might be there. "We don't want to go through a big slump because people aren't buying gingerbread men and pumpkin pies."

"We don't exactly have a big pool to draw customers from. Bald Eagle Falls isn't the biggest place."

"I know, but I think we still have untapped resources. Not everyone comes to Auntie Clem's. What are people buying in the city? What are they getting at the grocery store that they should be buying at the bakery? And why aren't they coming to the bakery for it?"

Vic sipped her coffee. Orange Blossom, having finished gobbling down his breakfast, sat back on his haunches and stared at them as he applied tongue to paw and washed his face.

"People who can eat gluten buy bread and baking at the grocery store because it is cheaper and convenient. Easier than making a separate trip to Auntie Clem's. And because of the stigma of gluten-free food being inferior."

Kicked into a higher gear by the caffeine, Erin's mind was already whirring, thinking about all the factors involved. "What if we sold bread to the grocery store? They could sell it off the shelves with their commercially produced stuff. People wouldn't have to make an extra trip. It would be right there."

Vic pursed her lips. "I'm not sure about that. If people don't come into the bakery, we can't up-sell. If they pick up a loaf of bread from the shelf at the grocer, how are we going to sell them cookies or cupcakes? Can we really stock the shelves at the grocery store too? That would be a lot of extra work."

"It would be. And we wouldn't be able to build a relationship or to up-sell… unless we sold cupcakes and cookies to the grocery store as well…"

Vic was shaking her head.

"Which would also be extra work," Erin admitted. "And if people didn't buy as much at the grocery store as we expected, Mr. Cooper would lose money. The margins are so thin, we couldn't afford to sell it to him much lower than we sell to bakery customers."

"I don't think you can be in both the bakery and the grocery store."

"No. You're right." Erin was quiet while she thought about other possibilities. Orange Blossom finished his bath and went over to Vic, rubbing up against her and yowling to be picked up.

"He's so demanding," Vic complained. But she put her coffee cup to the side to pick him up and cuddle him.

"That's because he's spoiled," Erin said.

"He is not!" Vic planted a kiss on the top of Blossom's head. "He was demanding even when you first got him. Before either of us had a chance to spoil him."

"That's true," Erin admitted. She eyed the clock on the kitchen wall. "I guess we'd better head out."

Vic gave Orange Blossom one more scratch and put him down. "Okay, Blossom, you'd better be good today. Marshmallow is here to keep you company, so no noise."

Orange Blossom stood looking at her for a minute, eyes intent and ears pointed forward. Then he turned and left the room. Erin got a carrot out of the fridge for Marshmallow and gave him his treat on her way out.

~

It wasn't long before Officer Terry Piper stopped by the bakery as he patrolled the neighborhood. Since it wasn't hot, his water bottle didn't need to be topped off yet, but Erin gave his partner, K9, a gluten-free doggie biscuit.

"How is everything today?" she asked Terry.

"Pretty quiet. Mrs. Sturm reported some vandalism last night, but I don't know if we'll be able to get anywhere on that. Kids, most likely."

"Vandalism? What happened?"

"Her car has been egged. No damage, just a mess."

Erin shook her head, thinking about the woman with the girlish blond pigtails and the people she had seen interact with Lottie. "You're probably right. Sounds like kids. Did she have any idea who it might have been?"

"Nothing too certain. Unfortunately, Lottie Sturm is... not well-liked among the younger generation."

Vic snorted. "Lottie isn't liked by a lot of people in any generation. If I had a nickel for every time she tried to stir up trouble..."

"I don't know if she tries to, or if she's just awkward," Erin said.

"She's not awkward," Vic said. "It's totally on purpose. She's a troublemaker. That's the kind of person she is."

"We really don't know anything about what kind of person she is. Some people say the wrong things and hurt people's feelings without meaning to."

"And you think Lottie Sturm is one of those people?"

Erin considered. "No," she admitted finally. "You're probably right. She seems to get a certain amount of enjoyment out of it."

Vic nodded vigorously in agreement.

"Regardless of whether or not she brought it down on herself," Piper said, "I've taken her statement and opened a file, and if the culprits are found, they will be dealt with. Other than that, it was a quiet night, and it's shaping up to be a quiet day." His eyes met Erin's. "No bodies. No twenty-year-old mysteries. Just the normal Bald Eagle Falls stuff."

"Good. I don't think I'm up for any more bodies. I'll stick to baking. That's what I'm good at."

"Well, I can't disagree with that," Terry agreed. He was eyeing a fresh batch of chocolate chip cookies that Vic was starting to lay out in the display cabinet.

Vic and Erin exchanged a look. "Do you want one?" Vic asked, eyes twinkling.

"I don't know, I probably shouldn't..." Piper patted his belly like he might be putting on weight. But if he was, Erin certainly couldn't tell. His police uniform fit him as neatly as it ever had and didn't pull or bulge around the middle.

"Oh, come on." Vic put one into a paper sleeve for him.

"With the amount of walking you do on a day of patrol? You'll walk this off easily. "

"I suppose." He took it when Vic handed it across the counter to him. "But even so, the sugar probably isn't good for me."

"It's gluten-free," Vic said with a wave of her hand. "That means it's good for you."

Erin opened her mouth to object that just because something was gluten-free, that didn't mean it was healthy. The cookies were full of refined sugar and flours, chocolate, and butter and were far from being a health food.

She saw the way that Piper was looking at her, expectant, waiting for the lecture, and closed her mouth. Was she that predictable?

"It's a dessert," she said instead. "As long as you don't go overboard, I don't think it will harm you."

"One little cookie never hurt anyone," Vic declared.

"Well…" Erin couldn't help objecting to this. Her muscles tensed up in spite of the fact that she was just talking to her friends. "If they're allergic or intolerant, then one cookie could cause damage, even an anaphylactic reaction—"

"Terry's not allergic, though."

"I know that. I mean that if he was…"

"I'm just going to eat this cookie," Terry said.

Erin looked at him. He took a bite of the warm cookie, leaving a smear of chocolate on his lip. The tension drained out of Erin and she laughed weakly.

"Okay. Good. And you two quit teasing me."

They both grinned like kids caught with their hands in the proverbial cookie jar. Erin shook her head.

The bells on the front door chimed, and Erin turned to greet the next customer.

CHAPTER 2

The fixer sat across the table from his boss. The man was physically unimposing, but if he could pay, that was the only thing that mattered.

"You found her?" the boss asked.

"Of course I found her. It wasn't hard. She's not in hiding."

"If you could find her, so can someone else."

He ran his fingers through his hair. "Sure. Anyone who is looking and has a little experience and the right tools could find her too."

"Even though you didn't know her name…"

"A name is nothing. Just one piece of the puzzle. If you have enough of the other pieces, you can figure out the solution."

The boss's eyes flicked around him, and he lowered his voice so it was almost a whisper. "Then I need for her to… disappear."

The fixer sat back in his chair considering the boss's words. "And by disappear, you mean…?"

It wasn't that he hadn't ventured over the line before. He worked outside the law at least as much as he worked within it. But if the boss was looking for a permanent solution, the fixer wasn't so sure. He would charge a much higher price, but he was also taking on a lot more risk. Was he willing to put his own tail on the line?

The boss scratched his head, twisting his face into a grimace. There was a long silence between them. He looked around to be sure no one was paying them any particular attention. Eventually, the boss wet his lips and cleared his throat. But he continued to speak in a whisper.

"I don't want her dead," he said. "That wouldn't be right. But if she disappeared, fell off the grid…"

"Why would she do that?"

"Maybe… she had to go into hiding."

The fixer thought about this, rolling it around in his mind and trying to formulate a plan. "Why would she go into hiding?"

"Why does anyone go into hiding? Maybe her boyfriend is abusive. Maybe she stole something. Maybe she was in danger. Be creative. Sometimes people leave just so they can start over again somewhere else."

"But how would I make any of those things happen? If you really do want to drive her into hiding, and you don't want her… dead… then making her decide to disappear… that's a lot more difficult than trying to warn her off or to blackmail her. I'm not sure how to work that."

"You've done well until now. I thought you were pretty competent."

The fixer was encouraged by these words. He did his best. He was willing to outwork everybody else to get the results his bosses needed. But he wasn't sure this current boss quite understood what he was getting into.

"You do know what family that boyfriend is part of, don't you?"

The boss narrowed his eyes. "Are you telling me you're afraid of some two-bit Tennessee family?"

"I didn't say I was afraid of them." But of course, any contact with organized crime made him nervous. He didn't like to be put in the line of fire of family business, big or little. "But it isn't like dealing with one person or one family. This is an organization. If we interfere with the girl or with her boyfriend, we're going to have targets on our backs and a lot of people looking for us."

"Are you saying I should be getting someone else for this job?"

The fixer chewed on his lip and ran his fingers through his hair again. "I have to think it through. We need to come up with a plan here. Something that makes sense."

"I don't need anything complicated. The fewer details I know, the better. Just make sure she goes into hiding where no one is going to find her."

"What's the payout for making her disappear permanently?"

The boss studied him carefully. "You understand that I don't want her dead. I'm not saying hide the body where it won't ever be found. I'm saying don't kill her."

"Killing her is not part of the deal. That's agreed."

"Not just that we haven't made it part of the deal. But it can't happen. I don't want her death on my conscience."

"Yes. Agreed. That's understood."

The boss looked down at the top of the table, scarred by many hands and nails. Using his body to shield anyone from seeing what he was doing, he traced invisible numbers with his index finger. The fixer watched the numbers and counted the digits. It wasn't a windfall. It wasn't the type of money he could retire on. But it would be enough to live in comfort for a while and not have to survive hand-to-mouth.

How far was he willing to go for that kind of money?

How much was he willing to put on the line?

It had been a while since Vic and Erin had gone out together to eat, just the two of them, so when Vic suggested a girls' night out, Erin accepted. She knew that Vic didn't have many other friends. Even though Vic was a fun, friendly, compassionate girl, she wasn't well-accepted in Bald Eagle Falls. The town was part of the Bible belt and, while the women there weren't any more perfect there than anywhere else, they were judgmental of the moral wrongs they saw or imagined. And Vic being a transgender girl meant that they would not have anything to do with her socially. It would have made for a lonely existence without Erin and Adele around or being able to go into the city for larger gatherings. And of course, she had Willie too, but he was out of town attending to some unnamed business. Erin wondered fleetingly what he was up to. But Willie was Willie, and he kept his business dealings pretty close to his chest.

They decided to go for Chinese, where they hadn't been for a while. Willie preferred the 'meat plus three' at the family restaurant, or maybe the hot chicken at the BBQ.

Erin watched Vic struggling with her chopsticks, a w-shaped wrinkle of concentration between her eyebrows. Vic looked up and saw Erin watching her, which made her drop the mouthful she had finally managed to wrangle.

"Shut up," she said sheepishly, "I can do a lot of things, but chopsticks are not my forte!"

"You're doing fine. You just need a little practice and you'll be an expert."

"At home, we always used forks when we went out for Chinese. It never even occurred to me to use chopsticks."

"You can use a fork here if you want to."

Vic always had before. But she shook her head. "No. I want to learn how to do this. Eating with chopsticks is different than eating it with a fork. I want the authentic experience."

"Okay. You're doing fine, so don't mind me."

Vic nodded and went back to work. Erin ate her meal slowly. She didn't want to be done when Vic was still trying to get her first few mouthfuls down.

"How's the research going?" Vic asked. "Did you mind being taken away from it tonight?"

"No, not really. I keep running into dead ends and I just get frustrated. Other people seem to manage to find long-lost family members, so why can't I?"

"You've just started. Sometimes those searches take years, you know. Decades, even."

"Don't tell me that!" Erin's heart sank. "That was pre-internet. Now, it should just be a matter of doing a few searches, and then… bingo, here's your new family!"

"Even when you know someone's name, it can be hard to find them on the internet. Not everybody even has email or social accounts. Some people who do still don't leave any tracks. And since you don't even know her name…"

Erin shook her head and wound noodles around her chopsticks. "How can I not even know my own sister's name? I mean… not even her birth name. How do you begin a search when you don't even have a birth name? Every time they talk about tracing adoptees on TV, they always say 'her birth name was…' Where do you start if you don't even have that?"

"I wish I could tell you. Usually there is a friend or family member who knows the history. Or hospital records. Or an attending nurse. Pretty hard when you don't have any of those things to start with.

"Everybody who knew anything is dead. The hospital only keeps five years' worth of records, and even if they did keep them longer than that, they've had black mold and a fire. Not just one or the other, but both!" Erin sighed in exasperation. "If I believed in God, I'd think he was trying to tell me not to look any further. Every time I think I found a way to track her down, it's blocked."

"God will make a way for you." Vic gave her a mischievous grin. "If there is a God."

"I can't just sit back and rely on some power of the universe to take over and direct my life." Erin used a pot sticker to wipe up juices on her plate. "If I did that, I never would have gotten anywhere in my life. I haven't gotten where I was by sitting still."

Vic gazed at her for a minute. "No… but you didn't get the

bakery because you decided that was what you wanted to do and saved up and bought it."

"No," Erin admitted. "I just took the opportunity when it was presented to me. I thought this was my one chance to do what I always wanted to and make gluten-free baking for people with dietary restrictions."

"But you don't think an opportunity like that was more than just chance? Maybe fate? Or God? Or the universe?"

"It wasn't chance or God. It was Clementine. I guess she knew how much I liked it when she ran the tea shop. She didn't have any other living relatives. So she left it to me." Erin shrugged. There was nothing coincidental about that.

"I'm not convinced it wasn't by divine design. How do you explain the fact that you wanted to start a baking business and that's the opportunity that Clementine gave you?"

"I hadn't ever thought I'd be able to start a baking business. I just liked making gluten-free food for friends and clients who wanted it. I liked baking because I liked working with Clementine when I was a little girl. It's no coincidence or design. It's just history."

"Okay." Vic gave a wide shrug. "Whatever you say, Erin. It was all just you and Clementine and your history together. I just think it all fits together rather nicely. That doesn't always happen, you know. I liked hunting when I was little, but if my Uncle Archibald left me a hunting lodge, I wouldn't run it. I'd just liquidate it and get out of there."

"It's not the same."

"No. Because for *you* it was meant to be."

When Erin got home, she invited Vic to join her for the evening, but Vic sighed and shook her head.

"No, it's okay. You've got things to get done tonight, I'm sure, and we need to get to bed soon."

Having to start baking bread before dawn, they always tried to be early to bed and very early to rise. Erin sensed that Vic had other things on her mind.

"Are you sure? We can talk if you want. I don't have anything that has to be done tonight. Just taking care of the animals and making my lists for tomorrow."

"Goodness, if you don't have your lists made yet, I'd better leave you alone for sure. You'll need at least a couple of hours for that."

"I'm not that bad," Erin protested. "No more than an hour, I swear."

Vic laughed.

"Really, though, Vicky. If you want to talk, or just sit together a while…" Erin couldn't quite bring herself to use the local 'set a spell.'

"We just had dinner. I'm talked out. Thanks, though."

"Okay. Have a good night. I'll see you in the morning."

Vic nodded and headed for her loft apartment. Erin shut and locked the door. Maybe she'd read a bit before bed. Or have a long soak in the tub. Or look over Clementine's genealogy books for some tiny clue that would help her to find her sister.

But as she had told Vic, she still had to take care of the animals, feeding them and changing their litter. And she needed to write up her lists for the next day.

She had just finished changing Orange Blossom's and Marsh-mallow's litter and was again considering the idea of a nice hot bath when the doorbell rang.

Erin checked the peephole before opening the door. There had been too many threats to her life over the last year to be casual about opening the door. But she only needed a peek to see that it was Terry Piper. She opened the door and invited him and K9 in.

"Your light was still on, or I wouldn't have stopped," Terry said. "You aren't headed off to bed yet?"

"No, not yet. I can visit for a bit. I still have to write up some lists—and no comments from the peanut gallery."

He grinned. "You're not *that* bad."

"Saying it that way makes me feel worse than when Vic wise-cracks about it. I can't help it if lists make me feel good. Call me weird, but it's my way of calming down and getting everything out of my head so I can sleep at night."

"If you can multi-task, we can visit at the same time as you are writing. Then you don't lose any time because I'm here. Or you'll lose less, anyway."

"Sounds good."

They both sat down. Neither of the animals had had much attention, with Erin being out to dinner and then working on other things, so they both wanted her attention. Marshmallow hopped over and started nibbling at her bare toes and Orange Blossom jumped up beside Erin onto the arm of the couch, keeping a close eye on K9. Erin laughed. She gave Orange Blossom an ear scratch and patted Marshmallow with her foot. It was going to be a few minutes before she would be able to get started on her list.

"Vic said you've been looking for your half-sister," Terry commented. "Any luck?"

"No. She was asking me about it tonight too. But I'm really not getting anywhere. I kept putting it off over the holiday season, because I always had so much going on and wanted to be able to really give it my attention, but I feel like I've lost momentum by not getting right onto it."

"It's been twenty years. It's not like a few more months makes that much difference."

"Logically, that makes sense, but that's not what it feels like."

"You're not getting anything from the hospital or government searches? I thought you could search adoption records now."

"If you're the adoptee, yes. But you have to have standing in the file, and that's only the adoptee and the birth parents. Biological siblings are just like the public. No access."

"Oh. Well, that's not too helpful."

"No. I thought getting my own DHS records was hard, but that's nothing compared to the roadblocks I'm running into here."

"What about court records?"

"What?"

"Court records are public, for the most part."

"Wouldn't that be just the same as the adoption registry information?"

"No. I don't think so. You should be able to do a search."

"How? Is it a name search? Because I don't know what her name was either before or after adoption."

"Normally, yes, but I think you can get paper copies of adoption orders for a certain window of time. If you had all of the adoption records for the year after she was born... would that do it?"

Erin nodded slowly. "I guess it's a start. It would at least reduce the pool from all of the residents of Tennessee to everyone who was adopted during that period."

"Only half of them."

"Why?"

"Because the other half are boys."

"Oh! Duh. Of course. Still, it's going to be a lot of names to sift through, isn't it?"

"It shouldn't be too bad. Just this county, girls, the year after your sister was born. It should be a fairly small set."

"That's a really good idea. I'll see what they'll let me do next time I go to the city."

"What about adoption reunion boards? It seems like they're all over the internet."

"It all seems a little daunting."

"I could help you with it, if you like. I don't think it would be too hard. And it can't hurt anything. Just putting your name on a forum with the information that you know. Place, hospital, birth date. A lot of people don't have any more information than that."

"Maybe you could use some of your police databases," Erin suggested.

"And what would I look for? Search DMV for all women with that date of birth? There's no guarantee that she still lives in Tennessee or has a driver's license. You didn't stay here. You moved to Maine, and all over the east coast. At least I had a name when I was checking your background. Even then, you weren't so easy to keep track of when you kept changing it."

Erin could feel herself blushing. She shrugged. He had asked her before about her past, but there were plenty of things from her past life that she just wasn't willing to have to tell him about. A person was entitled to a little privacy.

Orange Blossom had settled in beside Erin and was purring happily and Marshmallow was sprawled on top of her feet. Erin picked up the notepad that Vic had given to her for Christmas and opened it up to list everything she needed to remember for the next day. Terry bent down to scratch K9's ears, then leaned back in his seat, relaxing.

"I have an ulterior motive to helping you find your sister."

Erin didn't lift her eyes from the page. "Mm-hm?"

"You realize that if she is found, she's entitled to half of the Plaint estate?"

At this, Erin did look up. "What?"

"Her father was Adam Plaint."

"Well, yes. That's what it looks like, anyway. Obviously, no one has done a paternity test."

"Assuming her parents had a pretty good idea about when they had been with each other, your parents were both pretty sure she was not your father's."

"Right." Erin nodded, saddened by this. As excited as she was to find she had a sister, it would have been even more amazing if she had been Erin's full sister.

"Well, if Adam does prove to be her father, then half of Trenton's estate would go to her. He died intestate, so it goes first to his parents—who we now know are both dead—and then to his siblings. The sister, Sophie, is dead. That leaves Davis and your half-sister, who is also Trenton's half-sister."

"Davis can't inherit Trenton's estate anymore, can he? He's in prison."

"That doesn't stop him from inheriting, unless it can be proven that he had something to do with Trenton's death. And so far, all we have on that front is speculation."

The fixer presented his thoughts to his boss and waited for his feedback.

"These all seem half-baked," the boss said finally, shaking his head. "What are the chances that any of these approaches are going to work? We can't leave it to chance."

"If you don't want her killed or kidnapped, then everything else is just chance. All I can do is give her a push in the right direction and see how she responds. I'm usually pretty good at reading people, figuring out how to influence them. But some people... Even when you think you've found the right trigger, they still don't respond." He shook his head, his mouth twisting into a bitter grimace. "*Some* people are extremely stubborn and can't be blackmailed or bullied."

"Kidnapping is no good," the boss said, shaking his head. "It could take months, even years, to get everything sorted out. We can't keep her under wraps for that long. It has to be voluntary. We need her to go into hiding and to stay there."

"So you don't have a problem with any of the plans I've outlined? I can't guarantee the success of any of them, but one of them... it only takes one of them to work."

"We've both dealt with this family before." His boss shook his head in disgust. "You know she might respond exactly the opposite way to what you expect. If she's anything like the *other one*..."

"I can't make any promises. There is only one permanent solution, and you said no to that."

"It needs to be soon," the boss said, ignoring the suggestion. "It won't be long before they manage to trace her."

He nodded and stood up. "Okay, then. I'll do my best to get her out of the way."

"Do it," the boss said. "Make sure it works."

 rin measured orange zest into the muffin batter, the sharp oils tickling her nose.

"So you're still looking for her?" Vic asked.

Erin focused her attention on Vic, trying to pick up the thread of the conversation. But they hadn't been talking about anything. There was only one person that Vic could have been referring to, though, only one person Erin was looking for.

"Yes, Terry gave me some other suggestions of places to look or get searches. I kept running into dead ends."

"You think it will work? You'll be able to find her? Even though you don't know her name?"

"I don't know." Erin gave the batter a few stirs and looked at her recipe card. "I hope so. I'd really like to. Terry seems to think that it's possible. But after all of the issues I have had dealing with DHS and government agencies, I can't let myself get carried away. Who knows what problems I could run into."

Vic was quiet. She turned on the mixer for the cookie dough and didn't try to carry on the conversation over the loud motor. Erin looked over at her. Vic's usually sunny disposition seemed to have been dampened. She stared into the mixing bowl as if reading tea leaves, her expression dour. Had people been saying things to her again? Erin policed the customers who were prone to say rude or ecclesiastical things to Vic, trying to make sure that Auntie Clem's was a safe place where Vic didn't have to worry about being attacked for being transgender.

Or was there something else on her mind?

"Have you heard from Willie?" Erin asked.

Vic looked at Erin with a jerk, startled as if she hadn't even known Erin was in the room. "What? Oh… no, not really. He's sent me a few texts, but we haven't had any real conversations. He did say that he might not be able to call me much while he was out of town."

"But everything is okay?"

"Sure. Everything is fine."

"I just wondered. You seem like you're sad or worried about something."

"What do you think she's going to be like?"

"Who?"

"Your sister."

"Oh." Erin pressed her lips together, thinking about it. She'd had a lot of different foster siblings over the years, all different personalities. Some had been angry or cruel. Others had just drifted through like ghosts, barely registering in Erin's world. A precious few had been friends, or closer, like family. Like Carolyn. But Erin hadn't stayed in one home for long, never more than a year or so. She had learned to be like the ghosts, not investing anything in the relationships. Just drifting through the homes, trying to remain invisible. "I don't know, Vic. I've never had a biological sister. I don't have a clue what she'll be like. Will she be like my mother or Adam Plaint? Aunt Clementine? Me?" She shook her head. "I really don't know what to expect."

"Do you think you're going to be close? Keep in touch?"

"She's the only family I have, so I hope so…"

She saw Vic's lips form a protest, and then Vic turned off the mixer and the kitchen seemed unnaturally silent. Vic pulled off the mixing bowl and started to form teaspoons of dough into balls.

"I mean she's my only biological family," Erin said. "Of course I have other family. The homes I grew up in. My friends." She tried to give Vic a reassuring smile. "You and the animals. You're my family too. Just a different kind of family. The kind you choose."

"But you'll have more in common with a biological sister. I've read those studies. Twins separated at birth, and how alike each other they are when they are reunited. All the funny quirks that are actually family traits."

"But those are identical twins. This sister of mine… she's eight years younger. And we don't even have the same two parents. We only share one parent, so our shared genetic traits are more like… one quarter instead of one hundred percent like identical twins."

"I know with my family, though, siblings and cousins… when we get together at family reunions or funerals, there are family traits. Things that automatically connect you. Like magnets. They draw you together. You have more in common than strangers."

Erin felt a little thrill at Vic's words. She longed for that attraction. For people who were somehow the same inside as she was. Some person who wouldn't find her strange or an outsider, but who would connect with her like Erin never had with any friend or foster family.

"Those are people you grew up with," she reminded Vic. "The reason you're alike is that you were raised in the same social structure."

"Nurture, not nature? I don't know. I don't think so. Some of it. But there is something, like a pattern in a tapestry, a common thread. There's something more than just being raised in a similar way in a similar place."

Erin stirred sugared cranberries into the batter. She needed to focus on her work, or she was going to be behind before they even opened. "I'd like to think I'm going to find something like that with my sister. But I'm not counting on it. I don't think… I don't think shared genetics are going to make us the same in nature."

Vic rubbed the back of her arm across her forehead. "Blood is thicker than water."

"Think about Trenton and Davis," Erin said. "You've heard Melissa say how different they were. We saw it ourselves, even if we only saw Trenton briefly. Those two boys couldn't have been more unlike. Trenton was a bully. Good at everything. The Midas touch. And Davis was the opposite. A victim. Depressive. Unpopular. An addict. They didn't even look anything like each other. Not only that, they hated each other. Davis killed Trenton. Plotted it out and killed him, not just an accident or heat of the moment. What if my sister is like one of them?"

Vic tossed her head. "Well, maybe…"

"I hope she's someone who can be a friend," Erin said, "but I'm not counting on it."

CHAPTER 6

The fixer knew going in that it was risky. They were talking about mob, even if it was only a small Tennessee clan. They might not have the reach of some Italian or Asian connection, but their bloodlines ran through most of the families in the county and it was impossible to know who was connected or could be leaned on.

He watched the young man for a few days. Robert Dyson was not at the top of the organization, but he was son, brother, and nephew to members who were. Bobby himself was a small-potatoes street soldier who still needed to make himself. A man couldn't just rely on his father's high position to get him a place in the Dyson clan. He was far below a hundred men who didn't even bear the Dyson name. But they'd worked to earn their positions, and so far, Bobby boy simply swaggered, expecting to be given everything.

The fixer watched for the right time and opportunity. Bobby had his coterie of admirers, people who hoped to ride his coattails in his ascent up the ladder, and the fixer needed to catch him alone to do his job.

Subtlety wasn't his strong suit, but he suspected it wasn't Bobby's either. Maybe the Dyson clan had become too inbred, knocking off a few IQ points with each new generation until it seemed that only the grandfather's generation had the smarts it took to run anything in the organization.

So Bobby found the fixer in the hall outside Bobby's apartment, banging on the door late at night. Bobby looked him up and down, the sneer becoming more deeply ingrained in his smooth face.

"Who are you? What are you doing here?"

The fixer turned slightly toward Bobby, allowing a little sway and sloppiness in his stance. "Where is she?" he slurred slightly, motioning to the closed, locked door. "I thought Charlotte was supposed to be here tonight."

Bobby Dyson looked confused. "She isn't here. She's out with the girls tonight."

"I know," the fixer agreed with a leer. "The girls." He snickered and snorted. "That's what she tells him."

"Tells who?"

"You know." He gave a broad wink. "Her old man. When she needs to get out and have a little fun. He doesn't exactly give her everything she needs to put a smile on her face."

Bobby was having obvious difficulty working through the clumsy innuendo. Too much to drink at the pool hall before making his way home, shaving even more IQ points from his already low score. He inserted his key into the apartment door lock, a process that took multiple attempts between his double vision and the shakiness of his hands.

At first, the fixer thought Bobby was just going to go into his apartment and shut the door, forgetting all about the conversation. But Bobby waited, motioning for him to enter. *Come into my parlor, said the spider to the fly.*

"You're friends with her?" he asked. He blinked, trying to focus.

"Friends…?" the fixer let the word hang. "Well, you could call us friends with benefits. But it's more about the benefits. She has plenty of friends."

Bobby's face flushed red. He was finally getting it, starting to put the pieces together. He would confront her the next time he saw her. Hit her. Threaten her with his mob connections. He owned the city. He had friends everywhere. There was nowhere safe for her to go.

And if she were smart, Charlotte would disappear. A girl like she was shouldn't need to be told to make herself scarce more than once.

He drifted toward the door, still open.

"What are you talking about?" Bobby demanded, still trying to make all the connections. "You don't know her. I've never even seen you before."

"If she's not here, I know where to find her," he said. "It's not like it's the first time I've been *one of the girls.*"

Bobby threw a punch, but the young soldier was drunk, and his girlfriend's alleged paramour was only pretending to be, so Bobby couldn't land a blow.

"What's up with you, bro?" taunted the fixer. "It's not like a girl would look at you twice, if it wasn't for your money. That's all she wants. You should have known from the start she'd be fooling around on you."

Bobby came after him again, flailing like an untrained child.

The fixer easily avoided Bobby's flying fists and drifted out the door, leaving Bobby screaming incoherently behind him.

CHAPTER 7

I think I know your long-lost sister.

Erin looked at the words on her phone screen, not quite believing it. She'd placed messages on a number of adoption reunion boards, but she hadn't actually expected to get any hits.

And there was no guarantee that it was a hit. *I think,* not *I know.* It wasn't her sister writing back that she'd been looking for Erin. Would her sister even know about Erin's existence? Had she been told? Had her adoptive family been told?

It was probably nothing. How many adoptions had there been in the state? Just because the responder knew a woman who had been adopted around the appropriate time, that didn't mean she knew Erin's sister. It could be almost anyone.

Erin thought about whether to answer. What was the point in pursuing the poster? What were the odds it was legitimate? It could be some creep who wanted to meet her somewhere quiet. A predator.

Erin closed her email, checking her social networks instead. She only had a few quiet minutes for lunch, she didn't have time to be answering random emails. She picked up a grilled tomato sandwich.

"Are you okay?" Vic asked.

Erin wondered how she knew. Had Erin gone pale? Could Vic tell how hard Erin's heart was beating?

She hadn't expected to find anyone so quickly. She wasn't ready for it yet.

"Uh, yeah. I'm fine."

"You look like you just swallowed a live frog."

Erin laughed. "Just a weird message in my email. Whatever. Lots of creeps out there."

"Nasty pictures?" Vic suggested.

"Uh… no. It's nothing. No worries."

"If it's someone in town, you should let Terry know."

Erin shrugged. She made a quick conversation switch. "So Willie's back tonight?"

"No… he said he got held up. Going to be a few more days."

"Oh, I'm sorry. Are you okay with that?"

"Going to have to be." Vic gave a shrug. "He'll get back as soon as he can."

Bobby Dyson was in a state by the time his girlfriend got home from her evening out with the girls. As soon as she opened the door and walked into the apartment, the fixer heard Bobby snort and awaken, and then the screaming started.

"Where have you been? You think you can just treat me like this? Taking off and hooking up with some other man? Nobody does me like that!"

"What's your problem, Bobby? Are you drunk?"

"What's my problem? What do you think? You're running around all over town and you think I won't find out about it? Who do you think you're dealing with here? What exactly makes you think I'm just going to sit back and take it?"

"Bobby…" her voice was pitched low and soothing. "What's the matter? I told you I was going to be out with the girls tonight. I'm not cheating on you!"

He cursed her up and down, calling her every name in the book.

Meanwhile, the fixer was listening from outside the apartment door, leaning with his ear against the wall to try to catch every word.

"If you're going to treat me that way, I'm leaving." There was a snap in her voice. All of the soothing calm was gone.

Bobby swore even more at this. There was a crash from within the apartment. The fixer got closer, his whole body tense. Everything was going to plan, but if Bobby ended up killing her, that would screw everything up. He didn't fancy having to go to the boss to tell him that.

"Let me go, Bobby," the woman warned, her voice getting strident. "You take your hands off of me."

"You're not going anywhere. You hear me? You're never leaving here again!"

More sounds of struggle.

The fixer touched the doorknob. He was prepared to pick it, but he didn't think Charlotte had locked it. It turned smoothly and silently in his hand. Not that silence was needed this time. The screaming that was going on within would mask any small creaks and squeaks the fixer made.

He followed the noise of the struggle, the argument now going hot and heavy. Then he caught sight of them. If he'd imagined that Bobby was simply holding on to his girlfriend's wrist, he was wrong. He had both hands on her, and she wasn't just standing still and taking it. The two grappled, crashing into walls and furniture, kicking and clawing, neither one sparing the other because of tender feelings. But Bobby's superior strength was gradually overcoming the woman's desperate struggles. He managed to pin her against the wall. Then, holding her there with his body, he put one big hand around her throat, squeezing her windpipe and then the carotid. A few seconds without oxygenated blood to the brain, and she would be unconscious, unable to fight back against him any longer.

Her eyes glazed.

"Let her go, Bobby!" the fixer yelled.

Bobby was so startled by the unexpected voice that he released Charlotte, whirling around to face this new threat.

"Who are you?" he demanded, staring into the eyeholes of the fixer's black balaclava.

"I'm here to stop you from killing your girlfriend."

Bobby's brain was stuttering, trying to work through the possibilities and figure out what this strange man was doing in his apartment.

"Get out of my house! I'll call the cops."

"You'll call the cops with your girlfriend unconscious on the floor?"

Bobby's eyes went to the woman, who was not unconscious and was only now realizing it, coming back to herself.

"Who the—"

Maybe he was starting to put the clues together, figuring out that the man in the balaclava might be the drunk he'd been talking to the night before. But before he was able to finish the sentence, Charlotte's leg snapped out, and she kneed him, aiming straight for the groin. She wasn't fast enough and telegraphed the move, and Bobby was able to turn his body slightly so that she only kneed him in the leg, making him grunt with the impact instead of disabling him. Bobby grabbed her again, spinning in a circle to throw her down, but she clawed at him as he tried to put her down, pulling him off balance and making the two of them fall together, right through a glass coffee table.

The fixer winced as they both went down and glass flew everywhere. He took a few steps closer, fearing the injuries he would discover. The woman was struggling. He grasped her by the arms and pulled her to her feet. She didn't ask him who he was. Her eyes were wide with shock. Like Bobby, she'd probably spent half the night drinking, and she wasn't able to keep up with all that was happening. Bobby was still at first, then he reached behind him, and the fixer was sure he'd broken a vertebra or otherwise injured his back.

But Bobby brought his hand back out from behind his back holding a baby Glock. He pointed not at the masked intruder who had come into his apartment, but at his girlfriend.

If she were killed, the contract was off, the fixer's boss had made that clear. The fixer reacted as quickly as he could, pulling his own gun and aiming for center mass.

When he pulled the trigger, the effect was instant. Bobby lowered his gun, eyes glazing and mouth opening. He took a couple of spasmodic breaths, but it was obvious that the body's rhythm had been disrupted and, in a few seconds, all movement ceased.

Charlotte shouted at the fixer. She shoved him and ripped the gun out of his hand, her eyes wide with shock and horror.

"No! Bobby!"

She was on her knees over the man who had, just moments earlier, been trying to kill her. She laid the gun down on the floor as she held him, feeling for some sign of life.

"Lady, you'd better get out of here," the fixer told her. "If someone didn't call the cops when they heard you fighting, they surely will have now."

"You killed him!"

"I was never here. But everybody in the place heard the two of you fighting."

She didn't understand right away. "I didn't kill him! You did."

"They're going to come after you. They're going to be here within five minutes, so if you don't want to be cooling your pretty behind in prison for the next twenty years, I'd get up and get out."

"No."

He stared back at her and she didn't waver. For a minute, he thought she was going to hold firm. She really wasn't going to leave, but would wait by her boyfriend's body until the police came and arrested her.

Then she finally broke eye contact with him and looked around the apartment.

"Nobody heard," she disagreed. "Even if they did, nobody called the cops. They know better."

The fixer raised his brows, which was, of course, useless because the mask covered his expression. "They know better?"

"Everybody knows who Bobby is," she insisted. "No one is going to risk turning him in to the cops. We've fought before, and no one has ever called the police."

"Somebody will have heard the gunshot. It's pretty obvious how this argument ended."

"No," she told him again. She stood up and dusted crumbs of the tempered glass table off of her pants. Shocked sober, her brain was in high gear. "I do need to get out of here, just in case. But nobody is coming." She cocked her head for a moment. "No sirens."

The fixer stared at her. That was one cold broad. She had turned off horror and sorrow and was operating purely on logic. She looked around. He didn't realize what she was looking for at first, and then saw her purse where she had put it down on the counter when she came in the door. She picked it up and slung it over her shoulder.

The fixer tried to work out what she was going to do. If framing her for murder didn't keep her away, what would?

She gave the fixer one last long, appraising look, and then she was gone.

CHAPTER 8

Eventually, Erin broke down and told Vic about the possible tip she had received on the adoption reunion board.

"I don't know what to do about it."

Vic rolled her eyes and shook her head. "What do you mean you don't know what to do about it? You know exactly what to do about it. Answer them and get more information. You're not going to know if it is her or not without doing some more investigating. So find out."

"I know… I should… but I'm not so sure I want to find out now. What if it isn't her? What if it is her? What if we hate each other? Davis and Trenton hated each other, and they grew up together. They should have had a good relationship."

"I think it's *because* they grew up together that they hated each other. Trenton was the golden boy and Davis never measured up. And Trenton was a bully. Not exactly conducive to a good relationship."

"What if we don't get along?"

Vic raised her hands in a shrug. "Does it matter? Do you get along with everyone as soon as you meet them? Some people you need to get to know. And some people are always going to rub you the wrong way."

Erin's stomach roiled and twisted. All her life she had wanted a family. Ever since she had lost her parents when she was eight. She'd suddenly been cut off from everything and everyone she knew, shoved into alien environments and left there to sink or swim. How many years had she dreamed that it was some mistake and one or both of her parents would find her and take her home and they could be a family again?

Even before that, growing up as an only child, she had dreamed of having a baby brother or sister to help take care of and play with. Now she was finally on the brink of getting what she wanted, an actual biologically related sibling, and her brain was shutting down.

"I think I'll go to bed. I don't feel very good."

"You can't just avoid it, Erin."

Of course she could.

Erin had lots of experience with avoidance.

Erin sat at the kitchen table with Vic, going through her notes and sketches.

"I was thinking about what we talked about. That we don't have the time or resources to be supplying bread and baking for the grocery store as well as Auntie Clem's."

Vic nodded. "Good. Because I think we'd need at least another three people to stock the grocery store. If they sold well. And if they didn't, then all of our work would be for nothing. Not really a good business plan."

"Yes. I think we need to keep it to what you, me, and Bella can do for now. I can't really afford to be paying for more staff."

"Yeah."

Erin paused, tapping her pen to her chin. She looked sideways at Vic. "Has Bella used the commode yet?"

Vic laughed. "She won't even look at the door to the stairs, let alone go downstairs and use the loo. Don't bother asking her to run downstairs to get you something, unless it's just because you want to see that panic-stricken look on her face."

"I've told her that there isn't anything scary down there. Everything has been cleaned up, and it isn't like it was a horrible bloody death in the first place. It was really a very clean murder, when you think about it."

"Yeah… but I don't think she cares how bloody it was. It's the ghosts."

"There are no ghosts."

"She's sure Angela Plaint is down there, if not the entire Plaint clan. Doesn't matter that their bodies have been properly buried in consecrated ground. She's convinced that their spirits are stuck downstairs."

Erin shook her head. "I suppose I should be glad she even agreed to work for us. It's amazing she would even come into the bakery, if she's that terrified of restless spirits."

"You shouldn't mock what you don't understand," Vic warned.

She said it deadpan, and Erin studied her, trying to figure out if she was joking or serious. Even though Vic said she didn't believe in magic or ghosts or anything other than God and spirits either going to heaven or hell, her actions suggested she wasn't quite so sure. Erin decided to drop the subject altogether and go on.

"Where was I?" She scanned her notes. "Right. No more staff. Not yet. But I was thinking about the restaurants. How when Davis went to the family restaurant while I was there, he was so disgusted that they were using store-bought, mass-produced white rolls. He said that when he got The Bake Shoppe reopened, he would talk to them about a contract to supply them with good quality rolls and bread."

Vic nodded. "That would be nice. The store-bought stuff just doesn't measure up to handmade. But wouldn't that be just as much work as supplying the grocery store?"

"I don't think so. Not if we're careful. We can start just by supplying them with a gluten-free option. They can have frozen rolls and other bread products available for when someone orders them. Then we can look at offering them an upgrade on their meals. You can have turkey salad on brown bread, or you could pay a dollar fifty more and get it on an artisanal multigrain, hand-crafted, roll."

"Work our way in."

"Right. People get exposed to it as an upgrade over regular bread instead of thinking of gluten-free as an inferior replacement. They maybe decide that was a really good bread and stop by Auntie Clem's to pick up a loaf when they've got company over. And we can scale it over time. There's more room for profit if it's a premium product. We can see how it is succeeding before we have to scale up our man hours."

"Does that mean—"

The doorbell rang. Erin looked at the clock and got up. As she walked into the living room, Orange Blossom was jumping up onto the couch to stick his head out through the curtains and have a look to see who had arrived. He meowed loudly a few times.

"Who is it, Blossom?" Erin asked him. "Is it our friend Terry?"

She looked out the peep hole and saw that it was. She opened the door to let Terry and K9 in. Orange Blossom promptly arched his back and frizzed out his fur, hissing at K9 as if he were a dangerous intruder, instead of a friend that visited them regularly several evenings a week. Erin laughed and shook her head.

"Don't pay him any attention. Come on in; have you had anything to eat?"

She knew that even if he'd had supper, he would still have bread and jam, so they automatically headed for the kitchen table. Vic swiped Erin's papers into a pile and put them on the sideboard.

"Look who's here. How's it going, Officer Piper?"

Terry grinned at her. "Everything is fine, Miss Victoria."

Erin shook her head at their mock formality and got out some leftover rolls from the bakery and a selection of Jam Lady condiments.

"I searched that name for you," Terry said, after a couple of bites of bread. He wiped crumbs from his mouth. "Did a little bit of background on her."

Erin felt like her heart would stop. She put her hand over her chest and forced herself to breathe. She knew that Terry was waiting for a proper answer from her, but she was unable to formulate one right away. She got K9 a biscuit from the cookie jar and handed it to him. K9 lay down with it between his paws to eat it. Orange Blossom was sitting in the doorway watching him with haughty disapproval.

Marshmallow lolloped past Orange Blossom and circled the kitchen. K9 looked up and gave a little woof of interest, which Marshmallow ignored. He acted as if he had no idea that dogs and rabbits were naturally predator and prey, acting instead as if K9 were just another piece of furniture. He approached Erin and snuffled at her pant leg.

"You want a treat too?" Erin asked him, laughing. She got a stick of celery out of the fridge for him, and soon Marshmallow was crunching away at it. Erin looked at Orange Blossom. "What about you, silly cat, are you going to ask for a treat?"

Orange Blossom hunched his shoulders, a quiver running down his back, and disdained Erin. She shrugged.

"Oh, well."

Terry and Vic were both looking at Erin. Terry took another bite of roll. "Did you hear what I said?"

"Who did she ask you to look up?" Vic asked, when Erin didn't answer right away. "That name she got from the reunion bulletin board?"

Terry nodded. "Charlotte Campbell," he pronounced. "Do you want to know?"

Erin sighed. She swallowed, hoping her stomach would stay still and not misbehave. "I suppose."

Terry pulled out his notepad and flipped back to find the right page. Erin doubted that he actually needed to look at it to tell her what he had found. It was not complicated.

"The birth date matches. That's really the only thing we have that shows it could be her. Everything else on the birth certificate changes with her adoption. We can't tell what her birth name or place were. You'd have to go back to the court documents to hopefully find out more details there."

"So it's a 'maybe,'" Erin observed. "It could be her. But it could be someone else who just happens to have the same birth date too. And there's bound to be a few of those in Tennessee."

"Right. It's a good starting place, but you'll have to find out more information to prove anything."

"Are you going to contact her?" Vic asked.

Erin knew she should sit down at the table to join Vic and Terry, but she was too anxious to sit still. She pretended instead that she was just standing up to watch the animals and get them their food.

"I don't know."

"You have to at least contact her to see if she's the right person. And if she is... you'll want some kind of relationship with her, won't you? You'll want to get together and compare notes," Vic persisted.

"I'm not sure."

Terry frowned. Both Vic and Erin caught the subtle tightening of his mouth and wrinkle between his brows.

"What is it?" Erin asked.

"I told you I did a little background. More than just pulling up her DMV to check her date of birth."

Erin took a couple steps closer to the table. Her voice was lower, like it was a secret and she didn't want anyone else to overhear, when it was just the three of them and the animals.

"What else?"

"She has a record. Just petty stuff."

"Anyone could have a record..."

"Anyone *could*," Terry agreed. The way he looked at Erin

made her wonder again just how much he knew from her past. She had used different names in different places, across several states, and he had told her once that he'd had trouble following the thread, just as Alton had.

"But...?" It was Vic who prompted Terry to go on. Erin wasn't at all sure she wanted him to. She didn't want to know what kind of trouble Charlotte had been in. She didn't want to hear that the whole thing was just a scam. What would be the point in pretending to be someone's long-lost half-sister? It wasn't like Erin was rolling in dough. Well—maybe she was rolling in dough, but not in cash. Terry's sharp eyes caught Erin's brief smile, and he cocked his head slightly, trying to analyze it. Erin didn't fill him in on her erratic train of thought.

"Charlotte Campbell has some involvement with an organized crime family here in Tennessee."

Erin suppressed a curse. She took a couple of slow, even breaths. "You have organized crime here? I thought most of the crime in these parts was just vandals and moonshiners. Nothing serious."

"Don't get me wrong, it's no mafia. But there are a number of families that have been involved in some pretty nasty stuff for a number of generations... as far back as the civil war, some of them."

"Which one is this Charlotte part of?" Vic demanded.

"Dysons."

Vic, her complexion naturally fair, went a shade whiter. "The Dyson Clan? How did she get involved with *them*?"

"I don't know. There's only so much information I can get from official sources."

"You don't want to get involved with this," Vic told Erin firmly. "She's probably not really your sister, but even if she is... stay away from her. You don't want to get tangled up somehow with the Dyson clan."

Erin felt the first stirrings of curiosity, but also something else. One of her foster mothers had observed once, 'if you want Erin to do something, the surest way to get her to do it is to tell her not to.' Rebellion rose up in her at Vic's words. Charlotte was Erin's sister. If Charlotte were in trouble, maybe Erin could help her out. How bad could some backwoods Tennessee family really be?

"They're not really organized crime," she asserted, even though she knew nothing more about them than what Terry had just said. They were just an old Tennessee family with a bad reputation.

"Maybe not like *The Godfather*," Vic said, "but they're still some nasty people with deep connections all over these parts."

"You didn't say there was anything serious in her background," Erin said to Terry. "Right? Just minor stuff."

"Yes… but being involved with these people… there may be a lot more going on than has made it to her official record."

"But you don't know that. And you don't know how she's involved with these guys. She might have been adopted by someone in this Dyson family, right? She can't help that and it doesn't mean she's a bad person."

"No one is saying she's a bad person," Terry said, holding up one hand to stop her. "What we're saying…" He looked at Vic to make sure they were on the same page. "…is just that you don't want to get involved with this family."

"So you think I shouldn't contact her? That I shouldn't meet her, just because of the family she is in?"

Terry looked again at Vic, squirming. It was unusual for him to be at a loss for words. "I don't know, Erin. I wouldn't want you to get mixed up in anything."

"Just by talking to her and finding out if she's really my sister?"

"It sounds perfectly safe, I know. But I've seen innocent encounters turn into something else. I'd hate to see you get hurt."

"These are bad guys, Erin," Vic chimed in. "I grew up around them. Knowing who they were and what things they were involved in. Maybe it's not the mafia, but they're the closest you're going to get to it in these parts."

"You're the one who's been telling me I should get in touch with my sister. That I should do whatever I could to find her and not just forget about it. You were the one talking to me about how she was going to be like me, she was going to have more in common with me than any random friend. So if she's like me, she's not going to be involved in anything dishonest, right?"

"I don't think you can go that far. I don't think you can be sure. Not if she's been raised by these guys."

Erin shook her head in frustration. She looked at Terry. "You must know something. Was she raised by them? Or does she have some other connection with them?"

"All I can tell by what I was able to pull up was that these convictions on her record are gang-related. She is associated with the Dyson clan. Whether that means that she was in the wrong place at the wrong time, or that she's actually a member of the family, I can't tell."

Erin threw herself into her work at the bakery. If there was one thing she was good at, it was avoidance. She didn't know yet what to do with the information that her sister might be in some organized crime family, so she ignored the issue and pretended not to care. Vic didn't say anything to her about it, but Erin knew from Vic's glances when she thought Erin wasn't looking that Vic still wanted to talk to Erin more about it, to persuade her that the best course of action was just to leave Charlotte Campbell alone.

Erin looked up at the jingle of bells on the front door, and saw Mrs. Foster, Peter's mother. She had Traci, the baby, with her, but it was afternoon and the other children were still at school. Traci started begging for a cookie, and Erin got one out from the display case and handed it to her so that she and Mrs. Foster would be able to talk.

"She's getting to be such a big girl!"

"She sure is," Mrs. Foster said. "She's growing like a weed. It's a good thing we have lots of hand-me-downs, or I'd have trouble keeping her in clothes!"

Erin packaged up the bread and other baked goods that Mrs. Foster selected. "Do you find that your kids are a lot alike?" she asked. "Do they share a lot of traits and interests?"

"Lands, no. They all come with their own unique personalities. Peter was never like this little one. He's the firstborn, and firstborns are always a little bit of a perfectionist, you know. He had a lot of health issues, but when he was feeling well, he was always quiet and eager to please. He's such a mature little man now. The little girls, they're more like each other than like Peter. Karen and Jody are so close in age, they're almost like twins. Take their cues from each other. They're both girly girls, all into fashion and Barbies. This one," Mrs. Foster adjusted Traci on her hip, "I think she's going to be a little tomboy. She's far more interested in trucks and climbing and creepy-crawlies than in dolls or dresses."

She picked out some muffins and Erin went over to the till to ring up the purchases. Vic was in the kitchen, taking some fresh rolls out of the oven.

"Why do you ask?" Mrs. Foster asked. "Just idle curiosity?"

"Oh… I don't know. I just wonder what it would be like to have a sister, I guess. What it would be like to find out that I have one now. If we didn't grow up together, if we weren't playmates like your little girls, then how much alike would we be?"

"You never can tell." Mrs. Foster shook her head unhelpfully. "Some siblings are so different, you'd never believe they were even related to each other. Others… they're so much alike in looks and in the way they act, you know without even being told that they're from the same family."

Vic returned to the front of the store. She smiled and greeted Mrs. Foster and Traci. Erin made change for the purchase, but her brain was rabbiting off in a new direction. What about looks? Would her long-lost sister be dark-haired like she was? Or would she be a blond or even a redhead? Erin's mother had brown hair, and so did Adam Plaint, so Erin assumed their child would have as well. Would she have the same delicate facial features as Erin and her mother? Or the coarser, more chiseled look that Adam and his sons had? Terry must have seen mugshots of Charlotte if he'd looked at her police record, but he hadn't said a word about whether the woman looked similar to Erin or not. Wouldn't Terry have said something if they looked remarkably like each other?

"Erin?"

Erin brought her attention back to Mrs. Foster. "Oh. Sorry. What?"

"I just wanted to thank you again for all of the Christmas treats. Peter was just in heaven to have a whole platter of different kinds of cookies and sweets to choose from this year instead of one bag of store-bought gluten-free cookies. It was so nice for him to be just like anyone else."

"You're welcome. I'm glad I could make it special for him. I remember my sister... my foster sister that was celiac. She always felt so left out. She would sneak foods that she knew were bad for her because she wanted so much to be a part of the social experience. She wanted to be just like everyone else instead of being left out and forced to eat unappetizing substitutes, if anyone even thought of her."

Mrs. Foster shook her head. "I can't imagine. I'm so sorry she had to go through that. I've tried to do everything I could to make things normal and happy for Peter. Staying up late at night after putting a fussy baby to bed, just to make him a half-decent loaf of bread."

Erin nodded. Her foster parents hadn't worked that hard to make Carolyn feel normal. Maybe a biological parent, one like Mrs. Foster, would have been able to reach her.

"I'm always happy to do something for Peter."

The bells tinkled again and, looking up, Erin saw Clara Jones enter. Erin looked at Vic in disbelief. Clara had only been in the bakery once or twice before, and then only to cause trouble.

Vic shrugged. She greeted Clara pleasantly, but her expression was guarded. Neither one of them had any expectation that Clara was there to buy a dozen cookies for the police department, where she worked as a part-time administrator for Terry, the sheriff, and Tom Banks.

"What can we do for you today?" Vic asked. "I'm afraid Terry isn't here, if you were looking for him to sign something…"

"I'm not looking for Officer Piper," Clara said. She waited for Mrs. Foster to pick up her bag and depart. She leaned in toward Erin. "You should not be using police resources for your own personal investigations," she warned. "Terry may look the other way, but I think if the sheriff knew, that would be a different story. And if someone further up the line figured out what was going on…"

"Who is further up the line than the sheriff?"

"The mayor, for one. You really want the mayor investigating Officer Piper for misuse of department funds? How do you think that would end?"

Erin swallowed. She hadn't really thought about the possibility that Terry could get in trouble for running background on Charlotte Campbell for her. He was the one who had offered. Terry was always conscientious about his time, and Erin was sure he would have conducted the background search on his own time, not the department's. As far as using department resources… she had assumed that they had a monthly subscription to the databases, not that they were charged per transaction.

"You'd have to bring that up with Terry," she said icily. "He knows all of the ins and outs of the system and the politics, I don't. I don't see why you'd come here to harass me about it."

"I couldn't believe it when I saw those printouts," Clara said, eyes glittering. Her smile made Erin think of a shark. "I couldn't think of what trouble the Dyson clan would be up to in our town."

"I'm sure I wouldn't know anything about it."

"He told you about them, didn't he? You being from Maine, I could understand you not knowing what you were getting into with this family, though I would think that someone like Victor, growing up in these parts…"

"Don't call me that," Vic growled. Her tone was hard and Erin could see that Clara was surprised, having miscalculated how far she could push Vic before the girl would snap. Erin knew that Vic hadn't even gone by Victor before transitioning, so it was doubly insulting. Not like she was just an acquaintance who had forgotten what Vic's preferred name was, but making it obvious that she was intentionally misgendering her.

"Well, I'm sure sorry," Clara said dramatically, clearly not one bit sorry for what she had done. "I can't keep straight what it is you want to be called…"

Vic's mouth was in a tight, forced smile. "Since you're not actually a customer here—"

"Oh, I'll buy something." Clara looked over the goodies in the glass-fronted display case. "How about some gingersnaps? I don't think you can do anything to ruin gingersnaps…"

Erin was relieved when the bells rang again, needing someone else there to help dissipate the tension. Clara turned her head to see who was coming in as well, but she didn't get the eager audience she was hoping for. Instead, it was Willie Andrews, who Clara knew would not hesitate to jump to Vic's side and champion her case. Clara's mouth pursed into a sour knot while she waited for Vic to count the cookies out into a paper bag. Seeing who was there, the corners of Vic's mouth curled up slightly, and she counted out the cookies even more slowly and deliberately.

"Hi, Vicky," Willie's voice was warm and pleasant, happy to see her after he'd been away on whatever business had taken him from Bald Eagle Falls. He only had eyes for her.

Vic passed the bag of cookies down to Erin, who rang them up for Clara, taking her time just as Vic had. Clara paid for them, then practically snatched the paper bag and made a dash for the door.

"If you know what's good for you, you'll stay away from the Dyson Clan," she warned. "You're not from around here, so maybe nobody has bothered to tell you." She looked at Vic when she said *nobody*. "You better stay out of the way of the Dysons.

Or you're going to end up in a heap of trouble. The trouble you could get in from the sheriff for wasting department resources isn't even close to what's going to happen if you get involved with that bunch."

The bells jangled wildly when she shoved the door open, sending them dancing. Then the door swished shut behind her.

Willie looked at Vic, then at Erin, his brows raised. His soot-stained skin made the whites of his eyes stand out even more, so he seemed almost comically surprised.

"Uh… what was that about?"

"It's a long story," Erin sighed.

Vic looked at her. "Can I tell him about it? Do you mind?"

Erin threw her hands up in a shrug. "No, I suppose not. Looks like it's on its way around town now anyway. By tomorrow, everybody will be in the know."

"It's Erin's new sister," Vic said. "She got a lead on the identity, but the girl is involved with the Dyson clan. Terry did a background on her. We've been trying to explain to her that she should just stay away from them, give up on pursuing this woman any further. But you know Erin. Once she gets an idea into her head…"

"I'm not stubborn," Erin protested. "I'm a perfectly reasonable person!"

Willie and Vic exchanged a look that said otherwise.

Erin rolled her eyes and shook her head. "I'm not stubborn. You can compare me to a pit bull all you like, but that doesn't make it accurate!"

Neither one of them said anything. Erin didn't have anyone to argue against if they wouldn't push back, so she let out her breath and tried to just let it go.

"Nice to see you're back in town, Willie. Need your water refilled?"

"No, it's good. I just wanted to see Vicky and make sure we were on for tonight."

"I'm free if you are," Vic agreed.

"Good. I'll come by tonight when you're off."

Vic nodded, a brilliant smile advertising how happy she was to have him home again. Willie turned his gaze back to Erin, his mouth twisting into a grimace.

"And the Dysons, Erin? You really don't want to get involved with them. When I was—I know some of them… you really don't want to be mixed up in anything to do with that family."

Erin arched an eyebrow. "Really. I'm sort of surprised to hear that coming from you."

Willie was taken aback. He blinked at her. "Why? What do you mean?"

"I mean, usually, that's what people are telling me about you. He has a past. He's been involved in things. He has some bad connections. And I never listened to any of them."

"Well… it's all true. I do my best to be an upright citizen, but if you were to start digging into my skeletons… well, you might be surprised."

"But I don't care about your skeletons. And I don't care about Charlotte's. All I care about is finding her and getting to know her. If she is involved with some of these bad characters, or wants to get involved with one, that's her business. It's got nothing to do with me." Erin hesitated to say anything else, then forged on. "Everybody is entitled to some privacy about their past. You don't know everything about me, and I don't know everything about you, and that's okay. We should be able to evaluate each other without all of that baggage."

Willie gave a nod. "Normally, I would go along with that. But we're talking about a brutal gang here. Really, you don't want to underestimate them."

Erin considered his words. She was beginning to wonder if she could be wrong. It wasn't like it was just one of them telling her to stay away from the Dysons. Everybody acted like they were bad news.

"I'm not joining this clan," she pointed out. "I'm not getting involved in anything shady. I'm just talking about meeting someone who happens to have a connection to them. Do you really think they're going to kidnap me and induct me into their dark practices?"

Vic snickered. "They're not witches, Erin. Just… criminals."

"Exactly. I'm not going to be committing any crimes. I just want to meet my sister."

CHAPTER 9

Erin did think things through seriously. She considered all of the warnings from her friends. Willie's warnings in particular, weren't to be ignored, she'd learned in the past. She wondered what dealings he'd had with the Dysons in the past. Had he done jobs for them? Fought them for some kind of territorial right? Maybe just known some of the clan kids his age when he was going to school?

In the end, Erin had to follow her heart. She couldn't go another twenty years without meeting her sister. Now that she knew Charlotte's name, she couldn't just erase her. She needed to meet her. She needed to know what her sister was like and what it was like to actually have a family relationship.

She had a phone number, but she couldn't imagine just springing the news to someone over the phone that they were siblings. Erin had no idea what Charlotte's past was, whether she'd had any other siblings or had grown up as an only child. Whether she had lost either of her parents. Whether she'd had good relationships or bad ones. It wasn't something Erin could just spring on her over the phone.

She left Vic and Bella to watch the store one Friday afternoon, and headed to Moose River to find her sister.

Would Erin recognize Charlotte? She should have asked Terry if he had a picture of her. But she didn't want any preconceived notion of what Charlotte looked like. She wanted somehow to recognize her mother or Adam Plaint in Charlotte's features. If Charlotte didn't look like either of them, could she really be the right person? There must have been other Charlottes out there. Plenty of people with the same birth date who could have been the missing sibling.

The information from the adoption board contact gave Erin a home address, but no work address. She had no idea what kind of work Charlotte did or what time of day she worked. She aimed for six o'clock, figuring that would give her time to get home if she had a nine-to-five job, but before she would have to leave for a night shift. Erin could be completely wrong. Charlotte could go out for dinner or drinks at six o'clock. But it was the best Erin could do.

The address was an apartment building, but Erin was able to get in without having to buzz someone from the lobby. She went to number 309 and took a few deep breaths before knocking on the door. Too quietly. She knocked again, rapping her knuckles sharply, then worried that it had been too hard and Charlotte would think it was the police. The police always knocked like they were going to break the door down if the homeowner didn't answer right away. Erin had been roused from a deep sleep by that knock more than once.

She waited, chewing on the inside of her lip, practicing in her head exactly what she was going to say if Charlotte came to the door. To begin with, there didn't seem to be anyone home. Erin knocked again, criticizing herself silently for even being there. She didn't know for sure that Charlotte was her sister. She didn't know what to say to her. She didn't know what she would do if they didn't have anything in common. If there was a long, awkward silence and she didn't know how to fill it.

There were footsteps within, and then the door was opened.

Not even a pause to check the peephole or call through the door to see who it was. Maybe Charlotte was expecting someone.

Erin could instantly see familiar features in her sister's face. How many times had she wished that she looked like one of her foster sisters or a foster mother? That she was the one who belonged instead of the ugly duckling. She scrutinized her face in the mirror and saw only the vaguest resemblance to her mother's features, and nothing of her father's. There was no extended family to review for inherited traits she might have that had skipped her parents' generation. No long-lost cousins to say she looked just like this aunt or that great-grandmother. The pictures in Clementine's genealogy were black and white, too fuzzy to make out details.

"Yes...?" Charlotte asked, giving her head an impatient shake.

Erin tried to pick her jaw up from the floor and come out with something coherent. It took a bit of stammering to get her greeting out.

"Charlotte? You must be Charlotte Campbell."

Charlotte gave a scowl. "Who are you?"

"I'm... my name is Erin. Price. I'm... well, I've been looking for you. Could we... sit down and talk for a few minutes?"

"I don't have the time right now, I'm getting ready to go out."

Probably that was just an excuse. Get rid of the crazy lady at the door and continue with whatever she had been doing before Erin arrived. Charlotte was in blue jeans and a black t-shirt that was too small for her. Erin could see the edge of a tattoo under the neckline of the shirt. She had scratches on her arms. Maybe she had a cat. She seemed far too young to be Erin's sister. Almost as young as Vic. But Erin had known that. She knew that Charlotte was eight years younger than she was. Barely an adult.

"I'm sorry... maybe tomorrow? Could we have coffee?"

"Coffee?" Charlotte shook her head irritably. "I'm sorry, who are you?"

"You don't know me, but you're..." Erin still couldn't bring herself to say it right out. She considered telling Charlotte the information she had, the date and hospital where she was born, so tiny, to a mother who had been brain dead for months. But surely no one had ever given her those details, so Erin didn't either, holding back.

"Yeah, I'm what…?"

"Are you adopted?"

Charlotte's eyes narrowed. She looked at Erin with new understanding, looking at her face, and then up and down her, making the same comparisons as Erin was. Petite build and pleasant, small facial features. Dark brown hair. The same eye shape.

"Maybe you'd better come in."

Charlotte opened the door wider and Erin entered. The apartment was small and sparse, but neatly furnished. Charlotte picked up a pair of socks and a few other things from the floor, giving an embarrassed laugh. "I'm really not that bad a slob, let me just pick these up…"

But it was obvious she wasn't a slob. For the most part, everything was put away in its proper places. It was a pleasant place, if a little bare. The type of place Erin would have lived if she weren't in Clementine's old house. The type of place she had lived many times.

"It's fine," Erin assured her. "It's not messy, it's just comfortable."

"Lived in," Charlotte agreed.

Erin sat down on a couch. She swallowed and tried again to find the natural way to start the conversation. "I'm not sure what to say," she admitted. "I guess… you might be my sister. I don't know. Maybe."

"Your sister." Charlotte shook her head. "But I don't have any family. Any biological family, I mean. Both my parents died in a car accident."

That part was true, at least.

"I know they did. But I was eight at the time. I survived the car accident. They put me into foster care."

"Foster care. Wouldn't they put you up for adoption, like they did me?"

"I was free for adoption… but people don't really want eight-year-olds. Infants, but not older kids."

"Eight isn't that old."

"No… I know other kids who got adopted. But mostly… if you're older than five… you're hard to place."

Charlotte's eyes searched Erin's face. "How do I know you're telling the truth? How do I know this isn't just some scam?"

"Well… I guess you don't. Not really. But I know… if you're my sister, your biological parents would have been listed as Kathryn and Luke Price."

Charlotte quirked her head slightly. A movement that was vaguely reminiscent of Erin's mother. "Listed as…?"

"I believe that your father was actually Adam Plaint. Not Luke Price. Making us only half-siblings."

"Adam Plaint. Who is that? Is *he* still alive?"

"No. He was… it's a long story. He was killed about the same time."

"So it's just you and me."

"On our mother's side, yes. If Adam Plaint was your father, then you have a half-brother as well. Older. His name is Davis."

Charlotte sat back, thinking about this. "All of this comes as a bit of a shock. I was always told I was an only child."

A sharp pain sliced through Erin's chest. Why had they told her that? What was the harm in sharing that she had a sister? They wouldn't have known about Adam Plaint being her father and having other children, but they knew about Erin. Erin was there at the hospital. In the car. They put her into a foster family. DFS knew very well that baby Charlotte had a sister. Did they think it would be more attractive to her adoptive parents if she were an only child? Maybe they didn't want to put pressure on them to adopt the two of them as a sibling group? Or had Charlotte's adoptive parents known about her sister and not wanted to tell

Charlotte about Erin? Had they wanted a child who was unconnected and would never go looking for her biological family?

"You're not alone," she told Charlotte.

"Of course I'm not alone," Charlotte snapped. "I've got my parents, friends, a boyfriend—" She cut herself off abruptly and shook her head. "This is too much."

She went into the little kitchen and in a minute was pouring herself a tumbler of amber liquid. "You want a drink? I can't do this without a drink."

Erin's whole body was tense, her stomach a lead weight. She shook her head. "No… I don't drink."

"Of course little miss goody two-shoes doesn't drink," Charlotte muttered.

Erin looked down at herself. Had she done something to make Charlotte think she was condescending or judgmental? Was it the way she was dressed? Something she had said? Erin had been through plenty of scrapes herself and, while she might not be tattooed or a drinker, she wasn't like one of the Bald Eagles church ladies, outwardly self-righteous and telling everyone else how to behave.

"I'm not… I just don't drink," she said lamely. "After our parents… the car crash… and I lived in foster homes where… I saw what it did to other people. I just… never wanted to take the chance."

She thought of Davis and his long-time addictions. Did it run in the family? Was Charlotte already, at this tender age, an addict herself? She had certainly been quick to go for the alcohol.

"I don't need your preaching. You don't know what my life has been like. Maybe you're fine to go through life without a little help, but I could use a little something to take the edge off now and then."

Erin opened her mouth to object, but Charlotte didn't give her a chance to talk.

"I'm not an alcoholic. I just have a drink now and then and I don't see anything wrong with drinking socially. It's what I do with my friends. So you can take your judgmental attitude and—"

"I just said I don't drink." Erin gave Charlotte a steely glare. One of the looks she'd been practicing for dealing with the Bald Eagle Falls ladies when they started preaching or harassing Vic. Both Adele and Vic had been helping her, encouraging her to be assertive and not worry so much about pleasing others or meeting with their approval.

And it worked. Charlotte stopped ranting and looked at her, cheeks flushing red. She took a steadying drink from the tumbler, looking embarrassed by her behavior.

"I'm under a lot of stress," she explained. "You're right. You didn't do anything to deserve me acting like that."

"I know this must be weird for you," Erin said. "Just showing up like this and telling you we're sisters. Especially when you didn't even know you had any siblings. I'm sorry… but I didn't want to do it over the phone or email. I thought that face-to-face would be better… and I wanted to see you. To see if there was… a connection."

Charlotte sipped her drink, still holding herself aloof. "And is there?"

"You really look like our mother."

Charlotte considered this, shaking her head. "I've never been told I look like anyone. I mean, people will say I look like my adoptive mom, but she's always very quick to tell them that we're not biologically related. Like she doesn't want them to mistake me for a blood relative. I've never… your face seems really familiar. It's weird."

Erin nodded. Seeing her own features and her mother's features in Charlotte's face was disconcerting. It had been years since she had looked anyone in the face who had resembled her so closely. It had been more than twenty years since she had looked a blood relative in the face.

"I know. It's weird for me too."

They were both silent for a few minutes. "So, you live around here?" Charlotte asked. "You don't sound like you're from these parts."

"I do now, but I wasn't raised here. I had a foster family who moved north, out of state, and they were given permission to take me with them. I didn't have any relatives here I needed to stay available to. So I didn't grow up in Tennessee, even though I was born here and lived here until the accident."

"So, was it just the one foster family?"

"Oh, no. There were a lot of foster families."

"Oh." Charlotte nodded. "Sorry."

"Don't be. It was fine. I got to know lots of different people… different places…" She didn't focus on the bad stuff. Never being able to keep any personal possessions. Never knowing if the family she went to was going to be nice or abusive. Knowing she was a throwaway no one ever really wanted. Charlotte didn't need to hear any of that. Not yet.

"Must be nice," Charlotte said. "You don't know how many times I wished I could get out of Moose River. How I wanted to be anywhere but here."

It seemed like an odd complaint coming from a twenty-one year old. What was stopping her from pulling up stakes and moving somewhere else? She obviously wasn't still living with her parents. She had a place of her own. She could have moved anywhere else she liked. Erin had disappeared and left her old life behind enough times to know that it wasn't that hard. Unless, of course, being part of the Dyson clan, Charlotte wasn't allowed to make her own choice in the matter.

There was a knock on the door, so sudden and loud that Erin nearly leapt out of her seat and Charlotte spilled some of her drink. Charlotte swore and shook her head.

"What is it now?"

She went over to the door, and this time she did look out the peephole before opening the door. She stood there with her hand on the doorknob, hesitating.

"Who is it?" Erin whispered.

There was another loud knock, followed by "Police, open up!"

Erin stood there with her mouth open, all of Terry's, Vic's, and Willie's warnings flooding her brain. Don't get mixed up with her. Don't go meet her. It was too dangerous to chance getting mixed up with Dyson clan business.

"What are you going to do?"

Charlotte threw a look over her shoulder, clearly irritated.

At the third knock on the door, so loud it sounded like they were already using a battering ram, Charlotte opened the door.

"You trying to get me in trouble with the landlord?" she demanded. "What's with all the noise?"

One of the uniformed cops grasped Charlotte by the arm. "Charlotte Campbell, you're under arrest for the murder of Bobby Dyson."

Erin's heart dropped to her stomach. The murder of Bobby Dyson?

"Murder?" Charlotte repeated, her voice going higher. "Of Bobby? What happened to Bobby? Why would I kill him?"

"Young Bobby isn't exactly known for his discretion. Maybe you decided you didn't like him fooling around on you and making it known far and wide."

The cop pulled Charlotte's hands behind her back to handcuff her, then checked each of her pockets and did a cursory pat down.

"Any weapons?"

"No. I'm sitting in my house visiting, why would I be wearing a gun?"

"Or maybe you don't have it because you left it at the scene."

"Left it at the scene? You think I shot Bobby? I loved Bobby, I'd never do that!"

"Yeah. I'm sure," he sneered.

"I'd never hurt Bobby! Do you have any idea what they would do to me?"

The cop chuckled. "Well, I don't imagine they'll be too happy about it, will they?"

It wasn't until then that the little knot of policemen seemed to realize there was someone else in the apartment.

"And who are you?" the cop in charge demanded, putting his hand on his holster.

Erin tried to swallow a lump in her throat.

"I'm—I'm Erin Price. I'm Charlotte's sister."

He blinked at her, frown lines appearing in his forehead and his mouth turning down. "Her sister? Charley Campbell doesn't have a sister."

Exactly how well-known to the police was Charlotte?

"We were separated when our parents died." Erin swallowed and licked her dry lips. "She was adopted. I wasn't."

The cop approached her, leaving the other officers to supervise Charley, securely handcuffed. He studied Erin's face, and nodded slightly, perhaps seeing enough similarities in their features to accept the explanation.

"Jack Ward," he introduced himself. "How long have you been with Charley today?"

Erin looked over at Charlotte. "Not very long," she said. "Just a few minutes."

"Where were you last night?"

"Uh—not here."

"That's not an answer."

Erin wasn't keen on telling the policemen any more about herself than she had to. She didn't need everyone knowing who she was and where she was from. And more than that, she wasn't sure she was ready to tell Charley where she was from. She didn't need the Dyson clan following her home.

She jerked her chin a fraction of an inch in Charley's direction. "I wasn't around here," she repeated.

Jack Ward apparently got her meaning. He scratched his jaw, looking from Erin to Charley and back again.

"You got yourself in a heap of trouble now, Charley."

"I didn't do anything."

"We've got enough to arrest you and search your apartment."

"You need a warrant!" Charley's face was bright red.

Jack Ward unfolded a paper and flapped it in her direction. "I have a warrant."

Charley fumed silently. Ward grinned at her. He walked closer to her. "I've told you before, Charley. You hang with these guys and you're going to get burned, sooner or later."

Ward had Charley escorted from the apartment. He motioned to Erin.

"If I could also get you to come to the station, Miss Price."

Erin's stomach was clenched in a giant knot. "I didn't do anything. I'm not under arrest."

"As you heard, Charley just killed her lover, and there is going to be maelstrom like you've never seen before when the rest of the Dysons find out. Every aspect of this investigation is going to be tracked and scrutinized. If you think I'm just going to let a potential witness walk off without being questioned…" He shook his head. "It's just not going to happen. So you can come voluntarily, or you will be compelled. It's up to you."

"I'm not a witness. I didn't even get to town until this afternoon."

"You can put that in writing, and when we verify it, you'll be on your way."

"This just all seems so…"

"It's a murder investigation, ma'am. If you've never been caught up in one before, then everything is going to seem a little strange. But that's just the way it works."

Erin kept her mouth closed and did not inform him that she had been involved in a murder investigation before. More than once.

The murder investigations that she had been involved in, though, had not been shootings. They had appeared to be accidents. The investigations had been stressful, but she hadn't been in imminent danger of being thrown in jail, even when she was a suspect.

She followed Ward out of the apartment. There were more

officers in the hall outside, and once Ward had escorted Erin out, they streamed in.

"My car is just parked down on the street—" Erin attempted to split away from Ward to go get her own vehicle, but he put his hand on her arm and held her back.

"We'll take you in. Once you're released, someone will drive you back over to get your car."

"But that's ridiculous, I can just drive it over…"

"No."

Erin again opened her mouth to remind him that she wasn't under arrest and could therefore do what she wanted to, but she closed it and breathed deeply instead. He was doing his job. He had a mobster who had been shot. Erin imagined that such a murder could result in retaliation against anyone who was suspected of having been involved, as well as having political ramifications, as Ward had suggested. He wasn't concerned with her convenience. He had a murder to solve while sitting on a powder keg.

Ward let go of her arm and let her walk beside him unrestrained.

"So you've known Charley since she was a baby?" Ward asked. "I never heard any whisper that she had a sister before."

"No. I never met her before. I didn't even know she existed until just a few months ago. Then I had to track her down… This was the first time I made contact with her. We've never met before, not even on the phone or email."

His brows shot up. "Well, this is quite the introduction, then. I guess you didn't know that she was involved with an organized crime family."

"I… kind of did."

"Kind of?"

"I had a friend check her out… you know, to see if her birthdate was right and make sure she wasn't just some online scammer… He said that she was involved with this family somehow, but we didn't know how. I thought… maybe her adoptive parents were part of it… something that wasn't really her fault. I thought maybe she just had some peripheral involvement."

"Her parents are good, hardworking folks who are heartbroken to have a daughter get involved with these guys. Charley is a wild child who's been nothing but trouble for them since she was a teenager."

A wild child? Erin frowned, thinking of Charley's apartment. It had been fairly neat and clean, not some rat-infested drug den. Charley wasn't passed out with a bunch of other junkies, spent after a night of riotous living.

"So her involvement with these guys…" Erin was reluctant to call them a gang or syndicate, or whatever they considered themselves. "That's because she's the girlfriend of one of them?"

Ward gave a bark of laughter. "You're not listening to me, honey. She isn't in the Dyson clan because she's Bobby Dyson's girlfriend. She's his girlfriend because she's in the clan." He paused for a moment, and amended his statement. "She *was* his girlfriend. Now that's all changed."

He opened the door of a dark sedan for Erin and she slid into it. He shut her door and walked around to the other side. When he got in, he didn't speak to her, but started the car with a scowl on his face, lost deep in thought.

Erin watched out the window at the unfamiliar city streets whipping by. She'd only left Vic to take care of the bakery for one afternoon. What if she weren't back there by morning? How was she going to explain it to Vic? And worse—to Terry? Ward had said that all she needed to do was to sign a written statement, and then she could go home. Erin could only hope that it would really be that easy.

CHAPTER 10

*E*rin finished writing up her witness statement, which was really no more than couple of lines saying that she hadn't ever met Charley before six o'clock and had no knowledge of what had happened before then, and then she waited for Ward to return to the room and tell her she could go home. She was tired, in need of dinner, and trying to figure out if she should drive back to Bald Eagle Falls or stay overnight and let Vic know that she wasn't going to make it back in time to open up in the morning. Vic could either keep Auntie Clem's Bakery closed for the day, or she and Bella could work out some arrangement that suited them.

But Erin really didn't want to leave Vic in the lurch, so once Jack Ward told her she could go, she would probably grab a burger at a drive-through and hit the highway. She might not get much sleep, but she could at least be there to lend a hand. With an extra cup of coffee in the morning, she should be able to function, at least.

There was a polite knock on the door and Ward entered, reading a sheaf of papers in his hand. Erin shifted in her seat to get up and he motioned her to stay put. He sat down across from her without looking at her, and continued to flip through the print-outs, absorbing whatever important information had been gathered. Erin's statement wasn't long, so she wasn't sure why he was still keeping her. It wouldn't have taken more than thirty seconds for him to read it and send her on her way.

Finally, Ward put the papers down on the table in front of him. He cocked his head to the side, looking at her.

Erin shifted uncomfortably. "What?"

"You don't exactly have a squeaky-clean record yourself, do you?"

Erin licked her lips. "I've never been convicted of anything. Unless you count parking tickets. And I've paid all of those."

He stared at her for a minute, letting the silence lengthen. "What makes you think this is a good time to joke?"

"I'm not. I'm telling you—I don't have a record. I don't have any criminal convictions."

"Maybe not. But you've certainly been investigated a number of times, on a number of different charges. Under a number of different names or identities."

"I haven't done anything wrong. It's not illegal to use an alias."

"You haven't done anything wrong?"

Erin shook her head. "None of those charges have gone anywhere. I haven't done anything."

"These accusations just keep popping up," he said sarcastically, "all by themselves."

"Misunderstandings. Or circumstances. There was never any real evidence against me for anything."

He looked down at his printouts. Erin swallowed and tried to keep her face open and unemotional. Yes, she'd been investigated in the past, but she'd always been proven to be innocent, or there hadn't been enough to proceed. He couldn't hold those charges against her.

"You've been investigated for murder," Ward pointed out.

"It's not like that. A woman died in my bakery from anaphylaxis. But it wasn't from anything I did. It wasn't even an accident, it was somebody else. And she went to prison for it. I was completely cleared."

He frowned, still reading through the pages. "If I'm reading this right… not once, but twice."

"It wasn't me either time. Just because someone uses my baking as a vehicle for poison, that doesn't mean I'm guilty of anything. If someone pushes someone else in front of your car and you run over him, are you guilty of murder?"

Ward gave a little smile. "I guess that would depend on the circumstances."

Erin's face warmed. "I didn't have anything to do with either one of those deaths. I didn't set them up, or hire someone, or do anything. I had no motive. They ate baked goods that I made. That's all. I had nothing to do with it."

"Your record goes back further than that. You weren't exactly pure as the driven snow before you moved to Tennessee were you?"

"I didn't have an easy life up north. I ran into trouble a few times. But I was never convicted of anything. You can call up any of those cops who had anything to do with me, and they'll tell you. I never did anything."

"Seems like maybe this rebellious streak runs in the family."

"I was never rebellious," Erin insisted. But even as she said it, she knew it wasn't true. No, she had never gotten into drugs or crime or other things she shouldn't have as a teenager and young adult. She'd known from an early age that she was going to have to be able to support herself once she aged out of the system, and had planned accordingly. But she had defied her foster parents. Many foster parents. She had never been able to believe what she was told and trust in adults who had more experience than she did.

Instead, she'd had to figure it out herself. She had to test the limits. She disobeyed. She did the opposite to what she was told. Sometimes the adults in her life were right, but sometimes they were wrong, and she never had figured out a way to tell which was which without testing it out herself.

"You weren't rebellious," Ward repeated.

"I was responsible. You feel free to talk to any social worker or cop who ever worked with me. I worked. I educated myself. I supported myself. I was no 'wild child' like you say Charley was."

"But it sound like maybe you lined your own pockets when the opportunity presented itself. Felt free to accept gifts that you didn't deserve. Took advantage of those who were vulnerable."

Erin clenched her teeth. "No. I didn't. I worked hard as a caregiver. I never talked anyone into giving me anything. Sometimes... people would give me gifts. Was I supposed to turn them down? I worked hard."

"I'm sure you did."

"If someone gave you a gift, you wouldn't accept it?"

"It's called accepting a bribe. No, I wouldn't."

"But it's not accepting a bribe if you're not a police officer. It's just someone showing gratitude. And why would you turn it down? Especially if you were struggling to make ends meet. I don't think it's fair to expect that."

"I doubt if you were on the skids."

Erin shook her head slowly. "You have no idea what it was like for me."

"I know that now you're a business owner. You've got your own shop. Sounds to me like you managed to make out pretty well."

"I have all that because my aunt died. I've got no one else left in the world, and she didn't have anyone else to leave it to."

"Except Charley."

Erin was taken aback. "Except Charley," she admitted. "But Clementine didn't know about Charley. I didn't know about Charley. No one knew about her."

"Why wouldn't your aunt know about her?"

Erin realized that Ward was missing big pieces of the puzzle. She sat back, letting her breath out.

"I really need to get back to my bakery tomorrow. Do you think we could arrange to discuss this some other time? Or over the phone? Or I can email you answers to your questions? I can't just leave my partner to take care of everything."

"This is a murder investigation, Miss Price. The first few hours of case are vital. We need to get all the information we can as quickly as we can. Maybe your information won't have any bearing on the case, but we can't know that until we hear it. Leave it to us to figure out what is important and what is not."

"I don't see how this has anything to do with the murder. What does my Aunt Clementine leaving me the bakery have to do with Charley allegedly killing her boyfriend?"

"I don't know. I won't be able to make connections until I have all of the details. Maybe you have motive to set Charley up. Maybe she was threatening to take your inheritance. Maybe the two of you aren't quite as buddy-buddy as you would like me to think."

"We're not buddy-buddy. We just met each other today."

"I don't know that. I don't have any proof of that. I'd like to hear about why you inherited this property and she didn't."

Erin closed her eyes and covered them with her palms for a few minutes, trying to rest her head and stay clear.

"Okay. I'll try to explain it as concisely as I can. Clementine never knew Charley. None of us did. Charley was born after the accident that killed our mother. Our mother was kept on life support in order to carry Charley to term. I don't think Clementine found out about what had happened to our parents until years later. I don't know for sure, because the journal is still missing. But she didn't take either of us in. She might not have ever even known about Charley being born; it took me a long time to get any information out of DFS, and that was years later. Clementine knew that I was still alive... or was last she had heard... so she left everything to me."

"Did Charley challenge the will?"

"I just met Charley today!"

"So you say."

"You don't have any evidence that we ever met before this. I've got a business to run. I barely ever leave Bald Eagle Falls for anything other than supply runs."

Ward looked at Erin for a long time. Erin didn't crack. There wasn't anything else for her to say. She didn't have anything to confess to.

"Do you think your sister killed Bobby Dyson?" Ward asked.

"How would I know? I don't know anything about her or about him. I didn't get to town until after he was killed. I'm not Charley's alibi. She never said anything to me about him. I never heard his name until you arrested her."

"You'd heard of the Dyson clan, though."

"I told you that. I had a friend run background…"

"If you had him run background, why didn't you listen to him when he told you to stay out of it?"

Because Erin always had to test it out for herself. She should have listened to Terry, but she figured he was just being an over-protective boyfriend. She should have listened to Vic, who had grown up hearing about the Dyson clan and had warned Erin not to get involved with them. But Erin figured she was a little bit jealous of Erin meeting her long-lost sister and didn't want to take the chance of losing her place as Erin's close friend and confidante.

And Willie… how many times had Terry told her that Willie might not be quite as trustworthy as Erin thought him? She'd heard, not just from Terry, but from others as well, that Willie was suspected of being involved in shady practices. That he would do anything for a buck. That he didn't care who he worked for, as long as he got his money. Maybe she should have listened to Willie. Maybe he knew more about the Dysons than the others did. Not just rumor and innuendo, but actual first-hand experience.

Erin rubbed her forehead. "I guess I just really wanted to meet my sister. I didn't see how that could be a problem. It wasn't like I was getting involved in anything with this Dyson gang. I just wanted to meet my sister."

"Next time, maybe you should listen."

Erin sighed and nodded. "Yeah. Maybe next time I will."

∼

Before Erin left, she was allowed to see Charley. She hadn't expected Ward to allow it, but he'd looked at his watch and considered the request, and eventually nodded.

"Sure, why not?"

"Really?"

"You're going to have to wait just a few more minutes. I need to make sure we're not interrupting the flow of an interrogation. Obviously, we can't just break in in the middle of something important."

"Aren't you the one questioning her?"

"No, I have someone else talking to her right now. We take turns. Have to stay fresh. Questioning a suspect can be exhausting and can take a long time."

Erin suspected that Charley did not get to take breaks. They would keep questioning her, trying to wear her down and tire her out and break her down until she confessed to what they wanted her to. Erin watched TV. She knew how it worked.

She looked at her watch again, worried that it was going to be hours before she got a chance to see Charley and was able to start on her way home. But it was only twenty minutes before Ward was escorting her to the interview room where Charley was being kept. The police officer interrogating her was pulled out and Erin was allowed to enter. The door closed, sealing them in. Erin felt like they were in an echo chamber. Every sound was too loud. They were bound to be recorded and observed.

"What are you doing here?" Charley demanded.

"I asked if I could see you before I headed for home."

"That was nice of you. Why?"

"I just wanted to make sure you were okay, and to make sure you could get ahold of me if you needed to. I don't know… maybe you don't care. But if you did want to keep in touch…"

"It would be nice to have a pen pal while I'm in prison?"

Erin gulped. The conversation was certainly not going the way she had expected. "No... I didn't mean that... I'm hoping this is all just a mistake, and they're going to let you go, and then we'll have a chance to get to know each other."

Charley shook her head. Her eyes were angry. Probably not even at Erin; she was wound up after having to talk to the police for hours on end. Looking more closely, Erin could see lines of fatigue around her eyes, and puffiness that suggested she had concealed bags under her eyes with makeup earlier in the day. If she'd already been sleep-deprived before the arrest, Erin could only imagine how exhausted she must be with several hours of questioning on top of that.

"You seem like a nice person," Charley said. "But I don't know you from Adam. You could just be someone the department planted to get my confidence. If you are legit, then I'm sorry. You just got me at a really bad time. Maybe some other time—some other lifetime—we could get to know each other. But for me now... it's just not going to work."

Erin nodded. "Okay. Just for the record, I'm sorry this is happening to you, and I'm not a police plant. If you change your mind..." Erin slid a slip of paper across the table to Charley. "That's my cell number. You can call me if you want to. Otherwise... I guess we just go our separate directions now."

Charley looked down at the paper. It was a while before she nodded and picked it up.

"Okay, sis. Maybe I'll call you sometime."

CHAPTER 11

Vic was writing up price labels for the display case. She looked over at Erin and caught her yawning again. Vic raised an eyebrow.

"You sure you're going to be able to manage today?"

Erin had gotten back to Bald Eagle Falls in time to start the early-morning baking at Auntie Clem's, but she hadn't actually had more than an hour or two of restless sleep before that. She hadn't even bothered to put on her pajamas, but had just fallen into bed. She had at least managed to get her shoes off. Orange Blossom had prowled around, walking overtop her on the bed and sniffing at the abundance of unusual smells that clung to Erin, snuffling and sneezing at her.

"I know, I know," Erin had told him. "I'll shower in the morning and these clothes go straight into the washing machine. Though her nose wasn't as sensitive as the cat's, she could detect a number of the smells from the police station. Her own sweat, smoke from Jack Ward, who had obviously sneaked out for a cigarette at some point before talking to her, leftover fast food dumped into garbage cans, the bodies and bodily fluids of various detainees Erin had been forced to sit with while she was waiting to make her statement. Even if there hadn't been anyone else there, the furniture itself seemed to have absorbed their odors. Erin had gagged more than once at the foul smells.

Vic had fed the animals in her absence, so they didn't need to be taken care of, but both Orange Blossom and Marshmallow had seemed to understand that something was going on with Erin and had given her extra attention.

"I'm fine," Erin told Vic, rubbing her eyes. "I'll have another coffee and that will keep me going."

"You've had enough coffee to float the Titanic. What you really need is sleep."

"I don't think I'd be able to get it now even if I tried. Don't worry about me. It's just a day like any other.

Vic carefully filled loaf pans with dough. "So, are you going to tell me how things went? I guess you guys must have gotten on pretty well, to stay out there talking so late."

"Well… no, not exactly. I'm not sure if I'll ever hear from her again."

Vic turned her head to look at Erin, puzzled. "What? But you were out there…"

"I wasn't so late because we were visiting." Erin sighed. She wanted to talk it over with someone, but she also didn't want to have to divulge what had happened. She wasn't exactly going to be able to keep it from Vic. She knew Vic would keep whatever she said in confidence. "I was there late because I was talking to the police."

"What?" Vic dropped the spatula she was using to scrape out the bowl.

"I… uh… Charley was arrested, so they were questioning me as a witness."

"Who's Charley?"

"Charlotte. My sister. Apparently, that's what she goes by."

"She was arrested? Your sister was arrested?"

"Err… yeah."

"What for?"

Erin swallowed. She pretended to be concentrating on the

muffin recipe she was assembling, even though she could have done it in her sleep.

"Murder."

"Murder? Who?"

"Her boyfriend, one of the Dysons." Though Vic hadn't asked, Erin knew what question would be coming next. "Shot."

Vic's mouth worked for a few seconds before she managed to get anything out. "Land sakes! She shot her boyfriend?"

"That's what the police think. I don't know. I barely met her. I… hope she didn't."

"Goodness, I hope not. I can't believe it, Erin. That's just crazy! I'm flabbergasted! I don't know what to say!"

Erin nodded. "That about covers it."

"What did the police want from you? They didn't think you had something to do with it?"

"I didn't," Erin asserted, "and they'll know that if they verify my alibi. I was here with you yesterday morning."

Vic nodded, her eyes wide. "Do you think *she* did it?"

"I don't know. They didn't exactly discuss any of the details with me. I didn't talk to Charley about it, before or after she was arrested. I'm afraid I wouldn't want to know the answer."

"Wow."

"You're nice not to say 'I told you so,'" Erin told Vic. "You all told me not to get involved with her after you found out she was involved with the Dyson clan."

"Well… yes. We didn't want you to get involved in anything nasty. But I don't think any of us imagined that there would be a murder the day you met her. We were thinking more about you being exposed to some disreputable characters. Not… being caught in the middle of a murder investigation."

Erin looked at the clock. It was just about time to turn the sign to 'open.' She looked sideways at Vic and caught her looking back.

"I know," she said. "But it's not like it's the first murder investigation I've gotten caught in the middle of."

Erin was dreading having to tell Terry about her first visit with her half-sister. She didn't know how she was going to explain how she had ended up at the police station giving a statement about her movements over the previous twenty-four hours. But as it turned out, she didn't have to bring it up with him.

Terry came into the bakery for a water bottle refill and a visit during the slow part of the afternoon. He took a seat at one of the small cafe tables by the front window. Erin took a deep breath and looked at Vic, not sure about how to proceed. Vic just gave her an encouraging 'get on with it' gesture. Not helpful. Erin prepared a pitcher of water and got a doggie biscuit out of the cookie jar on the counter.

She approached him, forcing a smile. "Hi, Terry. How is everything?"

"Everything is quiet here."

"Good! I know quiet is better in the police business."

"Things are not so quiet in Moose River; but I gather you already know that."

Erin's heart sank. She sat down on the chair across from him. She gave the biscuit to K9. "Uh… yeah. Interesting story."

"Jack Ward says hi."

"He seemed like a very competent policeman. I'm sure he'll have it all sorted out before long."

"He called the PD to ask about you. Imagine my surprise."

Erin swallowed. She wished she had brought a glass over for herself. "I didn't know he was going to call you."

"Would it have made a difference?"

Erin searched his face. He wasn't happy, that was clear. His jaw was clenched. His voice was flat and cold.

"I was going to tell you about it later on. Tonight. There wasn't any point in calling you last night, it was almost time to get up by the time I got back here. I didn't have the energy to do anything but fall into bed. But if I'd known he was going to call you, then yes… I would have called you while we were making preparations this morning. I didn't think anyone in Bald Eagle Falls was going to know anything about it if I didn't bring it up."

"I *warned* you."

"But I didn't do anything, Terry. I was just there. Not even when the murder happened, I wasn't there until hours later. At Charley's house, I mean. Not at the crime scene. I was just there to meet my sister."

"Who I told you was involved in organized crime."

"Would you have let that stop *you* from meeting a long-lost relative?"

Terry frowned. He took his time unscrewing the top of his water bottle and topping it up from the provided pitcher. A wave of relief washed over Erin. At least he hadn't just snapped back an answer without seriously considering it. She waited, giving him time.

"I don't have a long-lost relative," Terry said finally. "I can't imagine what it would be like to have a sibling I had never met before. But I know that if one of my brothers was in trouble… I would go see him even if I knew he was involved in something shady."

Erin breathed out a sigh of relief. "I didn't go there thinking that she was actually involved in anything like a murder. I honestly couldn't see how going to see her could be dangerous to me."

Terry opened his mouth to interject, but Erin held up her hand and went on.

"I just wanted to meet her. I wanted to talk to someone I was blood-related to. I haven't been able to do that since I was eight years old. I haven't had anyone. I never planned to get involved in anything she was involved in. I never thought anyone would be suspicious of me just for talking to her. Maybe that's naive, but what were the odds she was going to be arrested for murder the day I met her?"

Terry cracked a smile. "With you…?" he took a sip of his water. "I wouldn't even want to speculate."

Erin tried to look aloof, though her face was burning. "I've never done anything to actually get myself mixed up in a murder investigation. Except maybe for maybe Adam Plaint's, and I wasn't involved, I was just helping the police department with the information I had uncovered. You suspected me in Angela's death, but even you have to admit I didn't do anything wrong. It wasn't like I was holding drugs for someone and got accused of dealing. I didn't do anything, I was just in the wrong place at the wrong time. Or *she* was."

Terry was nodding. "I know. I know. But this time you did have warning. Because I warned you."

"You didn't warn me that she might be involved in a murder."

"Well… no. How could I, unless I was clairvoyant?"

"Exactly. No one could have expected it to happen. None of us could have predicted *that.*"

"Okay. Agreed."

Erin looked out the front window, but all was quiet on the street outside. Nothing for Terry to investigate. No approaching customers for the bakery.

"What did Jack Ward have to say to you?"

"He didn't know that you and I were… together. He thought he was just calling me to get the background of an ordinary citizen. To check in and see whether you were a troublemaker, or just someone that landed in the middle of things."

"And you told him…"

"The latter. You've never been a troublemaker, Erin… but trouble certainly has a way of finding you."

Erin shrugged helplessly. "I know. I don't know how. Maybe since the car crash… I'm cursed. Maybe it altered my magnetic field."

He raised an eyebrow. "That sounds suspiciously like some new age witchcraft. Did you get that from Adele?"

"No. I've never heard her talk about magnetic fields. She'd say my spirit or some such nonsense. But she knows I don't believe in that kind of thing."

Terry took a long drink of his water. He bent down to scratch K9's ears, which Erin recognized as a sign he was getting ready to leave.

"What exactly do you and Adele talk about when you get together?" Terry asked.

"I don't know. Just like anybody else. Things going on in our lives, around town, books, politics…"

"She's interested in politics?"

"Not particularly. Neither am I. It's just something we talk about in passing. What's going on in the world."

Terry nodded. "I'd better be getting back out on patrol." He stood up. "I assume you're going to be staying away from Charlotte in the future?"

Erin stood up as well. She bit her lip, considering. A shadow passed over Terry's face.

"You *are* going to stay away from her, right Erin?"

"She's my sister. You said if it was one of your brothers who was in trouble, you would still go see them."

He looked troubled. "I know, but I'm a cop. I'm trained to deal with things like that. I could offer advice and try to help out. What could you do to help Charlotte? You'd just be exposing yourself for no reason."

"No, not for no reason. Because she's my sister."

A couple of days passed uneventfully. Erin caught up on her sleep and followed her usual routines, glad to get back to normal, but still wondered about her new sister and what was going on with her. Charley hadn't called her, so Erin tried to just put her sister out of her mind, but that wasn't as easy as it sounded.

Then one morning when her phone rang and Erin glanced down at the screen to see who it was, she saw the words Moose

River Jail scrolling across. Her heart leapt—there was no one else it could be, it had to be Charley—but she felt anxious and queasy at the same time. The morning sales were still pretty brisk, and Erin looked at Vic, gauging whether she should answer the call or not.

"Go ahead," Vic said, jerking her head toward the kitchen in the back. "I can take care of things here."

"I'll just be a minute," Erin promised. She hit the answer button and ducked through the door. "Hello?"

"Yeah, is this Erin? Erin Price?"

"Charley? Are you okay?"

"Yeah, yeah, I'm just fine."

"I didn't think you were going to call. How is everything going? I guess you're still…"

"I'm still here," Charley confirmed the obvious. "My lawyer is working on getting me out, but they don't move quickly around here. They like to leave you here and give you a taste of what it's going to be like if you have to be incarcerated long term. Throw a scare into you. Pigs. It's just taking a little longer than I expected."

"Uh-huh…" Erin had no idea what to say to this. She supposed she should commiserate. Express sympathy. Tell her sister that she knew Charley wasn't supposed to be there. And that she would get out soon. But Charley knew that world better than Erin did, and Erin was sure she probably had a pretty good idea of what her chances and the timeline were without any false encouragement from Erin.

"You said if I needed anything, I could call," Charley said tentatively

Erin was pretty sure that wasn't what she had said. But it was an olive branch. Charley was reaching out to her and Erin wasn't about to slap her down.

"Is there something you needed?"

Maybe Erin could take her some muffins or other baking. Was that kind of thing allowed in jail? Did people really try to smuggle things in to prisoners inside a cake, like in the comics? Surely with the advent of x-rays and metal detectors, that kind of thing was antiquated.

"Yeah. It's just... I wouldn't ask, but I really couldn't think of anyone else I could trust. I don't have a lot of close friends. I mean, there are girls I hang with but..."

"Trust with what?"

"I don't have anyone to feed Iggy."

"Iggy?" Erin pictured a little black puppy or kitten. Charley had already been away for a few days, but maybe she had an automatic feeder for it that would last that long. Charley had thought that she would be back to take care of him, but it was going to be too long.

"Iggy is... my lizard. Don't gross out. He's not slimy or poisonous. But... he's going to need to be fed. No one but Bobby had a key to my apartment. Obviously, the cops aren't going to step in and take care of him. I'm lucky they didn't just turn him in to the Humane Society."

A lizard? Of course Iggy was a lizard. It figured that her prickly little sister wouldn't have a fluffy puppy or kitten. Or rabbit. Instead... a lizard. A cold-blooded reptile. Just like the guys she worked with.

"Uh... I don't know much about lizards."

"Everything is set up. Just make sure that his environmentals are all okay, give him some crickets... he doesn't need to be taken out for a walk or anything."

"Good, because I'm afraid I'd lose him. Uh... how big *is* this lizard, anyway. Is he... I mean, he's not too big if all he eats is crickets, right?"

"It's not a gila monster," Charley laughed. She sounded natural and friendly for the first time. Just a girl talking about her lizard. "He's a chameleon."

"Named Iggy? I thought he'd be an iguana."

"Yeah... it's sort of a joke."

"I don't know how big chameleons are. They're the ones that change color, right?"

"Yes. He's not big and he's not going to bite you. Is that okay? Do you think you could…?"

Erin thought about it. Of course she wanted to rush over and do something for Charley. It was the first opportunity she'd had to bond over something. But it was a couple of hours driving each way. She hadn't told Charley she lived in Bald Eagle Falls, and Charley had just naturally assumed Erin was in town.

"Yeah… I can do that. But I won't be able to get there until late. How do I get the key? You don't have a neighbor that can let me in?"

"No. You'll have to come to the jail to pick it up. Sorry about that. And go to the pet store for crickets because I don't have any at home. The landlord freaks out over me keeping *la cucaracha* in the apartment." Erin could practically hear Charley's eye roll. "So you can do it?" Her voice took on a plaintive quality. "I know it's a pain…"

She had no idea how far out of the way it was for Erin. But Erin wasn't about to tell her and make her sister feel guilty for asking. She'd wanted a connection, and now she had it. She would be the lizard sitter. If Iggy only needed to be fed every few days, then Erin would probably only have to do it once or twice before Charley got released or got out on bail. When Charley learned how far Erin had gone to take care of the lizard, she would be super grateful, and it would be the beginning of a warm, sisterly relationship for them.

"I'll do it," Erin agreed. "I'll get over as soon as I can. How late can I get to the jail to pick up the key? And what are the pet store hours?"

Charley let out a sigh of relief. She gave Erin the details, and Erin bent over the desk in her tiny office scribbling them down.

"Thank you so much for doing this," Charley said. "It's a big relief. I've been so worried…"

"Of course. I'm happy to help."

"Looks like my time is up. I gotta get off the phone. Do you have everything you need? You don't need to know any more?"

"How many crickets do I need to get? And do I just drop them into his cage?"

"Reptarium. Yes. You don't need a lot, just the smallest container. Just open the tank and dump them in. Make sure the dripper is working and his heat and humidity are okay—"

There was a growling voice in the background, and Erin knew they were kicking Charley off the phone.

"That's all," Charley's voice was fading as she was getting farther away from the handset. "It's not hard. Thank you, Erin!"

The phone connection was cut. Erin stood there for a moment with her phone still to her ear, as if Charley might come back and continue the conversation.

What had she gotten herself into? She knew absolutely nothing about caring for a chameleon. Charley might say it was nothing, but if Erin did something wrong and the lizard was sick or dead by the time Charley got out of jail, that would not be a good relationship builder.

Eventually, Erin lowered her phone and slid it into her pocket. She looked at the time, and started calculating in her head what time she was going to need to leave if she were going to get to the jail and the pet store before they closed, so she could take care of Iggy properly. Then she'd need to immediately turn around and return home in time to get the sleep she needed to be functional at the bakery the next day. She didn't have the reserves she needed to stay up late more than once in a blue moon.

"Is everything okay?" Vic asked, as Erin walked back out to the store front, her thoughts miles away.

"Yeah. Fine. Just... thinking."

"Who was that on the phone?"

Erin looked at the customers who were listening in. None of them knew anything about Erin's sister or what she had gotten herself into.

"That was Charley."

Vic's eyes widened. "Charley? What did *Charley* want?" Vic

carefully avoided the use of a pronoun so that no one could catch on that Charley was a girl rather than a boy.

"Uh… Charley has a… friend… who needs a babysitter. Just tonight. After that, Charley should be home."

Vic followed this easily. "This friend is… all the way *out there?*"

"Yes. So…" Erin looked at the time again. "I think I'm going to have to leave early today, so I can pick up a meal and the key, and still get home in good time tonight."

"Yeah. For sure. You just go when you have to. I can take care of things here for one afternoon."

"Do you want me to call Bella and see if she can come in?"

"No. Don't worry about it. We already have her coming in on the weekend, and that's more important. It's not like it's all day, and everything is already made. It's just the after-school crowd and clean-up."

"Are you sure?"

"Of course. You have to take care of Charley's friend. It's important."

"Okay."

Mary Lou looked at Erin and Vic, a little frown on her face. "Charlie who? What's this all about?"

"It's nothing," Erin assured her. "I just have a little errand I need to run. Nothing to worry about."

"Then why are you being so mysterious?"

Erin did feel a little like they were drawing attention to themselves by being so cloak-and-dagger. Would people really care if they found out that Erin had a half-sister who needed her help?

And that that sister was in a criminal gang?

And currently in jail?

Erin decided that there was no way she was going to let that gossip loose in Bald Eagle Falls. She would keep it a secret for as long as she could.

CHAPTER 12

*E*rin was relieved that everything was in order at the jail. They seemed to be expecting her, and she had only to show her identification to get the key to Charley's apartment. She had been worried that they would interrogate her and make her sign some kind of statement about why she wanted it. Maybe the police would even insist that she had to have an escort to go back to the apartment, so they could be sure she wasn't tampering with evidence. But the police had already had their chance to search Charley's apartment to their hearts' content, and if they hadn't found the evidence they were looking for, that was their own problem. The jail didn't appear to have any problem with Erin picking up the key, so she didn't argue with success, and just smiled and thanked them politely.

Charley had told her which pet food store to go to. Not all pet stores would have crickets. She followed the noise of their chirps to the back of the store, where there were various sizes of container and varieties of bugs in tanks. It felt a little like take-out for insects.

The girl who helped Erin out didn't look like she was old enough to be out of high school. She was completely relaxed and matter-of-fact about all of the creepy crawlies.

"I'm helping out a friend who's out of town," Erin told her. "I haven't ever taken care of a lizard before, so I'm a little nervous."

"It will be totally fine," the girl assured her. "What kind of lizard is it?"

"Chameleon."

"Oh, I love chameleons! You will too. Did she tell you what to get?"

"Just crickets. The smallest size container."

"Sure. These babies are gut-loaded and calcium-dusted, so they're all ready to go."

Erin had to look away as the girl dipped a little bowl into the tank full of hoppers and then snapped the lid into place.

"All safe and sound," the girl promised. "It's nice and tight and isn't going to pop open in your car. When you have the chameleon's tank open, just dump them in. Did she tell you what else to do?"

She ran through the procedures with Erin, and Erin was much more reassured than she had been after the hurried talk with Charley at the jail.

Erin wrote down all of the details for later reference.

"Can I call you if I run into any trouble?" she joked.

"Of course! Here." The girl picked up a business card and wrote her name and number on the back of it. "I'm Olivia. If you have any questions when you get there or something happens or seems wrong, just call me up and I'll be happy to help. Any time, day or night."

"Really? You're a lifesaver, Olivia. I'm Erin. Hopefully, I won't need you, but if something happens… I'm really glad I have someone to call."

"You could call your friend," Olivia suggested. "The one who owns the chameleon."

"No, she's… not available most of the time. She can call me now and then to check in, but I can't really call her or ask her any questions."

"She must be in the mountains," Olivia decided. It wasn't

really a question, so Erin wasn't actually lying by not telling her yes or no.

Erin was soon on her way back to Charley's apartment. There were no police cars outside like there had been when Charley was arrested. Erin had kind of expected there to still be one cop hanging around to keep an eye on the place, but if there was, he was well-disguised, because Erin couldn't pick out anyone she thought was a cop or who was paying more attention to her than they should.

The apartment door looked just as it had. No crime scene tape or notice telling her to stay out. Erin fit the key into the lock and slowly let herself in. She waited once the door was open, listening. She strained her ears for any sign that someone else was in the apartment. There was not a movement, not a breath that she could hear. The apartment smelled as if it had been shut up for several days, the air still and undisturbed. Erin hadn't noticed the smell of the lizard's cage the last time she had been there but, either because she was expecting it or because it hadn't been cleaned for a few days, she could easily detect it.

Erin followed her nose to the small study that had been converted into Iggy's room, with a screened reptarium full of green growing plants and environmental monitoring equipment. She followed the instructions that Charley and Olivia had given her, staring through the screen to find the green lizard before opening the door and dumping the container of bugs into a corner. She closed the door again.

Iggy was still. Erin waited for him to go after the bugs. He blinked lazily and one of his eyes seemed to follow her, independent of the other. *Ugh. Gross.* It was a minute before there was a subtle shift in his position and she thought he was aware of the crickets.

"Yeah, see? Hungry?"

She was used to her cat and her rabbit. She understood their body language and behaviors, the ways that they talked and responded to her. The chameleon was like an alien. She didn't know whether they responded to voices, or whether they responded more to smell or movement. Did Iggy know that she wasn't his usual caregiver? Did he know Charley and respond to her?

It happened so fast that Erin completely missed it the first time. The chameleon's sticky tongue shot out, and a cricket was gone. Erin blinked.

"Whoa. That was fast. You're like a frog."

He blinked his eyes one at a time. Slowly, as if mocking her. The next time his tongue shot out, she was expecting it. And another cricket was gone. She waited for him to eat more, but he didn't, he just stayed there clinging to the branch, rolling his eyes around in different directions. The only other movement in the cage came from the crickets, wandering around aimlessly, apparently unaware of the predator that lurked above them.

Erin looked at the thermometer and hygrometer to make sure they were within the limits that Olivia had recommended. The dripper and heater were doing their jobs.

"Your mom will be back in a day or two," Erin promised Iggy. "Just as soon as she can get out."

He didn't respond to her voice.

In spite of how interesting the reptarium environment and the lizard were, her eyes started to wander around the study, taking in other things.

She didn't mean to snoop. That wasn't why she was there. She was just there to take care of Iggy, but she thought maybe she should have a look around to make sure everything else was in order as well. She was there and she was the only one with a key, so she was the only one who could make sure that everything was as it should be while Charley was away.

There was a writing desk on one side of the room, the chair between the desk and the wall so that when Charley sat down to use it, she would be facing the chameleon's environment and be able to watch him. Erin thought about the way that Orange Blossom would come up to her little attic hideaway while she was at her writing desk or reading nook, wanting to know why she was being so quiet and why she didn't want to play. It seemed a little sad to have only a lizard, who couldn't do that, but who just crawled along branches flicking out his tongue at insects. But maybe it was different for Charley. Maybe she felt a connection with him even though he did look like something from another planet. Maybe she was allergic to animal dander, or had grown up with parents who were allergic, so she hadn't been able to have a warm-blooded pet that would be more responsive to her.

Erin looked at the neat, tidy desk. What did Charley write there? Letters? A journal? It had a warm feeling and Erin couldn't imagine Charley conducting gang activities from there, writing orders for other clan members or keeping a double set of books. What was Charley's role in the clan? Did she have a specific function? Was it a well-organized group, or did the members just have casual roles? Erin could picture herself sitting there writing out recipes or making her lists for the next day. It was well-lit and tidy, with all of the writing materials and supplies she would need close at hand.

No laptop. Did that mean the police had taken Charley's computer or that she didn't keep one? Or maybe it was in another room. She might watch DVDs or a subscription service before bed and have a laptop in her bedroom.

Erin made sure that she had properly latched the lizard enclosure and left the study. After a few seconds of hesitation, she went to the fridge. She wasn't snooping. She was there to help her sister out. Charley hadn't said anything about Erin taking care of anything else, but she had been worried about her pet and the conversation had been cut short by impatient jail staff. She hadn't had a chance to ask Erin to do anything else while she was at the apartment. But Erin was there, and she might as well check on other things that she could be reasonably expected to do.

She opened the fridge, expecting to find nothing but old takeout containers and half-empty bottles of condiments. But it wasn't empty and there wasn't a takeout container in sight. Not even a frozen dinner or deli package. Everything seemed to be home cooked.

Erin took out a small carton of milk and, after checking the expiry date, poured it down the sink drain. She poked through the produce and the cooked dishes in covered glass bowls, adding a few things to the green compost bin under the sink. She noticed that the garbage can was empty, and that gave her pause. Charley hadn't had a chance to empty the garbage when she had been arrested. Had she emptied it before then, earlier in the day? There was no garbage pick-up schedule on the fridge that would give an indication of whether it would have been normal for Charley to have taken out the garbage that day.

It occurred to Erin that she hadn't eaten supper or made any plans to. She'd been focused on Iggy's needs and hadn't even thought of her own. Should she go out to a fast-food joint before heading home, or would Charley mind if she helped herself to some of the food in the fridge before it started to go bad?

In a few minutes, Erin had a small plate of food warming in the microwave and pulled out her phone to check for any new voicemails, texts, or social media messages.

Charley was a surprisingly good cook. She'd missed her calling in choosing to be a mobster. She should have gone into the food services industry. Erin thought back to helping in Clementine's tea room. Maybe it ran in the family. Maybe it was one of those inexplicable family traits. An interest in food services. A talent for food preparation. Erin had always found it comforting to make food and had enjoyed making other people happy or more at ease by making them food. It wasn't just Carolyn's death that had prompted her interest in cooking for others. It had spurred an interest in gluten-free and cooking for other special diets, but years before that, she had spent happy hours as a child helping Clementine in the tea room. She could remember playing with child-sized dishes when she was little, pretending to serve her mother and being frustrated that she wasn't allowed to be involved in the cooking of real meals. She knew she could do better than her mother, who seemed to struggle with even the basic heating of prepared meals.

She washed up and put away the dishes she had used. The kitchen was well-stocked and everything seemed to be in its logical place. Erin picked up the small compost bin and poked around in the corridors of the building until she found a room with a trash chute and a larger green bin smelling of rot that she emptied the small bin into.

Erin looked at her watch. She had saved some time by eating at Charley's instead of having to find a restaurant or fast-food place. She could spend a few more minutes making sure that everything had been properly taken care of in the apartment before heading home, and she'd still have time to work on her lists for the next day before bed. She found that thought comforting.

There was a little more mess in Charley's bedroom than in the rest of the apartment. Evening clothes draped over the back of a chair instead of hung up. Makeup strewn over the top of a dressing table with a mirror. The bed had been made, but Charley had certainly not been drilled in making hospital corners or a military-tight bunk.

Erin sat on the edge of the bed and looked around.

Was Charley really a wild child? A mobster? Nothing in her rooms seemed to indicate anything other than a normal, everyday existence. She could have easily been an office or retail worker, restaurant cook or hostess. But a career criminal? Her apartment was nothing like what Erin would have expected from a mobster or a mobster's girlfriend. But then, what did she actually know about what a mobster's room would look like? If she was to go from TV, it could range from a rat-infested flop house to a sumptuous mansion a king would envy. What exactly did a Tennessee organized crime clan look like?

There was little to indicate that Charley had had a boyfriend. There was a picture of her with a young man on the bedside table, but there wasn't a lot of jewelry, wilting flowers, or other romantic keepsakes that Erin could see. A quick glance through her closet and drawers did not turn up any men's overnight gear. Not even a toothbrush or change of underwear. How serious could they be if he wasn't even sleeping over occasionally?

Erin's face flushed warmly even though there was no one there to see her embarrassment. Who was she to be making judgments over how serious Charley's relationship with Bobby was? It wasn't like Terry was spending nights at her house either. There was plenty of room for another person in the family-sized house, especially now that Vic had her own place over the garage. But she and Terry had kept their lives separate and had not taken that step. They were moving slowly, content, for the most part, to spend time together as friends and not to do anything that would have caused tongues to wag among the Bald Eagle Falls gossips.

$\mathcal{E}$rin texted Vic that she was on her way home. When she arrived, she parked her car in the new garage. As she walked across the yard, Vic stuck her head out the door at the top of the stairs that climbed the outside of the garage to her loft apartment.

"Hey, Erin. Everything go okay?"

"Yes, Iggy was fine and has enough bugs for the next few days."

"And he didn't gross you out?" Vic grinned. She was far less squeamish than Erin, having grown up farming, hunting, and fishing. Critters didn't bother her.

"No, he's pretty weird looking, but at least he wasn't slimy."

"Did he change color for you?"

"No. Just green while I was there."

Vic nodded. "Okay. Well, have a good night." She started to pull her head back.

"You got company?" Erin asked. Vic usually came over for a few minutes before bed if she was by herself. But if Willie was over, she didn't.

Vic gave her a grin. "Yes, Miss Nosy Parker. Willie's here."

"Hi, Erin." Willie's voice drifted out from behind Vic.

Erin smiled and gave a little wave. "Hi and good night to both of you. I'm going to have a bath and head to bed."

"And make lists," Vic added.

"And make lists," Erin admitted.

Vic withdrew and Erin went into Clementine's house through the back door.

She had bathed and was in her pink flannel jammies when she heard voices coming from outside. Not Vic and Willie out for a moonlight stroll, but shouts and jeers.

Erin hurried to the kitchen, nearly tripping over Orange Blossom, and peered out the window. She caught sight of a few dark shapes flitting across the yard, and then they were out of view of the kitchen window. Erin opened the back door. Willie was coming down the stairs of the garage apartment at a run.

"Willie? What happened? What's wrong?"

"Stay inside, Erin. Call Terry."

"But what—"

"Stay inside."

Erin closed the door and locked it. She couldn't see what he was doing through the little arched window high in the door, and when she went back to the kitchen window, it was just in time to see him step out of view. Erin swallowed and concentrated on doing what Willie had said. She dragged her phone out and hit the speed dial for Officer Terry Piper.

"Piper. Oh, hi, Erin."

"Terry, something is wrong. I don't know what's going on. There were people in the back yard. And then Willie came out, and he said to call you."

"There was someone in your back yard?"

"More than one. I saw at least three."

"Stay inside."

"Willie already told me to. I locked the door. What's going on?"

"I don't know yet. Did he lock the apartment door?"

"No, I think he went after them. He was outside…"

"Of course he did," Terry grumbled. "Okay, stay put, I'll be there in a shake."

He must have put a call out to the rest of the police department, because Tom Banks pulled up in front of the house at almost the same time as Terry pulled in behind the garage. Both got out and took a look around the yard. Erin saw Willie join them. When they walked toward the back door, Erin opened it and stepped out to meet them.

"What is it? What happened?"

"It's nothing," Terry said, "just a little vandalism." He gestured toward the garage and walked with Erin toward it.

"Heard car doors slam," Willie growled. "Didn't even see the car before they were gone."

Even with the security lights turned on, Erin couldn't see the mess of the raw eggs until she got up close to it.

"If you've got a pressure washer, we should clean it off before it dries. Even just a garden hose…" Terry suggested.

Erin felt distant and removed from the situation as she went into the garage and got the little pressure washer she had picked up at a Black Friday sale after Thanksgiving. Terry took it from her and set it up outside the garage. His eyes flicked over her.

"You're going to catch a chill. Go put on a coat."

Erin looked at her pink pajamas. She had slipped sandals on her bare feet. "I'm fine."

K9 snuffled around and made an irritated huff when he sat down, disappointed at the lack of excitement. Tom was taking pictures of the vandalism. When he finished, he nodded at Terry. Terry aimed a stream of water at the mess and washed it off. Vic stood at the top of the stairs until he was done, then joined them.

"Who was it?" Erin asked Willie. "Why would anyone do something like this?"

Everyone was silent, looking at each other but not answering. Willie cleared his throat.

"They were shouting slurs," he said. He indicated Vic with his eyes, and Erin understood without his saying anything more that it was prejudice about Vic's gender identity. "I didn't see them clearly enough to identify who it was. Young people. Probably out drinking. Bored. Looking for trouble."

Erin shook her head. She looked at Terry. "Do you know who would do something like this?"

"Sure, I know a number of people who would do something like this. But I don't have any evidence of who it was. You don't have any security cameras, do you?"

"No."

Maybe Erin should have anticipated it. Vic hadn't exactly been welcomed with open arms by everyone in Bald Eagle Falls. Erin had already had rocks thrown through the window and an attempt to burn her house to the ground. It shouldn't have taken so long for her to figure out that she might benefit from a few security cameras.

"It's okay," Vic said. Her face was pale. "It doesn't matter who it was. It was bound to happen sooner or later. If we react to it, it will just get worse."

Erin scowled. She hated for Vic to think that it was acceptable. People might not choose to like or be friendly with Vic, and that was their right. No one was universally liked. But it wasn't okay for them to yell slurs and vandalize her home.

"I'll get cameras this weekend," she promised. "The guys can help install them, right?" She looked at Terry and Willie for confirmation.

"I can install cameras," Vic said with an offhanded shrug. "I just don't think... well, it's not like they tried to hurt me. If we overreact, they'll just think I'm a good target."

"Installing cameras isn't overreacting," Erin said firmly. "I'm worried about security. If these guys come back again, I want to be ready."

"If you want to upgrade your security, you can do a few other things," Tom said. "Put the security lights on a motion sensor. Put alarms on your doors and windows and keep it armed at night or when you're not home. You two ladies both live alone..."

Even though they were on the property and always in and out of the house, they did live separately. If someone broke into Vic's loft apartment in the middle of the night, or into the main house, the other would never know it.

Erin nodded. "Yeah. You're right. I should probably get something over at Adele's in the cottage as well. She's even more remote than we are."

"She's not going to like that," Vic said.

"No, probably not. But I wouldn't want anything happening to her, either. People might not realize that she's... you know what... but she's still isolated, and kids might not like the fact that she's taken over their old hangout and keeping an eye on things out there."

Vic sighed. She rubbed her bare arms. "I just hate that we have to change anything because of people like this."

"I know," Erin agreed. She thought about Charley living alone as well. With her enemies, why hadn't there been security measures at her apartment? Erin hadn't even needed to be buzzed in at the lobby door, and there was only a single lock on the apartment door. Was Charley so sure of her position in the Dyson clan that she had no fear of anyone breaking in when she was away or when she was home alone?

"You can file your reports in the morning," Terry said. "You ladies need to be up early, so you'd better get off to bed."

Erin yawned, but at the same time, felt wide awake. Her brain was going to take a long time to settle down. "I don't know if I can. Are you on call tonight?"

Terry shook his head. "I'm off. Tom's on. But you can still call me if something happens. You never use the dispatch line anyway." He smiled, showing that this was not something that bothered him. Just a statement of fact.

"Okay." Erin hesitated, then gave him a brief hug. The various badges and equipment on his uniform poked uncomfortably into her, but she ignored it. "Thanks for coming. I'll see you tomorrow."

He gave her an extra squeeze and let go. K9 whined, looking at Terry.

"We'll do one patrol around the house and yard and then we have to go," Terry told him. "If there's anything to find, you'd better find it."

He gave K9 a hand signal and let him lead the way. K9 smelled the remains of the smashed eggs on the ground and started to cast around for a scent trail. Erin knew that the perpetrators had escaped in their vehicle, so K9's search was unlikely to turn up anything of interest. Terry knew that too, but K9 wanted to do his job, and it was always possible that one of the young people had dropped something in the dark. A set of keys or a wallet with identification would be nice. Erin watched them for a few minutes, then waved at Terry.

"Night, Vicky. You be okay? Do you want to come sleep in the guest room tonight?"

Vic looked at Willie. "I think… are you going to stay?"

Willie nodded. "I don't like to leave you alone after this. I'll hang out tonight and make sure nothing else happens."

"Good." Erin nodded. "Thanks."

"What about you? Are you going to be okay alone?"

"Sure. It was Vic they were targeting, not me. They probably didn't give me a second thought."

"All right. See you in the morning."

"Bright and early," Erin agreed.

It might take her a while to get to sleep, but she was still going to have to be up in the morning.

~

The boss was not pleased with the way things had gone down.

"What were you thinking? The idea was to get her out of town and into hiding, not arrested for murder! How did this happen?"

The fixer raised his hands in a placating gesture. He looked around at the other tables, making sure that no one was listening in.

"Things didn't go to plan. Obviously. But I handled it the best I could, and the result is, she's out of the way. That's what you wanted, isn't it?"

"That's what I wanted? No, it's not what I wanted. I wanted her to quietly disappear. How do you think she's going to disappear when she's in the system? Got guards over her day and night? If they're able to get her name, they'll trace her here. Just like that. She's got a great big neon sign over her now. And if they find her, then I lose out. Understand?"

The fixer considered this, examining the situation from several angles.

"You've worked on these things before," the boss growled. "You've got experience. So why are you behaving like such an amateur?"

"Give me some time to sort it out. You want her to get out."

"Of course I want her to get out. Having her behind bars doesn't help anything."

"Maybe if she gets out, she'll run."

"She should," the boss agreed. "They've got enough on her, she's got to know that they've got enough to convict her and keep her behind bars for twenty years."

"Less than that for manslaughter," the fixer disagreed. "They won't convict on intentional murder. Anyone looking at that apartment or hearing about the fighting will know it was in the heat of the moment."

"Manslaughter, then."

"If she lives long enough to be convicted. Because the clan can't be too happy about her killing Bobby. Getting her out puts her back in their sights too."

"I don't want her killed. I just want her gone."

The fixer cleared his throat. "I can't be her guardian angel. If you want her out of jail, there could be consequences. I can't stand up against the whole clan. I'll do my best to get her to run, but she might try to tough it out."

"She has to run."

"If she has any sense, she will."

"I don't care about sense. She *has to run.*" The boss spaced the final words out and bit each one off, making it a sentence all by itself. Has. To. Run.

The gears in his head were turning, and the fixer nodded, focusing on the whole machine. It was one of the strangest jobs he'd ever had. But that didn't mean he couldn't do it. One way or another, the girl would have to disappear.

"I'll get her out," he agreed, "and then I'll get her to run."

Erin looked at the phone and saw it was another call from the jail. It was, at least, a quieter hour at the bakery, so she didn't feel as bad about leaving Vic to handle the counter and ducking into the back to take the call. Melissa was there, and Erin didn't need all of the church ladies in town knowing she had a half-sister in jail. She knew it shouldn't matter. She should be able to just be who she was and not worry about if the ladies were judging her for her sister's sins. But the fact was, a lot hinged on Erin's reputation. There had been threats before that the ladies would stop coming to the store because of perceived faults, and Erin knew that the success of the bakery was tenuous. If it were black-balled because not only was she an atheist employing a misled youth, but she also had family in jail, she would have to pull up stakes in Bald Eagle Falls and find something else to do. And she didn't want to. She really wanted to make the bakery work.

"Hello?"

"Erin, it's Charley."

"Hi. I did get to see Iggy and gave him the crickets and checked everything out. He seems to be perfectly happy and healthy."

"Great, thanks. I really appreciate it." But Charley's words were cold and clipped, like she was just saying it out of duty and not because she really felt anything. Erin instantly felt disdained.

"Was there something else, then?"

"They've scheduled a bail hearing for tomorrow. That no-good lawyer must have finally done something right. I was starting to think he was taking his orders from the Dysons. So I might be getting out."

"That's great! I'm really glad to hear it."

But what did she need Erin for?

"I just wondered… I might need someone to pick me up. I thought I could buy you supper. You know, for helping me out with Iggy and everything. And… I've been thinking about the things you said about my biological family… I thought maybe you could tell me a little more about them. I haven't… I haven't ever had a biological connection with anyone before…"

Erin listened to the beating of her own heart. Charley was saying the right things, but Erin didn't feel any warmth from her. She had the feeling that Charley was only saying what she thought Erin wanted her to say. What did Charley really want?

"So… tomorrow? I won't be able to get there until later in the day. I have my work."

"You can't get off?"

"It's my own business, Charley, and I don't have someone who can step in and take care of things on short notice like that. We're on a shoestring as it is, and if I'm not there, I have to pay someone else to be there. I don't even know if our usual girl will be available."

There was silence from Charley.

"You can't expect me to just drop everything to be there," Erin said. "You could probably get a cab or a bus or another way home. Maybe you should do that instead."

"No. No, it's okay. I don't mean to be ungrateful. You've been really nice and you don't even know me."

"Okay. So late tomorrow afternoon is okay?"

Erin really wouldn't mind if Charley decided she could get a cab after all. It was a little silly of Erin to keep making the trip back and forth when it was a couple of hours each direction. She needed to tell Charley the truth about how far away she lived so she could be more reasonable.

"Yeah, okay. Late tomorrow afternoon."

"All right. Will you call me after you get bail, when you know for sure you're getting out? It would be silly for me to come pick you up if you didn't even get bail."

"I'll let you know," Charley agreed.

Erin went back to work and to explain to Vic why she would, once again, need to cover the last few afternoon hours while Erin ran back to Moose River.

CHAPTER 14

Terry insisted on taking Erin out for supper, and she should have guessed by how hard he pressed her even when she said she had other things to do, that he had a reason other than just the pleasure of her company.

She didn't want to tell him that she had to get ready to go out of town again to see Charley and help her out of a scrape. He would find out anyway, but she would rather he didn't.

The way he looked at Erin when they sat down at the table told her that he already knew far more than she wanted him to. She ignored the feeling and they studied the menus they already knew off by heart and ordered meat plus three, and they both pretended they were just there to have a pleasant evening meal. Terry waited until they received their dinners to start in on the conversation he had planned.

"I hear you're going back to Moose River."

"I guess you've been talking to Vic."

"Why is it I have to hear it from her instead of from you? Why weren't you the one to tell me?"

"I suppose because I knew you wouldn't approve. Vic wasn't supposed to run to you and tell you."

"That's not exactly how it happened. Why did you think I wouldn't approve?"

"Well, you don't, do you?" Erin challenged.

He looked back at her steadily and didn't disagree, nor did he reword his question. He just waited.

"You already told me you didn't think I should have anything to do with Charley. But I'm a grown-up. I can decide for myself who I'm going to see or not see, or what to do or not do. Charley needs me, so I'm going to go give her a hand."

"Charley needs you?"

"Yes. She asked for my help. So I'm going to help her. It doesn't have anything to do with the Dysons or this murder or anything else shady. I'm not getting into anything dangerous. I'm just going to help out a friend. Family member."

Terry leaned forward, ignoring his steaming food. "Erin. This is not good. I know your instinct is to believe that she didn't have anything to do with killing Bobby Dyson, but the evidence against her is overwhelming."

"Then why are they letting her out on bail?"

"They haven't yet. If they do give her bail, it's going to be high. How is she going to pay for it? I hope you're not mortgaging the house or the bakery to help her out."

"No!" Erin was horrified at the thought. Give up her security on the chance that Charley hadn't killed Bobby Dyson and wouldn't run the first chance she was given? The second thought that she had was how glad she was that Charley hadn't asked her to. She wasn't sure what she would have done. "No, she didn't even ask. She must figure she can make bail on her own."

"Or that someone else will put up the money. Maybe even the Dysons."

"Why would they put it up?"

"Because while she's in jail, they can't do anything about her. Once she gets out, they can put a bounty on her."

"They can't do that while she's inside?"

"Well..." Terry considered. "Not as easily. Not without being traceable. Anyone who kills her on the inside is likely to get caught. If they want to get away with it, their best bet is to get her on the outside."

"But why would she take it? Wouldn't she know she was walking right into a trap?"

"I don't know. Maybe she thinks she's smart enough to get away with it."

"She must have money of her own. The apartment she lives in isn't any flophouse. And if she works for the Dysons like Jack Ward claims, then she must make pretty good money. I always thought organized crime paid pretty well."

Terry nodded slowly and took a couple of bites of his meal. "You're right. She might be using her own money."

"All I know is, I'm not putting it up. She said she was going to get out on bail, not that she needed me to pay for it." Erin pushed peas around her plate. Her stomach was hurting and she didn't feel like she could keep anything down. "What kind of evidence is there? They wouldn't be releasing her if it was overwhelming, would they? If there was that much, wouldn't they just keep her without bail?"

"I imagine she's pulled some strings. It's pretty bad, Erin. She was heard fighting with Bobby. Her fingerprints are on the murder weapon."

"He was shot? Ward said the gun was left at the scene."

"That's right."

"If she's supposed to be some kind of organized crime figure, why would she leave the gun at the scene? Wouldn't she know better?"

"People do things when they're in a panic that they wouldn't do if they were thinking. Criminals make mistakes, or we'd never catch them."

"I guess." Erin ran her finger down the side of her glass, making a track through the condensation. "So you think she did it?"

"I don't think there's any question she did it. The only question will be what she's convicted of."

"But what if she *didn't?*"

"She did, Erin."

"You thought I killed Angela Plaint. But I didn't."

"I thought..." Terry trailed off and decided that whatever argument or clarification he was going to make wasn't going to get him anywhere in the conversation. "It's not the same at all."

"You could be wrong."

"Everybody could be wrong... but it's unlikely."

Erin was quiet, thinking about it. Terry was watching her between bites.

"Tell me you'll just stay out of it, Erin."

Erin shook her head.

"Erin!"

"I know. I'm stubborn. I should listen to you because you just have my best interests in mind." How many times had she heard those words from foster parents?

Terry nodded.

"But you said if it was your brother, you'd help him."

"You're going to keep holding that over my head, aren't you?"

"I don't know why you think I'd behave any differently."

"I have training. I have connections. I'm in law enforcement, so if I get involved in an investigation, it's a little different."

Erin shrugged. "I may not have any training, but I have some experience. And I care what happens to her."

"I don't like you going there by yourself and putting yourself in the middle of this thing."

"I need to. I'm sorry, but I'm going to pick her up tomorrow and do what I can to help her out. You can't talk me out of it."

Terry's mouth tightened. He stared down at his plate and continued to eat in silence. Erin picked at her food, but didn't really have any appetite for anything.

CHAPTER 15

Late the next afternoon, Charley climbed into Erin's car and sat back with a sigh. "I appreciate you picking me up, Erin. I really… don't have anyone else to call."

Erin resisted asking her about her adoptive parents or any friends that must have lived in the area. Or what about other members of the Dyson clan? Surely some of them must have been on Charley's side. Even if Bobby Dyson's parents blamed her for his death, there had to be others who didn't.

"Did you want to go straight to your apartment? Or did you need to run any errands first?"

"The least I can do is to take you out to dinner," Charley said. "Where do you like?"

"Uh… I don't really know what's around."

"Wherever you want to go," Charley urged. "It doesn't matter. We can head back to… what neighborhood do you live in?"

Erin licked her lips. Charley fiddled with the shoulder strap of her seatbelt.

"Where do you live?" she repeated.

"Bald Eagle Falls."

Charley stopped playing with the seatbelt and looked at Erin. "Where?"

"Bald Eagle Falls."

"Is that one of the new developments on the west side?"

"No. It's a town. In the mountains."

"You don't live in Moose River?"

"No."

"How far away is Bald Eagle Falls?"

"A couple hours."

"Why didn't you tell me?"

Erin gave an embarrassed shrug. "I wanted to help you out. So I… made the time."

"That's crazy! I wouldn't have called you. I thought you said you were here in town. I guess I just assumed. I've always lived here, I thought you had too."

"I wasn't raised here—"

"I remember that," Charley interrupted. "You said you'd been raised away from here, but then you came back. Here."

"Here… to Tennessee. You weren't born in Moose River. I just meant I came back to Tennessee."

"Well, this is a mess. I guess you can stay overnight on the couch, if you like. You can head back in the morning. If you need to work. If you can take a day or two off, you're welcome to stay. You don't have to do all that driving in one day."

"I need to be at work early. It's better if I get back tonight and get a few hours of sleep in my own bed."

Charley looked at her for a minute, then shrugged. "You can do whatever you want. But you have to eat. You like sushi?"

"Uh… no. Not big on sushi. Family Style? Chinese? Pizza?"

"Pizza," Charley decided. "And for that, we can just go home and order in. You'll want some time to relax, at least."

"Sure. Sounds good."

"But I'll need to stop at the pet store on the way, can we do that? Iggy can celebrate with some worms."

"Worms?"

Crickets had been bad enough. Vic and Charley might be able to stomach wrigglers, but Erin didn't want to see Iggy eat worms any more than she wanted to eat sushi. She was queasy just thinking about it.

"As long as I don't have to do it," Erin said.

Charley laughed. "I gather you're not a reptile person."

"I didn't mind Iggy, but the bugs…" Erin gave a shudder that made Charley snicker. "I have a cat and a rabbit," Erin said, trying to make a connection with Charley. "I never had any pets as a kid, but I've acquired two since moving to Bald Eagle Falls."

"And it doesn't gross you out to feed your cat meat or fish? It's no different."

"Uh… it's a little different. I don't feed him anything that moves."

"I bet he'd like it better if you did."

"He probably would, but I'm not going to try."

"It's the natural order of things," Charley pointed out. "Predators and prey. Survival of the fittest."

Erin glanced over at her, wondering if she had a similar view of the place for violence in human society. Since human society had always been violent, did that mean it was okay? Might makes right, so use of force and deadly weapons was perfectly natural and acceptable? Charley was looking out the passenger window and didn't catch Erin's look. Erin stared at the road in front of her.

Charley directed Erin to the pet store once more, and Erin elected to sit in the car while Charley went in to get Iggy's celebratory treat. She came out with the little takeout container in a paper bag.

"All done up tight," she promised. "No worms are going to escape in your car."

"Good thing."

She knew the way from the pet store to Charley's apartment fairly well and Charley only had to redirect her a couple of times. Charley called her favorite pizza place on the way, and they arrived there just ahead of the delivery man.

Inside the apartment, Charley put the pizza and the bag from the pet store down on the kitchen island while she kicked off her shoes and sorted through her mail.

"Make yourself comfortable," she advised. "You must be tired after working all day and then driving out here. You need to get some rest in before going back to Eagle whatever."

"Bald Eagle Falls."

"The backside of the mountain," Charley scoffed. "I don't know why you'd want to live somewhere so isolated."

"It isn't like I live by myself. It's a little town, but I have friends."

Charley sighed. "More than I can say."

Erin looked again at the pizza and the pet food bag on the counter. Her stomach felt like it was filled with worms. She wasn't sure she was going to be able to eat any of the pizza with the worms in such close proximity.

"You want to see them?" Charley offered, following Erin's gaze.

"Ugh, no!"

"Oh…" Charley picked the bag up. "I see. Did you know there are places you can order crickets or mealworms on your pizza?"

Erin felt dangerously queasy. "Uh, no. I don't think I'm going to be going for that. Your pizza place doesn't, right?"

Charley snorted. "No. Too bad, I could order for myself and Iggy at the same time! We could share a pizza…"

She laughed at Erin's expression and gave the bag a little shake. "I'm going to go see the little bug-eater and give him his treat. Come and watch if you want."

"I'll just wait out here."

Charley nodded and went into the study. Erin looked around the apartment. If it was a false front, a mask for what kind of person Charley really was, it was a good one. It certainly didn't look like the apartment of a wild, rebellious child. Nor did it look like anything she envisioned a mobster living in. It was perfectly normal and not too showy. There was no sign that she normally kept weapons, drugs, or large amounts of money there.

"Okay, let's eat," Charley invited.

Erin was startled out of her serious thoughts. She was about to say that she didn't know if she could eat, but when Charley opened the pizza box and the apartment filled with the fragrant smells of garlicky tomato sauce, pepperoni, and mozzarella, her stomach gave a loud growl and she realized she was more than a little hungry.

"That smells amazing! No wonder you like this place."

Charley nodded. She got out plates, and she and Erin each grabbed a couple of slices. They sat down at the table. Erin took a bite of the pizza and contemplated the pillowy, crispy crust. "Do they offer a gluten-free option?" she asked.

"I never asked. Why, you aren't allergic, are you?"

"No, I just—"

"Are you on one of those diets? Paleo or grain free? Caveman stuff?"

"If I was, I wouldn't be eating this. No, my bakery is gluten-free and caters to special diets. I'm always on the lookout for other opportunities."

"You're going to start selling pizza?"

"I already sell some pizza crusts. And pizza pretzels. But I should check with the local pizza joint and see whether they stock a gluten-free crust for special orders, or if I could supply them with frozen crusts so they could offer them."

"Oh. Cool. Good idea. So you can eat normal food, but you bake gluten-free just as a marketing plan? For commercial opportunities?"

"No, I just want to… make sure that people who do need to follow special diets can get everything they need right in town."

Charley looked up from her pizza and gazed at Erin. "Why?"

"I had a sister… a foster sister, I mean… She was celiac, and she did a lot of damage to her system because she refused to eat gluten-free. She couldn't stand to be different than everybody else and to have to provide her own food. It was more important for her to look normal than to stay well. I want the kids in Bald Eagle Falls to be able to eat where everyone else eats and to be able to order food that looks the same as everyone else's. And the adults too."

"Well, that's nice… but I don't know how you could keep a place like that afloat. In a little town? I don't even know how a normal bakery could stay in business."

"It's been okay, especially since… the previous bakery had to close. So we only have the one. People who want regular bread can get it at the grocery, but if they want fresh bakery bread and baking….. Auntie Clem's is the only place to go. And it's good food."

"Auntie Clem's? Is that the name of your bakery?"

"Yes." Erin took a bite of her pizza. "After my—our—Aunt Clementine. She used to run a tea shop there. She left it to me when she died. I didn't want to reopen the tea shop, but I thought I would take a run at seeing if a gluten-free bakery could make it."

"Huh." Charley chewed a mouthful of pizza thoughtfully. "I never would have thought of doing something like that."

Erin shrugged and looked down at her plate.

"Go ahead and ask," Charley said. "I can tell you're dying to."

"What?"

Charley just leveled a look at her and waited.

"Okay… did you do it?"

"No."

Erin was a little surprised at the denial. She'd expected excuses and explanations, not a flat-out no.

"You didn't have a fight with Bobby Dyson and end up shooting him?"

"I had a fight with him, sure. Bobby and me were always fighting. He was a passionate guy. But I didn't kill him."

Erin looked Charley in the eye. The woman's gaze didn't waver. But Erin did realize that under Charley's makeup there was something more than bags under her eyes. She hadn't managed to completely cover up a black eye. Erin remembered Terry's comment about the state of Bobby Dyson's room. It had, she guessed, been more than just a heated argument.

"Did he hit you?"

Charley touched the bruise briefly, as if checking to see if it were still there. "He was a passionate guy," she repeated.

"Was it self-defense?"

"I told you, I didn't kill him. I have an alibi, so they're not convicting me of anything."

"You have an alibi?" It was the first Erin had heard mention of this.

"Yeah. I was out with girlfriends. They'll confirm it. Like I say, nobody is railroading me for Bobby's murder. It wasn't me."

"Then how…? People heard you there. The gun had your fingerprints on it."

Charley raised her eyebrows. "How do you know that?"

"I… talked to Jack Ward."

"Why would he tell you my fingerprints were on the weapon? They're not going to reveal details like that to the public."

Erin wasn't sure what to say. Charley had already demonstrated some suspicion toward Erin, accusing her of being a police plant. How was she going to react if Erin told her that her boyfriend was a policeman and that he'd been in contact with Jack Ward?

"You're a terrible liar," Charley said, "so how about the truth?"

"I didn't say anything; how do you know if I'm a bad liar?"

"Because everything you think is written on your face. Haven't you ever played poker?"

Erin shifted uncomfortably. "I think I used to be a better liar. Or maybe it's just because it's you. I don't want to lie to you."

"Then don't." Charley's voice was stern. She looked Erin straight in the eye. "Obviously, you're not a cop, or you wouldn't be having any trouble telling me a believable story. So why would Ward be telling you any details of the case? Unless the two of you…" she held up two crossed fingers. "Maybe you had some extracurricular time away from the police station?"

"No. No, not Ward."

"Ah. Who, then?"

Erin dropped her eyes to her pizza, uncomfortable with the scrutiny. "I know the police in Bald Eagle Falls."

"And they thought they'd share the details with you."

"They didn't want me to come and help you."

"Because I'm a murderer. Already convicted in their minds."

Erin shrugged.

Charley shook her head. "Well, get this through your head. I have an alibi. Whoever Bobby was arguing with, it wasn't me. And if my fingerprints are on any gun there, it was a frame. Maybe there really was a gun with my fingerprints there. Or maybe the police just made it up. My gun is still here and I never touched any of Bobby's."

Erin was relieved. She glanced around the room. "You keep a gun here? Is that safe?"

"Yes, it's safe. That's how I keep myself safe."

"The police didn't confiscate it?"

"It's in a safe." Charley went suddenly still. For a moment, she sat there frozen, then she jumped to her feet and ran out of the room. She popped into her study, and was back a few seconds later, swearing like a sailor. "They stole my safe. Just grabbed the whole thing and took it with them! They can't just take my property!"

"If they thought it had something to do with the murder…"

"Something like what? They already had the weapon, why would they take mine, unless they wanted to screw with the evidence? They're going to swap my gun with the one at the scene, and say that it was mine all along. That's why Ward said it had my prints on it. Because they planted my gun!" She swore loudly.

"They wouldn't do that," Erin protested.

"Oh, they would do anything they could to get me permanently behind bars. Or in the ground. If they tell Bobby's family that I'm the one who killed him…"

Erin kept her mouth closed to prevent herself from defending the police a second time. She wasn't the one who was in Charley's position. Charley obviously knew the situation with the Moose River police much better than Erin did. Just because the police Erin knew wouldn't have ever dared contaminate evidence, that didn't mean that all police would be just as diligent and honest. Terry had leaped into action on a previous case in order to keep Alton Summers from being killed, even though he was a miserable specimen of a human being and continued to harass Erin. Summers had initially been hired by Clementine's estate to track Erin down, but after he spent his money from that job, he'd been back, trying to blackmail her into giving him more. Even so, Terry had been willing to protect him as a citizen, and Erin knew he would never do like Charley suggested and encourage the Dysons to take her out of the picture.

Charley started to pace back and forth, her movements tight and controlled.

"They wouldn't dare do anything without Dwight's blessing," she said, obviously talking to herself more than to Erin. "So it's him I've got to talk to. If I can. How am I going to get a call through to him?"

"You won't get anywhere without asking," Erin said.

Charley stopped and looked at Erin, looking baffled to find anyone in the same room as she was.

"Just ask. That's your suggestion? Just call them up and say I want to talk to Dwight Dyson."

"If he's the only one who can help you. What good is it going to do to talk to anyone else? Or to beat around the bush and try to get to him another way. If he thinks you might be Bobby's killer, won't he want to talk to you? To get your story?"

Charley laughed. "You know nothing about how it works in the family. This isn't about justice. It's about vengeance. And you get that wherever you can. If it looks like someone is unfaithful to the family, you get rid of them. It doesn't matter whether they really are or not. If people think that they are, that's more than enough reason to get rid of them."

"Call," Erin urged again. "What's the worst that can happen?"

"They know I'm here and come here and kill me. And you too, for good measure."

"Won't they already know you're here?"

Charley resumed her pacing. "Of course they'll know. They'll know I was getting bail. Either they pulled strings for me to get it, or they had someone keeping tabs and would know. They just watch for me to get back here. If they wanted to, they could already have come up here and killed me."

She stopped and looked at Erin.

"Does that mean they don't want to? If they wanted to, they could have done it by now?"

Erin shrugged and didn't point out that they might simply have wanted her to get nice and worked up first. Maybe they wanted her to fully realize what kind of trouble she was in before taking care of her. It wouldn't be quite as satisfying to just take her out at the first opportunity, without seeing that understanding on her face.

Charley picked up her phone from where she'd left it on the table beside her plate. Then she put it down. Then she picked it up again. She stared down at it in her hand. Finally, she started moving her thumb over the virtual keys. She put the phone up to her ear, and breathed out a long, heavy breath.

"This is stupid," she said quietly. "This has seriously got to be the stupidest thing I've ever done in my life."

After waiting for several rings, she apparently got an answer.

"It's Charley Campbell. I need to speak with him."

A pause while she listened.

"I need to talk to him. And he's going to want to talk to me. You know what happened, don't you? You think he's going to be happy if he hears that I tried to get ahold of him, and you wouldn't put it through? He's going to start by cutting off your fingers and feeding them to you. Is that how you want to die?"

Apparently it was not, because after waiting in silence for the next few minutes, Erin could tell by Charley's face that it was ringing again. She seemed to withdraw into herself. She looked lost and bleak. Erin wished she could give Charley a hug and make it all better. But Charley had gotten herself into something that a hug wasn't going to fix.

What about the police? Did they really want the Dyson clan to just murder Bobby's killer, eliminating the need for the state to do anything in regard to prosecuting her? It was much cleaner and cheaper if the Dysons would just kill each other. Or had they also stationed guards to watch for Charley, and to watch for anyone else who was watching for Charley, to try to protect her?

"Dwight." Charley's voice was hoarse, almost a whisper. "Yeah… it's Charley." She swallowed. "I didn't kill him. I swear it. You know I loved Bobby. I'd never do anything to hurt him. I'd never kill him. The cops are setting me up. I just got home, and they've taken my gun safe. That means they've got my gun, and they're going to swap it for the one that was found at the apartment and make sure everything points to me. But I didn't do it. I wouldn't do anything to hurt him."

She stopped speaking. Erin couldn't hear what was being said on the other end of the conversation. She pictured Dwight Dyson, a godfather with a Tennessee accent, sitting behind a big black walnut desk and giving Charley his theory of the crime.

"I don't know what happened," Charley said. "I don't know who it was. Some guy—I don't know. I wasn't even there."

Erin watched Charley, frowning, trying to follow everything that was being said when she could only hear half the conversation. It was like dinner theater, except that she knew gangsters could come through the door to end it at any time, and she and Charley had no way to protect themselves. She wasn't at home, there was no Terry Piper to save the day. Though they might actually have 9-1-1 service, and Erin could covertly call the police while Charley was on her call…

"Maybe it was a hit and it was meant to look like it was me. A frame. I was out with the girls…"

Erin slid her own phone out of her pocket. If she called 9-1-1, could they trace it to her location? Would they find her if she didn't say anything? How about if she texted? Could she text 9-1-1? Erin glanced at the apartment door. It was still shut. No intruders. No Tennessee mafia showing up to kill them. Had Dwight Dyson called them off when he took Charley's call, or did he want to hear it go down while he was still on the phone with her?

"You've got to believe me," Charley begged.

Her shoulders dipped down and her eyes closed. Erin thought for a moment she was going to faint, but then Charley lowered her phone and looked down at its blank screen.

"What did he say?" Erin squeaked.

"I'm supposed to go talk to him. He's sending someone over to take me there."

Then there was a knock on the door.

Erin and Charley both stared at each other, wide-eyed with alarm.

"It's them," Charley hissed.

"How did they get here so fast?"

"They didn't. They were already here. Just like I said."

She reluctantly went to the door, unlocked it, and turned the handle to face her visitors. Erin couldn't see the man clearly. The angle she was at to the door obscured most of her view. It took a minute for her to realize what was wrong with him. He wore a ski mask to obscure his face. Erin's stomach tightened, even more anxious than before. Wouldn't the Dyson clan soldiers be guys that Charley already knew? Why would he cover his face? And was it odd that there was only one of them? She had been expecting two, at least. The eye holes turned in Erin's direction for a minute, then the man took Charley by the arm and pulled her firmly through the door. Erin covered her mouth and tried to keep from screaming or calling out after her. But the masked man didn't take Charley away. The door did not shut again, and Erin could still see their figures in the hall. The masked man stood close to Charley, and his words were too quiet for Erin to make anything out. Charley's body language exuded confidence that Erin certainly didn't have. She suspected that Charley didn't either; it was just a bluff.

It was only a minute or two before Charley slipped back in through the door, alone again. She looked at Erin, her forehead wrinkled and sweat gathering at her hairline.

"What happened?" Erin asked.

"He told me to get out. He said the clan was coming after me and that I should run. Disappear. Never show my face here again."

Erin nodded slowly. She wasn't sure why that was so surprising. "Who is he, then? Not someone from the clan?"

"No. He's not."

"Do you know him?"

"He was—no. I don't. I have no idea who he is."

"Not a policeman?"

"A policeman wouldn't tell me to disappear. I'm on bail. If I disappear, they don't get to prosecute me. If they don't want the Dysons to kill me, then they want to prosecute me."

Erin's head was whirling. "Then who is it? Another gang? Do the Dysons have a rival? Or is it someone from your family that wants to protect you?"

"No, I said I don't know him. It isn't someone from my family."

"Should we go? Before the guys Dwight sent get here?"

Charley bit her lip, considering, then shook her head. "I'll look guilty to the Dysons. And I can't disappear that fast, I need to make arrangements—get money and ID. Make a plan. I can't just run out of here and be gone."

They both looked at the still-open apartment door.

"You should go," Charley told Erin. "You shouldn't be here when they arrive. I don't want you getting mixed up in this."

"I don't want to leave you like this…"

"Go on." Charley made shooing motions. "I shouldn't have brought you here in the first place. I wasn't thinking. Thanks for helping out with Iggy, but I think I'd better not call you again. It wasn't a good idea. We've lived this long without knowing about each other. I don't think we should talk to each other again."

Erin walked toward the door, anxious and uncertain. She looked back at Charley but, like someone trying to chase away a puppy, Charley again made motions for her to scram. As Erin walked down the hall, the elevator dinged and the doors slid open.

There were the men from the clan. Almost twins in appearance, tall and spare, with blond sun-kissed hair and freckled faces. They weren't in mafioso suits, but they weren't in shabby t-shirts either. They had on polo shirts and slacks with sharply-pressed creases. They moved with purpose down the hall toward Charley's apartment.

They obviously knew Charley by sight, because they didn't spare Erin a second glance. She walked right by them without either one registering her presence. Erin got on the elevator and, as the doors closed, watched them enter Charley's apartment.

Erin was in a daze as she rode the elevator down to the main floor and headed over to her car. She was completely unaware of anything going on around her. It was dark, and she should have been far more worried than she was about being alone in a strange parking lot in the city.

Someone hit her hard from behind, slamming her into the body of her car. Erin tried to fight her way free from the man's grip, but there was no use.

"Be still and I won't hurt you," he whispered in her ear.

Erin was sure that was what all muggers and rapists told their victims. *Be still. Be quiet. I'm not going to hurt you.*

"Let me go, or I'm going to scream."

"I know who you are, Erin Price, and you need to stay out of this."

Erin was paralyzed hearing her name come out of his lips. How would anyone know who she was? She wasn't from Moose

River. No one in Moose River knew her. Only Charley and the police. And Charley had said it wasn't the police who had warned her to run. Likewise, Erin didn't think the police would be whispering warnings to her in the parking lot.

"Who are you?"

"Did you hear me?" His arm was against the back of her neck, pushing her harder against the car. "I know who you are. Stay out of it. It has nothing to do with you. Go back home, and never come back here or make contact with Charlotte Campbell again."

Erin couldn't raise her voice to answer him. She was so shocked by the sudden attack that she couldn't think of what to say to him. She couldn't argue with him, couldn't figure out who he was. She couldn't put her brain into gear to figure out the best course of action. She just stayed there, frozen, pressed up against her car.

"I know where you live. I know who your friends are. You wouldn't want anything to happen to anyone you love, would you?"

Erin swallowed. "Leave me alone."

He gave her another shove. "Why do you have to be so stubborn? You just don't understand how this works, do you? You may fancy yourself an amateur detective, but you don't know anything. Stay away from Charlotte and just let things take their natural course. Quit poking around and stirring up trouble. Go home and make cookies."

*E*rin sat in her car and shook.

She told herself it was just the adrenaline. It would make anyone shaky. She'd been unexpectedly attacked and threatened, and it was only natural for her to react emotionally and physically.

She checked again to be sure the car doors were locked. Could she drive all the way back to Bald Eagle Falls without having an accident? Or should she call Terry or someone else for help? The trouble was, it would take anyone from Bald Eagle Falls two hours to get there, just to have to turn around and drive another two hours home. She couldn't sit there in the parking lot for two hours waiting. Even if Terry used his lights and siren, it was still going to take a significant amount of time for him to get there. Assuming he could get someone to cover for him if it was his turn to be on call.

Erin turned the key and tightened her grip on the steering wheel, trying to ground herself. She could drive home. There was nothing to it. The trip down the highway would be soothing. It was just what she needed to relax. She backed out of her parking space and focused on the journey.

The fixer watched Erin drive away, fuming to himself. Charlotte Campbell was supposed to run as soon as she got out on bail, and instead she had ended up meeting with Erin Price. One of the very people that the boss didn't want her near.

He continued to surveil the building, hoping to see Charlotte leaving with a hastily-packed bag. Her car was in its reserved space. Did she not realize the danger she was in if she stayed around? The Dysons would be out for blood. They weren't going to listen to any fanciful stories about the appearance of a mysterious stranger. They would simply put her in the ground for Bobby Dyson's death.

Instead of being rewarded with the sight of her emerging with her luggage and making straight for her parked car, the fixer saw Charlotte exit the building between two of the Dyson boys. There were no visible weapons trained on her, but she had undoubtedly been threatened and they would have whatever arsenal was needed to ensure her compliance.

The fixer was a little surprised that they would remove her from the apartment rather than just leaving her body there in a pool of blood. But they surely had a plan and were acting under orders. Charlotte Campbell looked as cool and collected as if she were headed out for a Sunday stroll in the park. Like a lamb to the slaughter.

CHAPTER 18

*E*rin was calm when she got home. The shakes had disappeared. But she didn't want to be alone and it was going to be hours before she was ready to sleep, which meant another caffeine-charged day at the bakery.

Willie's car wasn't parked anywhere that Erin could see, so she figured he must be off on a job. Willie always had something going on. Even over the Christmas holidays, it had been hard to get him to commit to a time when they could all get together. Erin picked up Marshmallow and cuddled with him on the couch. Orange Blossom yowled and complained and, after telling her all of his troubles, jumped up on the couch next to her and butted her with the top of his head, demanding that she give him just as much attention as she was giving Marshmallow. Erin rubbed and scratched both of them until they eventually settled comfortably against her, Blossom purring and Marshmallow flicking his ear every few minutes.

"You wouldn't believe the critter my sister has," Erin told them. "Green and scaly, eyes that go two separate directions, and a tongue that's twice as long as he is! What a thing."

With both pets quiet and content, Erin texted Vic and then Terry to see if they wanted to come visit.

Vic only had to cover the back yard, so she was the first to get there. She didn't bother knocking; Erin considered it Vic's home just as much as her own.

"You're back! How did everything go?"

Orange Blossom abandoned his place beside Erin. He jumped to the floor and stretched his back, then flopped over and offered his belly to Vic for a scratch.

"Watch out for his pointy ends!" Erin warned. Though, of course, Vic knew this as well as she did. Orange Blossom would tolerate a tummy scratch for all of about five seconds, and then would attempt to grab Vic's hand with his front paws while kicking with his back. An unwary victim would end up being raked with claws from all four 'pointy ends.' Vic gave Orange Blossom's belly one quick scrub, then picked him up to cuddle, and sat down on one of the easy chairs.

"So, Charley is out on bail? Everything is okay?"

"She's out, but everything is… pretty uncertain. I'm really worried about what's going to happen to her."

Vic frowned. "Why? What happened?"

Erin looked at her phone to read Terry's text response, then slid it away. "May as well wait for Terry, then I don't have to explain twice."

"Okay, sure."

They played with the animals.

"Did you eat?" Vic asked.

"Yeah… pizza." Erin tried to remember how much of it she had eaten. Had she even finished one slice? It had been good pizza, but once their conversation had turned to matters of Charley's safety, Erin wasn't sure she had eaten anything more. She shook her head. Either way, she wasn't hungry. She didn't need anything else before hitting the sack. "Where's Willie? Not around today?"

"No. He had an *important* job. Not sure what, but he didn't know when he would be back."

"Out of town, then?"

"I guess so."

Erin stroked Marshmallow's long, velvety ears. "He doesn't tell you what he does?"

"Sometimes. It just depends on what kind of job it is, I guess. There are plenty of times he'll tell me who he's working for and what he's doing for them. But other times it's confidential... I just don't ask. He tells me what he wants to offer."

Erin supposed it was no different from Terry with his police work. Sometimes, he had no qualms telling Erin about what he was up to. Other times, he had to protect the privacy of the citizens he served.

There was a soft knock on the front door, and Vic got up to answer it, depositing Orange Blossom on the couch beside Erin so she wouldn't get clawed up when Blossom spotted K9 and decided to make his disapproval known.

Terry entered and settled on the couch with Erin, giving her a hug and then touching her cheek with the back of his fingers. It was one of those rare occasions when he was wearing a t-shirt instead of his uniform. Obviously, not on call.

"You're pale. Too many late nights?" he asked.

"I guess, yeah."

"I figured you'd be heading to bed. You're going to get sick if you keep staying out late."

"I can't get to sleep yet. Terry... do you know any more details about Bobby Dyson's murder? Or could you get more?"

He settled back, the cleft in his chin more pronounced than usual. "I thought you were going to leave it alone."

"I'm not," Erin said, surprising herself with the vehemence in her own voice. "The more people tell me to stay away from it, the more sure I am that there's something going on. It wasn't Charley. She's being set up."

Vic and Terry both shook their heads automatically. But they didn't know anything. They just didn't want her looking into it.

"I know you're worried that I'm going to get mixed up somehow with this Dyson family. I get that. They're... scary.

They're dangerous. But I'm not doing something that's against their interests, I want to find out who really killed Bobby."

"What makes you think it isn't Charley?" Terry asked. "She was heard there. Her fingerprints are on the weapon. You can't get much more certain that that."

"But what if it's a setup? What if the female voice the neighbors heard wasn't Charley? What if the gun was a plant? What if the police are setting her up?"

"Contrary to what you see on TV, that's not something that's usually done," Terry said. "Sure, half the people who get arrested are going to tell you they were set up or that drugs or weapons found in a search were planted by the police, but that doesn't make it true. Most police officers would never consider tampering with evidence."

"But that doesn't mean it never happens. And with cases that do involve criminals who keep getting away with breaking the law over and over again, don't the police get more and more frustrated? It would get more and more tempting to do something about it to get the person put behind bars."

Terry shrugged. "Again… TV. Do you think I would do that?"

"Get tempted? I don't know. You're human, so I assume you could be tempted just like anyone else."

"I just do my job. It isn't my job to ensure convictions. Just to make sure that there is enough evidence to perform an arrest. If they get off, that's not on me. That part isn't my job."

"I just want to know what else you know about Charley's case. You talked to Jack Ward, right? So tell me what you found out. Were there any other fingerprints on the gun?"

Terry hesitated. He looked at Erin and at Vic, then down at K9. "Yes, there were unidentified prints on the gun. Most of them too obscured to get a good match. The ones that were clear had not been identified. But it takes longer to get a hit when you don't have a short list of suspects to compare it against. It isn't like you can just pop it into the scanner and have an identity ten minutes later. Not usually."

"Was the gun registered to Charley?"

"No. Still registered to a previous owner. It changed hands a number of times, and the final owner never registered the change of ownership."

"So it wasn't Charley's."

"They can't prove it was Charley's. That doesn't mean it was not."

"She said her gun was still in the gun safe in her apartment. But the safe wasn't there, so the police must have confiscated it in their search."

"Which would be within their rights. They would need to catalog any firearms and to account for any that might have been registered to her."

"Did they take her safe? Was her gun still inside?"

Terry gazed at her. "I'd have to ask Jack Ward. That's not the kind of thing he would just offer up to me in casual conversation. And by now, he's probably heard about the connection between the two of us, so he's not going to want to divulge details to me that he knows are going to get back to you."

"She says they're going to swap her gun for the one that was found at the scene. As proof that it was her."

"They can't do that when the other gun has already been logged and its serial number noted."

"Then don't you think it at least points to the fact that it wasn't Charley? If it was her, why would her gun still be at home? Whose gun did she use?"

"There's nothing to stop her from owning more than one gun. If I was going to kill my boyfriend, I would choose the unregistered gun over the one registered in my name."

"But they don't think it was premeditated, do they? She didn't go there to kill him."

"We don't know that. If he was cheating on her—and from what I understand, there's no question of that fact—that might be exactly why she went there."

"What if it wasn't her he was arguing with? If he was cheating on her with other women, couldn't it have been one of the other women who confronted and killed him?"

"Witnesses say it was Charley. I'm sure the Moose River police department will be getting whatever surveillance video is available inside and outside the building."

"If they just heard her, it could have been someone else. They might have just assumed it was her. They probably didn't hear Bobby calling her by name…"

"Erin… you're so determined to prove that it wasn't Charley. But what if it was?"

"I just… can't believe that." Erin closed her eyes, trying to separate her emotions from the facts of the case. "My parents… they're gone. Maybe their deaths were accidental, but if they'd made better choices… maybe they'd still be around. I just found Charley. I don't want to lose her. And I don't want to think that she's a murderer. I want… a sister."

She let out a long, shaky breath. "Before I left her place… a couple of the guys from the Dyson gang came to get her. And someone… threatened me to stay off of the case. Someone who knew my name."

"What do you mean, someone?"

"He came up behind me, so I didn't see him. It was a man. Bigger than me. Strong. But I never saw him."

"He knew you?"

"He called me by name. He knew I was from Bald Eagle Falls. He knew I was a baker."

Terry scratched the back of his neck, frowning. "Those are all basic background, but it's still disturbing. He would have to know who you were to look you up. And you aren't known in Moose River. Or at least, you weren't. You were questioned when Charley was arrested, so your name is on the police records. They could have a leak."

"Did you recognize his voice?" Vic asked.

Erin tried to replay it in her head, and immediately shook her head. "No. He was whispering. So I couldn't recognize it."

"Words he said? Phrases? Diction?" Terry interrogated.

"No… not that I can think of. It was all so fast. It's not like it was a long conversation. He just told me to stay away from Charley. To stop causing trouble."

"I'd tell you that myself if I thought it would do any good," Terry said in a teasing tone. Erin knew that he was partially serious. He had told her and would probably continue to tell her the same thing, but Erin had already proven that she wasn't going to listen to his warnings. It was a source of frustration for Terry, but Erin couldn't make herself abandon her sister just because her friends were worried she was going to get in some kind of trouble.

"I don't know who it was," Erin said. "But it did kind of freak me out. I guess you're right about the police knowing who I was, and maybe someone leaking the information… I was afraid it was someone I knew here in Bald Eagle Falls."

They were silent, thinking about it. They'd all had run-ins with various members of the community who were not as welcoming or pleasant as they ought to be. But no one was going to start throwing accusations around.

"You're sure it was a man?" Vic asked.

Erin looked at Vic, disconcerted. The crisp line that she used to see between male and female had blurred since she had met Vic. Her experience with Vic and the few things that Vic had shared about her growing-up years and her gender identity made Erin reluctant to classify anyone's gender without knowing how they self-identified.

"Uh… no. I'm assuming it was the same person who warned Charley to get out of town before the Dysons showed up, and I thought that he was a man. But I only caught a glimpse and he was wearing a mask.

Terry's expression was almost comical. Erin realized she was telling the whole story out of sequence and he was getting more frustrated and angry with each revelation.

"Oh… uh, yeah… Somebody came to Charley's apartment… and…"

"And warned her to get out of town," Terry finished. "A man with a mask, apparently."

Erin nodded.

"What kind of mask?"

"Like a ski mask. I could just see the eye holes."

"And possibly that it was a man."

"I thought so, yes."

"Height? Build?"

"It was just a glimpse, across the room, through a doorway…"

"You saw him near a doorway? Did his head reach the top?"

"No. Just… average height, I guess. A strong build… you know, not blocky or paunchy, but… not slender."

"All pretty average. That's not very helpful in identifying him."

"I know. I wish I could tell you more…"

"Any tattoos? Anything else that would help identify him? Something you'd recognize if you saw again?"

"No."

Terry pondered the clues they had. "So he warned Charley to take off before the Dysons showed up. And he told you to leave town, to go home and forget about her."

"So it doesn't sound like he was aligned with the police or the Dysons, does it?" Erin said. "That's what I can't figure out."

Erin pulled out her phone and looked at the screen. She told herself she was only checking the time, but she was checking to see whether Charley had called too. Charley had said she wasn't going to involve Erin any more, because she didn't want to put her in harm's way. But Erin was hoping she would have changed her mind. Surely she would want to tell someone about what happened when she went to see Dwight Dyson, wouldn't she? If she were still alive to tell the tale.

"What is it?" Vic asked.

"I was just hoping… Charley would have called me. I wish I knew if she was okay."

"Are you afraid that this masked man might have done something to her?"

"No, the Dysons. She was going to talk to one of them... I don't know if he's the head of the family, or Bobby Dyson's father, or both. But she said the only way she was going to be able to convince them that she hadn't killed Bobby was to talk to him face-to-face."

"That's a pretty dangerous proposition," Terry commented.

"I know. She was pretty scared about it. But she figured if she didn't talk to him, they were going to kill her anyway. So I guess... she really didn't have much choice one way or the other." Erin rubbed her forehead. It was pulsing with fatigue. "I just don't know what to do. It's not like I can call the police to tell them what happened. She doesn't want the police involved. And I can't call the Dyson family to see what's happened. Charley said not to contact her again. But how can I go through life not even knowing if she's alive or not?" A few tears escaped Erin's eyes and dripped down her face.

Terry rubbed her back. Orange Blossom squirmed away from Vic and jumped back up onto the couch, where he climbed over Terry and Marshmallow to reach Erin and bump her face with the top of his head. Erin scratched his ears, sniffling.

"This has been really hard on you," Terry observed. "I never expected it to turn into something like this."

"You guys all said to stay away from her when you found out about the Dysons. I guess I should have. I would have been better off not knowing what was going on."

Neither of them argued with the statement, but they both looked sympathetic.

"Should I call her?" Erin asked. "Do you think it would be okay?"

"If she told you not to... maybe you shouldn't," Vic said tentatively.

"How about Jack Ward?" Erin appealed to Terry. "Do you think we could call him tomorrow and see if he knows anything? Maybe he'll give you a little more information about the murder... and he could check in on Charley, see if she's okay?"

"I suppose we could check," Terry conceded. "But don't expect to be able to get anything out of Ward. Chances are, he's going to keep his cards pretty close to his chest."

"Okay." Erin rubbed her eyes. "I just hope she's okay."

There was a tap at the door, and the three of them looked at each other, startled. Terry put his hand on his holster, which he was wearing even with his casual clothes.

"It's not Willie," Vic whispered, "he would have let me know if his plans changed."

It was too late for casual visitors. Terry got up and moved to the door. He checked the peephole and his stance relaxed. He opened the door and ushered their visitor in with a half-smile.

"Adele!" Vic, unencumbered by animals, jumped up to greet her.

Erin made a little gesture indicating that she would get up, but Adele motioned her back. "No need. I just saw your light on and popped in to make sure everything was okay. You're not usually up this late."

"I just got back from Moose River," Erin explained. She looked at her phone, and realized that quite a bit of time had elapsed since she had made it home. It was getting very late. "Oh... a while ago."

"You're okay?" The tall, spare woman peered at Erin, looking like she didn't quite believe it. "You look a little piqued."

"Things are... not so great. I'm tired and I'm worried and I'm hyped up. My heart is still pumping like a train engine, I don't know how I'm going to get to sleep tonight."

"Let me make you some tea," Adele said, heading into the kitchen without an invitation. "Do you have any herbs?"

Orange Blossom jumped down, figuring that anyone in the kitchen was fair game for him to beg for an extra treat. Erin moved to get up to help Adele, but Terry sat back down beside her, taking her hand to keep her seated. "Stay and relax. I'm sure she can find her way around. You two both need to relax and get some sleep before work."

Vic shrugged. "I'll just take an Ambien and be out like a light."

"I'd be too dopey if I did that. I'd be hung over." Erin knew her limits. She had a few herbal sleeping remedies, but anything pharmacy grade would still affect her in the morning.

She could hear Adele putting the kettle on the stove and opening various cupboards to see where everything was.

"Should somebody be keeping an eye on her in there?" Vic whispered anxiously. "What if she… makes a potion?"

"A sleeping potion?" Erin suggested, trying to keep a smile from her face.

"No… I don't know, something else…"

"You're the one who said that witches don't actually perform magic," Erin pointed out.

"I know that… but she could still make something that… affected you the wrong way. She could poison you."

"With a policeman right here?"

"She could poison him too."

Terry shook his head. It was clear from his expression that he was also trying to keep from smiling at Vic's concerns. "I won't drink anything, Vic. You and Erin can have it. I don't need to be up as early as you do. I still have plenty of time to get to bed."

"I'm not drinking it!" Vic insisted.

"Why not?" Adele was standing in the doorway. "Do you really think I would try to poison or magick you, Victoria?"

Vic turned a brilliant red at having been overheard. "No! No, I know you wouldn't do anything, I just mean… I just was worried that… I don't know, you're not exactly *licensed*."

"Does someone need to be licensed to serve tea now? I wasn't aware of this new requirement."

"You can serve the tea," Erin laughed. "But it looks like you and I will be the only ones who are having any."

"I'll have it ready in a minute. Just waiting for the kettle to boil."

"Thanks, Adele. That's really nice of you."

"Just want to do right by my boss. She's a pretty nice person, you know."

Adele disappeared back into the kitchen. Vic covered her face and then dropped her hands back down to look at Erin. "I'm so embarrassed!"

"I don't know why you're so worried about Adele. She's never done anything to hurt any of us."

"It's the way I was raised. I guess I still have a few prejudices I didn't realize I had," Vic admitted.

In a few minutes, Adele brought a tea cup to Erin and sat down with one of her own.

"Try to let your troubles go," she advised. "Release them… tomorrow morning when you are refreshed, things will not seem as bad."

Erin nodded. "Yes… things are always worst at night when you're tired."

"Let it all go tonight. Tomorrow is another day."

Erin smelled the tea before sipping it. There were many tins, bags, and boxes of teas of all kinds in Clementine's cupboards. Clementine had been forced by her poor health to close the tea shop, but that had apparently not stopped her from enjoying a wide variety of teas herself. When Erin closed her eyes and breathed in the aroma, she could see her younger self helping Clementine in the tea shop when her mother left her there for Clementine to keep an eye on. Erin loved to identify each of the teas by smell, and was right ninety-nine percent of the time.

"Is it okay?" Adele asked softly.

"Chamomile and lemon balm," Erin guessed. "Good Night Tea." She opened her eyes again.

Adele smiled broadly. "Yes, that's right. You know your teas."

"The nose knows." Erin tapped the side of her nose and took another breath of the steam before bringing the teacup up to her mouth to have a sip.

CHAPTER 19

Erin and Vic had a bit of a rough morning getting up and getting prepared to open. Erin was still tired and found that it made her clumsy as well as a little bit irritable. Part of her irritability also had to do with her concern about Charley, and the fact that she still didn't even know whether Charley was alive or dead.

Vic seemed better-rested than Erin, though she too seemed a little thick-headed, having to write some of her labels twice and to pull out the calculator for math she could normally do in her head. Together, they managed to bungle their way through the pre-opening routine and eventually the morning rush as well. They normally took their lunch early, and Terry stopped by to see if he could take Erin away for a few minutes. She promised Vic she would be back soon, and went with Terry to the police department in the Town Hall. Terry closed the door to his office and turned on the speaker phone to call Jack Ward.

It didn't take him long to get past the receptionist, and then they heard Ward's gruff voice over the speaker.

"Jack, it's Terry Piper in Bald Eagle Falls. I've got Erin Price with me."

Ward grunted. "You got something for me?"

"Actually, we were hoping for a little information from you."

"It's still an active investigation," Ward said, his words clipped and impatient. "I don't have anything to share with you."

"Erin might have a few things that you are unaware of," Terry said. "But she would like a little information in return."

"It's not a two-way street. We can't release anything to a civilian."

"Which is why I'm the one calling you," Terry said. "I figured you might be able to tell me…"

"Not when it's going straight to the ears of the public," Ward countered, not giving an inch.

"Do you know where Charlotte Campbell is this morning?"

There was silence for a moment while Ward considered the question. Erin could hear papers being moved around.

"Why do you ask?" Ward asked cautiously.

"Charlotte was visited by a couple of the Dyson boys yesterday. Erin was concerned that something might happen to her."

"Then why did Miss Price not call emergency or call my number yesterday?"

"I didn't know what to do," Erin protested. "She called them and was okay with them coming over… so I didn't think it was an emergency. I didn't know what to do."

"You should have called me anyway. I'll have someone follow up with her, but it's a little late now. If she was in any danger, it's way too late to do anything about it now."

Erin's stomach was tight, cramped up with the fear that Ward was right and it was too late to do anything for Charley.

"There was apparently another man who came by Charley's last night as well," Terry informed Ward. Erin put her hand out to stop him, not sure she wanted anyone else to know about the masked man, but Terry ignored her and continued on. "He told Charley to get out of town, and Erin to go home and stay out of the way."

"Not bad advice for Miss Price," Ward grumbled. "Who is this guy?"

"Erin doesn't know. He was wearing a ski mask. But he knew her name and where she was from."

"It's a small community. Wouldn't take much to find out who she was. Are you okay, Miss Price?" His voice was still gruff, but noticeably softer. "Did he hurt you?"

"No, I'm okay," Erin found herself choking up at his more sympathetic approach. "He grabbed me and pushed me up against the car, but he didn't really hurt me. Just scared me."

"You should have called me. You'll need to file an official report."

Erin shook her head. "An official report of what? Like I said, he didn't hurt me, and I don't know who he is."

"It's still an assault. Did he threaten you? That's a second charge."

Erin tried to remember all of the man's words to her. "No... I don't think he said anything that would be considered a threat. He said he knew who my friends were. Told me to go home and stay away from the investigation."

"Like I said, that's good advice."

Tears escaped the corners of Erin's eyes. She wiped at them, trying not to let Terry see she was crying or to sob or sniffle so that Ward would be able to hear. Terry reached over and rubbed her shoulder, which didn't help stanch the flow of tears.

"Jack, how sure are your witnesses that it was Charley they heard fighting with Bobby Dyson?"

"It was Charley. She was well-known to the neighbors."

"It couldn't have been another woman? Bobby Dyson might have been seeing others."

"Of course he was seeing others. But they didn't come to his apartment. Charlotte was his official girlfriend and the others were kept out of sight."

"That doesn't mean one of them couldn't have shown up."

"We're sure it was Charley," Ward said flatly.

"She said she had an alibi," Erin protested. "She said once you checked her alibi, you'd know it wasn't her."

Ward's derisive snort carried over the phone line. "Her iron-clad alibi? Yeah, that's not going to hold any water."

"You think it's fabricated?" Terry guessed.

"She and her girlfriends were out enjoying chimichangas and margaritas. We have independent verification until about one in the morning. After that, everything falls apart. The party broke up and went their separate directions. Charley has a couple of the ladies saying that they went out together for a nightcap at that point, and then she went back to her own apartment to hit the sack."

"So she does have an alibi," Erin asserted.

"Until one. After that, no one saw Charley with the others. No surveillance cameras. No waiters or bartenders. Just her girl-friends. She's asked them to cover for her."

Erin recalled how Charley had said she had no other friends. But apparently, she'd had friends that night. Maybe they figured they'd done enough for Charley and she couldn't tap them for anything else.

"Charley Campbell killed Bobby Dyson," Ward growled. "She did it and we know it. The judge was stupid to grant her bail, but sometimes judges can be bought. The Dysons aren't exactly short on cash."

"You think the clan paid her bond?" Terry asked.

"I don't know whether they paid it, or whether she paid it out of her own ill-gotten gains. Either way, you can bet it was origi-nally Dyson money. And either way, she was stupid to bond out. She would have been a lot safer in isolation at the jail than on the outside."

Terry cleared his throat. "Is there any way you can follow up and find out if she is okay today?"

"I already said I would. You should have called last night."

"Yes," Erin agreed in a small voice. "I guess I should have."

When Terry hung up the phone, he looked at Erin. "Are you okay?"

"I guess… it's been harder on me than I thought. I know Charley and I have lived completely different lives, and I've only had a few days to get to know her a little… but I let myself get attached to her. She's my sister."

"It's been quite a whirlwind. You haven't really had time to sort out how you feel."

"Yeah."

"I'll take you back to the bakery. You probably have low blood sugar too, and that doesn't help anything."

"Do you think… Ward will be able to find her? Do you think she's okay? He's right, I should have called someone last night. But she didn't want me to, and these Dyson guys only showed up because she had called them. It wasn't… exactly an emergency."

"You could have called me. Especially when this guy approached you and tried to scare you off."

"I thought about it. But I just wanted to come home. If I'd called you, I would have had to wait there for hours. I wanted to get out of there as fast as I could."

He nodded. "Understandable."

Terry delivered Erin back to the bakery, with strict instructions to Vic that Erin was to sit down and have something to eat, no matter how close it was to the lunchtime rush. Vic took the direction seriously, going immediately into mother-hen mode and not even letting Erin prepare her own lunch.

Terry looked satisfied with Vic's compliance, but he didn't leave to recommence his own duties immediately.

"Is Willie around today?" he asked casually.

"He should be," Vic confirmed. "But he hasn't stopped by or contacted me yet, so he might have been held up."

"He was out of town yesterday?"

Vic nodded as she prepared a sandwich for Erin. "Yeah. Some emergency call."

"You don't know what it was about?"

"He doesn't give me details." Vic looked at Terry, her gaze stern. "And that doesn't mean he's up to anything he shouldn't be. It just means he's a private person and he likes to keep his business to himself."

Terry opened his mouth to answer, but Vic beat him to the punch.

"He's got mining claims that could be really valuable, and if word got around town about what he was taking out of which mines…"

"So you think he was at one of his mines yesterday?"

Vic made a face and put the sandwich in front of Erin. "No, I don't think he was at a mine. He's got a lot of other work he does too for other people. One of them called him and needed him."

"Did you see him take the call?"

Erin was starting to get the feeling that there was something more going on than Terry just asking how Willie was doing and when he'd be back in town. Vic's expression was suspicious.

"Did I see him take the call? Why? He got a call. He needed to go out of town to deal with a problem. You think it's something else? You think he's cheating on me?"

"No. Not at all. I was just curious. I just wondered if he seemed concerned. Or if it was just something routine. Willie's a bit of a loner and I like to keep an eye on him. After he disappeared last year, with that knock on the head…"

Erin saw the words hit Vic like a blow. All of the anxiety she had suffered when Willie had dropped out of sight and then when they found evidence that he had been injured flashed across her face in a microsecond. She put her hand on the counter to steady herself.

"It's nothing like that. If he's away for too long and doesn't text me, I'll get in touch to make sure he's okay. I was there when he got the call. It was just a job. Nothing for either of us to be worried about."

"He didn't seem like he was concerned about it?"

"No. Not at all."

"It seemed like it was just a routine call, not anything that was too difficult or worrisome?"

"Right."

"But he said it was an emergency call?"

"I don't know whether he said emergency. It might have been urgent or important."

"So not routine, but not something that upset him."

Vic scowled and shook her head. "I have no idea why you're interrogating me over this. Do you think something happened to him?"

Terry weighed his words. Erin munched on her sandwich, knowing she had to eat before they opened up again, which would have to be soon. But she hardly tasted what she was eating and couldn't have said what was actually in the sandwich later. She just forced it down, focused on Terry's strange behavior.

"It's not so much that I'm worried about something having happened to Willie," he said slowly. "It's just that I know he has family connections in Moose River, and with all that's going on there at the moment..."

"Wait." Vic faced Terry straight on, her expression thunderous. "Wait just one dang minute here. Family connections in Moose River? What's going on? You think he's one of the Dysons?"

K9's ears were up and he stared at Vic as if waiting to be given the word to take her down. He'd been trained to identify threats, and he obviously didn't like Vic's angry tone.

"I don't *think* he's one of the Dysons." Terry licked his lips and kept his gaze focused on Vic. "I know."

Erin gasped out loud. *Willie?* What could he possibly have to do with the Dyson clan? He'd always been kind and courteous to Erin and Vic. She knew that Terry was overly suspicious of Willie's activities, but she'd always just figured that was jealousy.

"He's not!" Vic insisted.

"His mother was a Dyson. You think I'm making this up? You wonder why Willie is such a pariah around Bald Eagle Falls? You think it's just because he works odd jobs? People have good reason for being so suspicious of him. You've heard him admit to being involved in shady dealings growing up. I'm not just making this up, Victoria. He should have told you where he came from a long time ago."

Vic shook her head. "I don't care. I didn't care where he came from before, and I don't care now. I don't judge anyone because of the family they came from. He can't help who he was born to or how he was raised. All he can control is the life he lives now. And you know he's a good man!"

Terry reached for K9, scratching his ears and the scruff of his neck, motioning for him to sit. K9 relaxed his alert posture, letting his tongue loll out in a doggie grin.

"I've said before, Willie has certain skills that I would trust my life to in the right situation. But he also has a past and a present that he keeps well-hidden. He's not open about everything he's involved in, is he? He doesn't tell you where he's going or who he's working for or what type of job he's going out on. He keeps that all under wraps."

Vic swallowed as she tried to come up with an argument, but she just shook her head. "I know what kind of man he is."

Terry stood there silently, letting Vic think about it. Giving her some time to let it all sink in. He took a step toward the door, having gleaned everything he could from her. He still had other work to do. He looked back at Vic.

"And is he the kind of man who would tell Erin to get out of a dangerous situation and to come home?"

$\mathcal{E}$rin and Vic looked at each other for a long moment after Terry was gone. Erin guessed they had similar expressions. Mouths open, eyes wide, skin pale. They were both shocked at the suggestion.

It was Vic who broke the silence. "Could it have been him, Erin?"

Erin tried to replay the one glimpse she'd had of the man through the doorway. She tried to remember the feel of his hands and the timbre of his voice. But it had all been too quick. He'd been well-disguised and he hadn't given himself away.

"I don't know. I can't rule him out. I didn't get a good look. I just... don't know."

"I can't believe this."

"That Terry would accuse him?"

"That Willie didn't tell me. Why wouldn't he tell me his mother was a Dyson? Why didn't he tell you, when we were talking about Charley being in the clan?"

"I don't know. Maybe it was just like he said, that he wanted privacy. He didn't want to be judged by his upbringing or who his family was. He wanted to be his own person and live his own life, the way he wanted to."

"He could have! I wouldn't have judged him! Heaven knows, my family ain't no gathering of saints."

Erin put her plate into the sink. It was time to open up again for the lunch rush. The conversation would have to wait until a more appropriate time.

"I'm sure he would have told you in time. He was just waiting until he was comfortable with it. He was just waiting for the right time to let you know."

Vic's face looked pinched and pale as she followed Erin to the front of the bakery. Erin turned the sign to *Open* and unlocked the door.

Mary Lou brought over a fresh batch of Jam Lady jams to add to their stock. The jams sure helped to sell bread, and vice versa. Erin and Vic knew the Jam Lady's secret—that it was actually Mary Lou's husband who made them while Mary Lou acted as the distributor and kept the maker a secret—and neither had ever breathed a word that would even hint at the truth.

"I figured you were about due for a new shipment," she told Erin, holding up the flat of jars. "How's your inventory?"

"You're right, as usual," Erin assured her. "Thanks."

Mary Lou gave Vic a frozen smile and smoothed her form-fitting blazer over her hips. "And have you heard anything from your family, my dear?"

Vic stared at her. "Have I heard anything from my family? No. Why would I?"

"I just thought that with all of the trouble going on, they might have stopped by to see you or gotten in touch with you by phone or email…"

"All of what trouble?"

Mary Lou looked from Vic to Erin and back again. "Well, I… you are from Moose River too, aren't you?"

Erin looked at Vic, stunned. Was everybody in on the inside track of politics and society in Moose River except for her? Vic had said nothing about being from Moose River.

"I'm from *outside* Moose River," Vic corrected icily. "My folks have never lived in town."

Mary Lou gave a little laugh and shook her head at this.

"Well, outside Moose River, then. It's all the same. I just thought that with a murder happening, and the threat of violence between the clans…" she trailed off, letting Erin and Vic complete the thought.

"What's she talking about?" Erin asked Vic. "Am I that dense? I don't understand."

Vic stared down at the baking in the display case. "I'll tell you later. For now…" she raised her voice so that the rest of the customers could hear her clearly. "Thanks for the jams, Mary Lou. Did you want anything from the case?"

Mary Lou took her time looking over the baked goods on display. "Everything always looks so good here." She smoothed her jacket again. "Of course, I can't eat any of it, or it would go straight to my hips. But the boys would like something, I'm sure. Oh… why don't we go with chocolate chip? Always so good with a glass of cold milk."

"Certainly," Vic agreed.

Mary Lou was looking around the store to greet the other patrons with a smile. While she always made Erin feel welcome and included with her friendly manner, she had never quite extended the same courtesy to Vic. She didn't give her the same smile, the same thanks, the same effort at being pleasant. Erin realized that Vic was giving Mary Lou a baker's dozen, and made a motion to stop her and remind her that Mary Lou always requested an even dozen so that the desserts would split evenly between her husband and two sons. Vic smiled and raised a brow at Erin and with an expression of mischief, slid thirteen cookies into the bag for Mary Lou.

Erin stifled a giggle. She was tired and stressed and if she started laughing, she wouldn't be able to stop.

"Is there anything else?" she asked Mary Lou, calling her attention back to the transaction.

"Oh, no. That's all I need today."

They settled up the bill, and Mary Lou went on her way with the thirteen cookies. Erin shook her head at Vic. "You're incorrigible."

"Mary Lou was being very kind to inquire about my family," Vic said. "Of course I would want to do something nice for her."

Erin shrugged, baffled by whatever had passed between Mary Lou and Vic. There would be a story coming later, and Erin wanted to hear it.

"Has Erin Price been take care of?" the boss demanded. "I wanted her kept out of this situation. Now she's walking all over it like chickens scratching in a yard. For an outsider, she has certainly managed to muck things around."

"She's taken care of," the fixer assured him. "She's been warned off, and both Terry Piper and Jack Ward are doing their best to pull her back. She's not going to cause any more trouble."

"I wish I could believe that. The woman is relentless. She's determined not to leave things alone until I'm completely ruined."

"It's just coincidence. She's not going to be a problem anymore."

"Better not be. And what about Charlotte? Where is she?"

"Well…" the fixer grimaced at that. The one question he couldn't answer. "I did get to her ahead of the Dyson gang, but not by much. Told her to get out of there and not come back. But she didn't have time to get packed and get out before they got there."

"And now…? Where is she now?"

"I'm sure we'll turn her up before too long. She's too important to just leave hanging. There will be too many people looking for her."

"That's not an answer. Dyson got her? And did what? Is she still there or back home?"

"She's not home. The cops are looking for her. I haven't found anything out yet. I'm doing my best to monitor what's going on, but people don't exactly trust me."

"You're not particularly trustworthy."

The fixer snorted. "I'm a lot more trustworthy than you!"

The boss didn't disagree.

CHAPTER 21

So explain to me what Mary Ann was going on about today," Erin told Vic as they cleaned up, preparing to leave.

"Oh, Erin… you don't want to hear all about my family's dirty laundry."

"Their dirty laundry? What kind of dirty laundry? And how would Mary Lou know about it?"

"Because it's been going on for generations. And when something has been going on for that long, word spreads, and people know."

"What's been going on for generations? I'm at a definite disadvantage as a newcomer in these parts."

"Except you're not, you're part of the community too. You just… don't know what you don't know. If your parents had raised you here, you'd know all about it too."

"But they didn't. So you're going to have to fill me in."

Vic sighed. "Well… you know Victoria Webster isn't my birth name."

"Of course. I know that."

"There's a reason I didn't just change my given name. Victor was my middle name, and I always liked Victoria. But I also changed my last name, from Jackson to Webster."

"Right. So you wouldn't be as easy to track when you ran away."

Vic nodded. "But not just because my family objected to me being transgender."

Erin slowly washed the dishes, scrubbing them under the warm, soapy water.

"What is it about the Jackson family, then? It's an old name in these parts. Pretty common."

"Yeah. There's lots of us around, and everyone is related to everyone else on the mountain."

She waited. Vic could dance around the issue all day for as long as Erin continued asking her questions. She wasn't going to get to the crux of it until she decided it was safe to do so.

"The Dysons and the Jacksons have been rivals for a long time," Vic said finally. "They've been fighting each other for generations."

"Like a feud?"

Vic shrugged. "Like a feud. Or like two mafia families fighting for territory. It's like with Romeo and Juliet, you don't get to choose which family you're a part of. You're just born into it, and there you are. You have to live with it."

"Is that why you were so surprised to hear that Willie was a Dyson?"

"That's just one more curve ball. I don't know what to say, Erin. Your sister… she's one of the Dysons. She's my mortal enemy. Stupid, I know, but that's the way it's been for years. You can't just change that kind of thing on a whim. You can't just say 'Oh, she seems nice, so we'll accept her as one of us'."

"So do you hate her?"

"Me?" Vic laughed. "No, not me. How could I? She's your sister. I can't hate anyone who's part of your family. But my fami-ly…? Yes. They can hate her. They're not going to give her a chance, they're just going to hate her."

"Even though she killed Bobby Dyson? Or they think she did?"

"That's just the way it is with a rivalry like this. Even if she killed Bobby Dyson, Charley is still a Dyson herself, so we hate her. *They* hate her."

"That's crazy." Erin shook her head, putting the pans on the drying rack and grabbing a few more to scrub off. "I couldn't hate anyone without even meeting them. What about your religion? Doesn't Christianity say you're supposed to love everyone?"

"Everyone but the Dysons," Vic agreed. "They wrote that part into the Bible themselves."

"You can do that?"

"No. You can't do that. I'm joking."

"So... all this time... I thought you grew up on a farm shooting varmints and climbing trees. Are you telling me you hunted the Dyson family? That you learned to shoot so you could fight this feud?"

Vic looked troubled. She set out the clean and dry cooling racks for the next day.

"No, it wasn't like that. I *did* grow up on a farm. I haven't ever shot a person, only squirrels and coons and such. But I always knew we were part of the Jackson clan and that we were enemies with the Dyson clan. If we ever ran into Dysons at school or in town... there was tension. Nobody killed anybody, not while I was around, but we didn't have anything to do with each other. And the politics... I always knew my uncle was a big boss in the clan. I never really understood what that meant. Just that we showed him respect. People didn't go around talking about whatever the clans are involved in... protection scams or drugs or black market weapons... but even when I was little, I knew that... a lot of what the grown-ups said had double meanings. One thing to little ears or outsiders, and something different to the adults who were in the know."

Erin couldn't fathom being part of a big family organization like that. Most of the families she had been a part of had been very small and insular. Sometimes there were aunts and uncles and grandparents, but she was a foster child, so she wasn't treated like a real family member. There had been many times when she'd been shipped off to a respite family so that her foster family could entertain the extended family. The real kids stayed home and the foster kids were sent away.

"So… have they called you like Mary Lou said?"

Vic didn't answer right away. "I'm still estranged," she said finally. "Most of them don't want anything to do with me."

"Most of them," Erin repeated. "What about Jeremy? Has he called?"

"A couple of times. Since we got back in touch at Christmas, you know."

"I know," Erin agreed. She remembered the joy Vic had greeted her brother with. The exuberance of her reunion with him after being away from each other for months, shunned by a family who wouldn't accept her gender identity. What kind of sense did it make to be involved in whatever organized crime they were involved with, and yet to shun a person for being a girl? "Has he been in contact with you in the last week or so? Since I met Charley?"

"Well, yes."

"And…?"

"I wouldn't ever do anything to put you or your sister in danger, Erin. I swear it. When Jeremy started nosing around, asking questions that were none of his business, I told him so. I told him to just take a hike if he was going to interfere with my friend's family. You're family to me, Erin. You took me in when my family of birth wouldn't have anything to do with me. So you're my first priority. I chose you to be my family."

Erin felt a little twinge of guilt at Vic's words. She felt guilty for going against what Vic had told her and seeking Charley out anyway. Vic, Willie, and Terry had all told her to stay away from Charley and the Dysons. They all had different reasons, different kinds of experience with the Dysons, but they had all seen trouble brewing and warned her to stay away. And Erin hadn't. She had chosen her sister, someone she didn't even know, over friends who had stuck with her through thick and thin and three murder investigations.

Erin wiped her hands on a dishtowel and gave Vic a hug.

"I'm glad you're my family too. I know I haven't always been the best friend…"

"What are you talking about? You have been the best friend. Every minute!"

"Not when I went to see Charley…"

Vic brushed that away with a gesture. "I'm not enemies with Charley. I'm not enemies with anyone. My family can choose to ignore the Bible if they want. But I'm not going to live like that. I'm not going to live my life under the thumb of some criminal organization. I can't help where I was born. But I can help where and how I live now that I'm an adult."

They looked around the kitchen to make sure everything was ready for the next day, then turned toward the door together.

"You never knew Willie was a Dyson?" Erin asked.

Vic laughed. "No. I suppose I should have guessed. Aunt Angela said he was no good. That should have been my first clue. But I never asked him anything about his family, and have only gleaned a few bits and pieces about his past. Nothing clear. I never got why he was shunned in Bald Eagle Falls. I just figured… it was because of the way he looked, and that he didn't have a regular job."

"Do you think he knows you were a Jackson?"

Vic considered this. "Yeah… I'm pretty sure he does. I never hid my birth name from him. I'm sure I must have mentioned it at some time."

"What a rascal," Erin said. "He really should have told you. It's not fair that he knew who you were, and that you were supposed to be enemies, and that you didn't. He should have said something."

"I was okay with him knowing I was a Jackson… but that

doesn't mean he had to be comfortable with me knowing his roots. I knew he had secrets. And I'm pretty sure that's not the only one."

"You're a lot more forgiving than I would be."

"What about your boyfriend?"

Erin frowned. "What do you mean?"

"He did tell you he was a cop, right?"

Erin laughed. "Yeah, it might have come up in conversation at some point."

"And did you tell him everything about your past?"

There were a few seconds of silence. Erin swallowed. "The salient points."

"So the two of you are okay with not being on exactly the same page too."

"Uh… yeah, I guess," Erin agreed.

"Terry is willing to wait for you to tell him about yourself. Or to be kept in the dark indefinitely."

"It's not like I have this deep, dark past," Erin said. "He knows the basics. So do you."

"Uh-huh. But you're not ready to expose everything, are you?"

"No."

"I'm not going to insist that you tell me everything about your past. And I'm not going to insist that Willie tell me everything about his. We'll figure it out. We've got years to get to know each other."

Years. It was such a foreign concept to Erin. She didn't stay in the same place, associating with the same people for years. She stayed around for a few weeks, a few months, and then she would be off on a new adventure. She would leave everything behind, shed it like the skin of a snake, and start over again as a new person. The idea of staying in the same place and getting to know the same people over a period of years was a daunting concept.

"It's okay," Vic repeated. "We've got plenty of time."

CHAPTER 22

It had been such a tiring week that Erin was asleep the instant her head hit the pillow. Orange Blossom could make all the noise he wanted to, because she wasn't waking up again for anything.

So when she awoke to Vic shaking her, she knew she must have overslept. The alarm had probably gone off, and she had just slept right through it. She sat up abruptly, her heart thumping wildly.

"What time is it?"

"I'm sorry, Erin. We've got to go."

Erin looked at the clock and frowned. She hadn't overslept. It wasn't even time for the alarm to go off yet. She'd only been asleep for a couple of hours. She put her hand over her pumping heart and took a long breath.

"Vicky, are you sleepwalking? It's not time to get up."

"We have to go," Vic repeated. "You took so long to wake up, I thought I was going to have to carry you. Get up. I'll explain on the way."

She tugged on Erin's arm, and Erin slid her feet off the bed and got unsteadily to her feet. "What's going on? It's not time to get up."

"Get your shoes on." Vic grabbed Erin's bulky purse and chivvied her toward the bedroom door. "We have to go out. Come on."

"Is it Adele? Is something wrong?"

"It's not Adele. I promise, I'll explain. Just keep moving."

Erin rubbed her eyes with both hands as she stumbled down the hall. At the back door, she put her shoes on over bare feet, trying to process what was going on. Vic pulled her out the door and stopped to lock it and arm the new alarm system.

"The car," she instructed. "Let's go."

Erin led the way to the garage, blinking in the moonlight. She had no idea what Vic was up to. Where in the world were they going in the middle of the night. And how were they going to be awake enough in the morning to run the bakery?

Vic motioned to the passenger side. "You ride shotgun. You're not awake enough to drive yet. Did you take something to sleep?"

"No. I was just really tired. Can't we just sleep tonight and do whatever this is another day?"

"No. Get in."

Erin was already opening the door on the passenger side of her car. She hadn't ever ridden in the passenger seat before. She always drove. She settled in and Vic handed her her purse and made sure she had done up her seatbelt. They were on their way in less than a minute.

Erin yawned widely. "Now can you tell me what is going on? I don't understand where we're going in the middle of the night. Is something wrong?"

Vic nodded grimly. "Willie called me. Told me to get out of there and get you out right away."

"Why?"

"He didn't have time to tell me and I didn't ask. If he's a Dyson, Erin, and he says we're in danger, I trust he knows what he's talking about. I'm not going to wait around to find out the details."

"Where did he say to go?"

"I don't know yet. Just get out of the house and get out of town. I'll call him now and see if he can tell us what's going on."

Vic pulled out her phone and was fiddling with it while racing down the dark highway. Erin took it away from her and found the speed dial for Willie. She put it on the Bluetooth radio. They both held their breaths while they waited for him to answer. One ring… two… three… it went on and on, and Erin was waiting for it to disconnect or go to voicemail. Then there was a click.

"Vicky?"

"We're fine," Vic assured Willie. "We're on the highway. Can you tell us what's going on? Where do you want us to go?"

"Erin is with you?"

"I'm here," Erin acknowledged.

"Good." Willie's voice was relieved. "I was afraid I wasn't going to be able to get to you in time."

"What's going on?" Vic demanded. "Is it the Dysons?"

There was a pause while Willie thought through what it was he wanted to say. "Vic, I never told you, but…"

"I know. Terry told us. Your mother was a Dyson."

"Well, thank you Officer Piper… okay, well… Erin probably shouldn't be driving. Can you pull over for a few minutes?"

"She's not driving, I am."

"Oh. Do you even know how to drive?"

"Oh, please. I've been driving tractors and back roads since I was seven. I'm a good driver!"

"Do you have a license?"

"Willie, will you get on with it?"

"The two of you are in danger. Well, Erin anyway. The Dysons don't like her poking around Bobby's case, and—"

"And even though she went home when you told her to, they decided that wasn't enough."

For a few seconds, Erin thought they had lost the connection. There was dead air, with no response back from Willie. She looked down at the phone screen to make sure the call was still active.

"Willie?"

"What do you mean, when I told her to?" Willie demanded.

"You were the masked man, weren't you? It was Terry who figured it out—"

"What masked man?"

Vic looked over at Erin, who was finally fully awake and alert.

"The man who told Charley to run," Erin said, "and who told me to go home and stay out of it."

"That wasn't me. Back up. What happened?"

"When I went to Moose River to pick up Charley. She made bail, but she needed a ride and I still had her apartment keys. When we were at her apartment, a man in a ski mask came to the door, and he told her she should get out of Moose River and disappear. But she had already called the Dysons to try to explain to them, and they had men on the way. I left, but in the parking lot, he came up behind me. He told me to stay out of it and go home."

"It wasn't me." Willie reiterated. "What made you think it was?"

"It was Terry—"

"What made Terry think it was me?"

"The man knew me by name. He knew I lived in Bald Eagle Falls and was a baker. So Terry thought either the police department had a leak, or it was someone..."

"Someone who knew you personally. Like me."

Erin nodded mutely, even though he couldn't see her.

"You were called away right when Charley was released. I just thought..."

Willie was quiet for some time.

"Willie... I don't even know where you want me to go," Vic reminded him.

Willie gave a short laugh. "I don't either, so don't feel left out."

Erin had to smile at his dry sense of humor. She ran her fingers through her hair to tame it into some semblance of order. There weren't exactly a lot of places she could go, dressed in her pajamas, bed head and no makeup, with only the shoes on her feet and whatever was in her purse. And what about the animals? Someone would need to feed them. And open the bakery. It couldn't run without Erin and Vic opening up and getting everything ready.

"Do you know if Charley is okay? Or did they…?"

Willie made a humming noise, considering. "I'm not on the inside, so I can't tell you anything with certainty, but from what I can gather from the whispers I've heard, they've got her under wraps, but still alive. Her turning herself in to Dwight was either desperation to prove herself innocent, or an audacious bluff, but they don't know which yet." He paused a few seconds. "They're leaning toward a bluff, which wouldn't be good for Charley's health."

"We have to help her."

"There's nothing any of us can do, Erin."

"What about the police? If you know where they're holding her…"

"I told you, I'm not a trusted insider. They're not going to give me information like that. It's only luck that I know what I do."

"Do you really think they were coming for Erin tonight?" Vic asked. There was a quiver in her voice, the adrenaline of their escape affecting her.

"They were," Willie said flatly.

Erin shivered.

Vic reached over to rub Erin's knee comfortingly. "Can we meet you somewhere?" she asked Willie.

"Yes… Let's pick a random hotel in a random town along the way. Hillard Bluff?"

"Hillard Bluff," Vic agreed. "Is there a Best Western off the highway?"

"Yes. I'll probably get there before you, so I'll get a room. I don't want to be waiting around in the lobby." He cleared his throat. "I don't exactly blend in."

"Just dress like a construction worker," Vic advised. "No one will even notice you."

CHAPTER 23

Erin was self-conscious walking into a hotel in her pajamas, but there was nothing else for her to do. They couldn't stop somewhere to buy clothes and change in the middle of the night.

Vic caught Erin eyeing her clothes, and gave an apologetic smile. "I know. I got changed and then I hustled you out the door. But by the time I got you to wake up... I was really panicking about getting out of there fast enough. I didn't know for sure what was up, but I wasn't about to piddle around when Willie said to get out now." She swept her hands through her ponytail. "I really didn't take time to do more than pull on pants and a shirt."

Erin shrugged. Nothing could be done about it at that point. The important thing was that they were both safe for the moment. She wasn't sure whether she could say the same about Charley. Willie said she was still alive, but Erin wondered what kind of shape she was in and what she might have been going through.

The desk clerk made no sign that she noticed their attire or disheveled condition and merely directed them up to their room. Vic texted Willie from the elevator, and when they reached the hotel room, Willie opened the door and let them in. He stayed at the door and looked up and down the hall. He stepped back and let the door shut, and still stayed at the peephole looking out into the hallway. Eventually, he relaxed and joined Vic and Erin in the bedroom. He sat down on one of the beds and Vic joined him, cuddling up against him. Erin sat down on the other bed. Despite how fast her heart was still beating, she really wanted to lie down and go back to sleep. She rubbed her eyes and stifled a yawn.

"Doesn't look like you were followed," Willie said in a low voice. "Not up here to the room, anyway. There could still be someone watching the hotel and waiting for you to leave again."

"I didn't see anyone following us," Vic said. "They wouldn't know where we were going, so they would have had to follow us all the way from the house. There were lots of times on the highway when I couldn't even see any other headlights."

"I hoped that if I acted fast enough, I could get you out of there before anyone showed up."

Erin and Vic nodded.

Erin looked Willie over. She was used to his usual grubby appearance, his skin stained dark by the mining and processing work he did and his clothes frequently worn. He had done as she had suggested and dressed like a blue-collar worker, so he looked less like a homeless person and more like he was just in the middle of a dirty job.

Willie tapped the bill of his hat. "Sewers and sanitation," he pointed out. "No one wants to look too close at someone who just climbed out of a sewer."

Erin chuckled. "No, you're probably right there. How did you get your hands on that in the middle of the night?"

"Don't ask me any questions, and I won't have to lie to you."

"So what are we going to do now?" Vic asked. "We're safe, but what do we do next?"

"Best would be to get some sleep, if you think you can. We can try to sort things out in the morning."

Erin kicked off her shoes and lay down on the bed, looking at them. "What about the bakery? We have work."

"Tomorrow is Sunday," Vic said. "So, thank goodness, it's not a regular work day. If you want, we can just stay closed. If not, you could call Bella and see if she can manage it herself. It's just the ladies' tea. They all know where everything is and can help her get set up. There are enough cookies and treats in the freezer that she can put a couple of platters out and no one will be the wiser."

"Those are for an emergency," Erin protested.

Vic raised an eyebrow. "Uh… yeah," she agreed.

Erin's face warmed. Running for their lives didn't constitute an emergency? Exactly what was she saving them for? "Okay. I guess we can call Bella. She hasn't had to handle it on her own before, but she's been there enough times… and it's not like serving the rush crowd on other days."

Vic nodded in agreement. She followed Erin's example and pulled off her shoes. She lay down, and Willie stretched out behind her, spoon style. Erin didn't close her eyes. She was tired and hyped up at the same time. Vic looked back at her across the gap between the two beds, not closing her eyes either.

"Tell me about when you were a kid," Vic told Willie. "Since I know where you come from now, you don't have to worry about giving yourself away."

"You already knew where I was from," Willie said, his voice gravelly. "Bald Eagle Falls, just like I said. None of that has changed."

"What was it like growing up as a Dyson?"

"I don't imagine it was so different from growing up as a Jackson. My parents left Moose River before I was born. Wanted to get away from the clan. Be their own people and not have to worry about the politics or about having the cops on their case all the time."

"What did the family think about that?"

"No big deal, I don't think. Not everyone stays involved in family matters. Not everyone is made for it."

"Your dad was a trucker; what did your mom do?"

Willie grunted. "Dad was a trucker when he was employed, which was not very often. Mom did what she could from home.

Sewing. Laundry. Going out and cleaning houses when we could be left alone for a while. When we got old enough, we picked up after-school jobs to try to contribute to the household."

"How bad was it?" Vic asked. "Were you really poor?"

"Grindingly poor. We didn't have many clothes, always got made fun of for that. Why people think it's okay to make fun of those who have less, I'll never understand. Like poverty was a crime or a choice. Believe me, we didn't choose to live that way."

Vic shifted, reaching behind her to pat his cheek. "In a way, your parents did. If they'd chosen to live with the clan, you wouldn't have been poor. You would have had everything you needed."

"At a cost."

Erin closed her eyes, thinking about the hollowness in Willie's voice. Just what had he suffered in his life, first living without enough food or clothing and being bullied by Trenton Plaint or boys like him? Then leaving Bald Eagle Falls to strike out on his own.

"What did you do when you got out of school? You left Bald Eagle Falls?"

"Yes. I figured my parents had made the wrong choice. That they didn't know what they were talking about. So I went to the Dysons."

Vic caught her breath sharply. "You went back?"

"Technically, I didn't go *back* because I'd never been there before. But yeah, I went back to what my parents had abandoned, thinking that they were just naive and out of touch and I knew better than they did."

Erin closed her eyes. She wanted to block out the pictures and to see them at the same time. She didn't want to look at Willie, but to give him his privacy. Even though he was her friend, it seemed like a more intimate moment, one that he should have shared with Vic alone.

"How could you do that?" Vic asked. "You knew they were… criminals. Bad guys. That's not the kind of person you are."

"I was a teenager," Willie said. "Teenagers know everything. I wanted the money. I wanted the power and the respect. I didn't want to be looked down on anymore." Erin cracked her eyelids briefly to see him shaking his head. "I didn't want to be hungry anymore."

Vic turned over to face him. She put her arms around him and buried her face in his chest. She rubbed his back comfortingly. "I'm so sorry…"

"I learned pretty quick that there were worse things than being poor. And that being part of the clan didn't get me the respect I wanted. I was the lowest man on the totem pole. I knew nothing about the family or the way things worked. There were twelve-year-olds with more skill and experience than I had. People outside the family didn't respect me. Fear, yes. Plenty of people who would look away or kowtow to me. But real respect for me and my skills… no."

"How long before you decided to go back home to Bald Eagle Falls?"

"I had committed to… something like an apprenticeship or internship. I had to do my time so they could see what kind of an asset I was and how they could use me."

"For how long?"

"Five years. And after that, I was allowed to decide what I wanted to do. It wasn't easy, but I left it all behind. I decided my parents had been right in the first place. Better to be poor and be your own man. Better not to be a slave to the organization or to have to give up your standards and beliefs for theirs. I didn't come back to Bald Eagle Falls. Not right away."

Vic murmured a sympathetic sound. She continued to rub Willie's back and to hold him close. "What did you do, while you were apprenticing? Was it hard? Was it…?"

"I can't talk about it. I can't tell you what things I did or what I was involved with. You know the kind of people who run the family. You know what kind of organization they are and what they're involved in. An apprentice doesn't get to avoid anything. He has to learn the organization from the ground up."

Erin thought about some of the skills Willie had shown in the time she had known him and how Terry was so wary of him, never fully trusting him. He'd run away, a teen starving for attention as much as for food. He'd returned a man, with years of knowledge and experience in things he should never have had to witness or participate in. Erin was glad that he and Vic had connected. Vic was still way too young for him, but maybe he needed her inexperience and non-worldliness to balance his own cynicism and weariness. It shouldn't have worked between them, but it did.

CHAPTER 24

Erin had apparently fallen asleep sometime during the night or the early hours of the morning. She couldn't remember all that they had discussed during the night or when she had fallen asleep, but by morning they were all snoring away, exhausted by the emotion and the events of the night.

Erin was the first to awaken, and decided to take advantage of the fact to have a shower. The hot water felt good and the white noise of the droplets was soothing. She really needed it.

And whatever the reason for it, she was going to have a day off. A full day off, away from the bakery and thinking about how to keep it solvent.

But before long, her mind went to Charley and she lost her zen state, returning to full worry mode. They had to find Charley. They have to figure out how to help her. There had to be a way.

By the time she got out of the bathroom, all dried off and dressed again in her pajamas, Erin could feel the frown lines creasing her forehead. They couldn't afford to just let the hours drift by without doing anything. Vic shifted in her sleep, and Erin shook her arm.

"Vic. Vic, we should get up and figure out what we're going to do."

"Five more minutes." She sounded like a child trying to avoid getting up for school.

"No more minutes. You're getting out of bed right now, young lady."

Vic squinted in the bright light of the hotel room. "Are you channeling my mother?"

"That's right. Up and at 'em. Time's a-wasting. The early bird gets the worm."

"You are evil," Vic groaned. She stretched and sat up, rubbing both eyes with her fists. "What time is it?"

"Later than we ever get up for the bakery, so you shouldn't have any trouble getting up. You got to sleep in."

"I barely got any time," Vic objected. "I just barely got to sleep."

"We need to figure out what to do."

"Okay." Vic elbowed Willie none-too-gently. "Hey. Willie. Time for action."

"Five more minutes."

He'd obviously heard Erin getting Vic up. Vic laughed and attacked him, tickling and kissing him while he played possum, pretending he was still asleep. Eventually, Willie put an end to it, pulling Vic into a bear hug and kissing her firmly until she stopped struggling. He released her, and Vic got to her feet, face red, giggling at Erin. She disappeared into the bathroom.

Willie yawned and stretched. He cracked his fingers and his neck joints and ran his fingers through his close-cropped hair.

"I know you said you don't know where they have Charley," Erin said. "But can you find out? Can we figure out some way to help her? We can't just leave it up to the clan to decide that she was responsible for Bobby's death and execute her for it."

Willie ran his hand briskly over his head, back and forth, like he was trying to warm up his brain.

"Let me think about it. I need caffeine."

"I would offer to go down and get you some from the breakfast buffet, but I need some clothes."

Willie looked at Erin's pajamas as if seeing them for the first time. "Oh. Yeah, I guess we'd better get you something more appropriate. Did Vicky bring anything?"

"We didn't have time to pack," Vic said, coming out of the bathroom. "I barely stopped to throw on clothes myself. All we brought is what we've got on."

Erin lifted up her purse. "And this."

Vic looked at it. "Somehow, I doubt you've got a change of clothes in there."

"Uh… no." Erin dug around in it. "I do have breath mints."

They both looked at her.

"No toothbrush," Erin explained. "So…"

Vic laughed. "At least if we have to face down the Dysons, we'll have fresh breath."

"We are not facing down the Dysons," Willie said.

"I hope not," Vic agreed. "But how are we going to help Charley? I think we're going to have to talk to someone."

"Coffee first."

"And clothes," Erin added. She pointed at the in-room coffee maker. "We can start some coffee brewing here. But someone is going to have to pick up some real clothes for me before I leave this room."

Vic and Willie looked at each other. Vic looked down at herself, getting pink. "And I didn't do anything more than pull on the closest things I could find. I don't even have on a bra."

Willie shifted uncomfortably. "You want me to go out and buy Erin an outfit and you a bra?"

"No, I won't make you go bra shopping."

Vic was getting pink and Erin suspected that Willie would be too if she'd been able to see his natural skin color.

"You and me will go together. We'll check the gift shop first. See if they had some souvenir t-shirts. And hopefully some pants. Then we can all go together to get the sundries Erin and I need."

Willie nodded. "Okay."

"We can't spend too much time shopping," Erin worried.

"Popping down to the gift shop is fine, but going to the department store or mall for other things… I don't want to waste any more time than we have to. They could decide that Charley is guilty at any time. And then she could be gone before we have a chance to do anything."

"We won't waste time," Vic promised. "And Willie will be working the phone while we're getting what we need. Right?"

Willie raised an eyebrow. "Maybe if I can figure out who to call to get some help with this… situation."

"Charley called someone named Dwight. What about him?"

Willie shook his head. "I don't have an in with Dwight. He's way higher than anyone I have any connection with. Maybe someone on his staff would know something…"

Erin moved over to the coffee maker. "Okay, caffeine coming up. Get ready for it, because once you get this, you're not going to want to stop until everything is sorted out."

"That must be some magical coffee."

With coffee on board, Willie was functioning a little better, and was able to start putting together some plans.

"Dwight is Bobby's dad. He's also sort of the boss of the Dysons in Moose River."

"Like the Godfather?" Erin suggested.

"Well, more like one of his capos," Willie said. "But close enough. All you need to know is that he's important, high up in the organization, and he's dangerous. You can't mess around with this guy. Understood? There's no trying to trick him or lie to him. He won't take it."

"But Charley—"

"Charley went for broke. I don't know whether she was telling the truth or playing the biggest bluff ever. But we can't do that. We can't bluff our way into anything, but especially not into Dwight Dyson's inner circle."

"How are we going to—"

"Dwight has another son. Not a bigwig like Bobby was. Not wild and flamboyant like Bobby. Quiet and studious."

Erin and Vic nodded, listening intently, trying to memorize every word as if their lives depended on it. Because they probably did.

"Nelson, I can probably get in to see. I've helped him out with his computers. Other projects. Dwight wouldn't know me from Adam, but Nelson does."

"Nelson," Erin repeated. "That sounds good. And would he be able to help with Charley? Telling us where she was or even getting her out?"

"One step at a time. He's still living at home with Dwight, so there's a chance he would have heard something about what has been going on. For sure, he'll know that Bobby is dead, even if he's had his head in the sand about everything else. We'll start with that. Find out if he knows about Charley." Willie sighed. "I want to be able to play this like a chess game, staying four moves ahead of them. But I can barely even see what's on the board. It's frustrating."

"So how do we get in to see Nelson?" Vic asked.

"I'll call him… I'm going to need to offer him something of value. He's not going to let us just march in there and do whatever we want to."

"What's he into?"

Willie shook his head. "Computers, sound systems, drama. He's mostly a loner, but he gets together with some friends for gaming or putting on little plays."

"Kind of a geek, huh?"

Willie shrugged. "I'm not going to judge. If he's managed to keep himself separate from the family business, then good for him. Whatever it takes. If he had to lock himself in his room for the first twenty years in order to avoid it, then good for him."

"How about a double-date?" Vic suggested. "If he's kind of

awkward, then maybe if you just told him the four of us wanted to go out to dinner together…"

"No one said he was awkward. Being a geek is not the same thing. He doesn't have a steady girlfriend as far as I know, but that doesn't mean he doesn't know any girls. The drama clubs include a lot of women."

"Say we have a play we want to get produced and we want him in it?"

"I told you, we can't bluff our way into this. We have to have something of value to offer him."

"A way to avenge his brother," Erin said. "To impress his father and do something for Bobby."

Willie pursed his lips and raised both eyebrows as he considered this. "Not bad. And what do we actually offer him when we get there? We can't exactly say that we know what happened or that we can offer him anyone in place of Charley."

"No… we tell him we can get the truth from Charley."

"How are we going to do that?"

"She wanted the chance to tell Dwight her story. I don't know if he heard her out. We could get Nelson to listen to it, and then he'd be able to offer something to his dad. An alternate version of what happened. Even if Charley doesn't know who did it, if she could tell what she knew…"

"You're putting an awful lot of faith into the idea that Charley didn't do it. Are you really that sure?" Willie challenged.

"I can't understand why she would go to Dwight if she did. Why would she do that? Wouldn't she just run? Isn't that what you would do if you had this family after you?"

"What I would do and what some girl I've never met would do aren't necessarily the same thing. This kind of business attracts and rewards big egos. And people who have big egos think they can talk their way out of anything. What do you really know about Charley?"

Erin sighed. She scratched at a spot on her pajamas. "I wish I could get a chance to know her better. I really don't think she did it, Willie. She just wants to live her life. Why would she throw everything away like that?"

Willie didn't answer immediately. He took a sip of his coffee. "I think *you* just want to live your own life. You're putting your own motives on her. She wasn't raised in the family. She didn't just fall into it naturally. She had to join up. And this wasn't something that was planned. If she killed Bobby Dyson, it was in the middle of a big blow-up. If she was smart, she'd be arguing self-defense."

"But if she really didn't do it…"

"Then she should definitely be arguing self-defense and trying to get a deal."

Erin frowned. "No, if she didn't do it—"

"If she doesn't want to spend the next few years in court, and to be able to get off without prison time, she should be working a deal."

Erin felt a lot better once she had on real clothes, even though they were new and a little stiff and didn't quite fit her the way that her own clothes did. She might look a little juvenile in her touristy gift store t-shirt and pants, but they were better than walking around town in her pajamas.

When she and Vic got out of the department store with their unmentionables also dealt with, Willie was waiting in his car talking on the phone. Erin and Vic got in quietly and listened to Willie's half of the conversation, trying to analyze how he was doing with getting them inside the Dysons. Erin's stomach was tight with nervous anticipation.

"You know I usually don't get involved in this kind of thing," Willie said. "I keep my nose out of other people's business. But this is different. I actually know Charley's sister. If anyone can get the truth out of her, it's Erin."

There was a long pause while he listened to the voice on the other end, Nelson Dyson, Erin assumed.

"Would he still have her there if he'd gotten everything he wanted out of her?" Willie countered. "He obviously doesn't have everything he needs. And the longer he's got her, the hotter things get. The cops are looking for her. Other people are looking for her. It's only a matter of time until they come by there with a warrant, and then what?"

More waiting.

"Of course Dwight is careful. He wouldn't be where he is today if he wasn't. But this is your chance, Nelson. Your one chance to do right for Bobby and show your father that you're not second-best."

Erin and Vic looked at each other, gauging each other's reaction to Willie's conversation. Erin had a strange sense of being in an alien world. She'd always seen Willie as a blue-collar worker. He did his mining, he did odd jobs that involved physical labor, like moving boxes, painting buildings, and putting flyers on cars. She knew that he had advanced skills in caving and first aid, but those were hobbies, not a professional skill-set. Listening to him smoothly negotiating with Nelson Dyson was a freaky, out-of-body experience. She'd never even imagined him in that role before.

Willie started to nod. "Yeah. Yep. I know. I can't guarantee results, but this is about as close as I can get. Give me this chance. If it doesn't pan out, then nothing is lost, right? You're no further behind than you were to start with. It's not your job to get the story out of Charley, so if you can't, no skin off your back. If you do, though… Well, Dwight isn't going to ignore it, is he?"

Wrapping up noises from the phone, which Willie acknowledged, and then hung up. He looked at Erin and Vic.

"Okay. We're in. I just hope we're not jumping into a hornets' nest." He swallowed, lips tightening. "I want to keep you girls safe."

CHAPTER 25

*E*rin had been expecting a big house. The foster families she had grown up with had always lived in little places, relying on foster parenting checks to help pay the bills. She had worked in some bigger houses, cleaning or caregiving, and that was what she had pictured in her mind. A mob boss would obviously live in a big house. But she had never seen anything like the mansion that Willie drove up to.

There was a big gate with a guard booth. Willie handed over his wallet. "Here to see Nelson."

The guard took his time going over Willie's ID and checking it against his list, then handed it back and pressed the button to open the motorized gates. "You have a nice day, sir."

Erin thought she detected a sneer in his voice, but she couldn't think of anything that warranted his contempt, so she brushed the feeling aside. They drove down the long driveway, and then the house came into sight. It was at least as large as the hotel they had slept in. Erin stared, her mouth gaping open.

"That's... a house?" she asked weakly.

Willie nodded. The muscles in his jaw and neck were tight, belying his calm exterior.

Erin shook her head in amazement. A dozen regular houses could have fit into the same footprint.

"How many people actually live here?"

"Good question. Dwight and his second or third wife and her kids. Nelson. I think there are a couple of grown daughters. Household staff. Security. Gardeners and groundskeepers. Whatever soldiers or guests he has at any time. All in… somewhere over fifty, I would think."

At least it wasn't just Dwight and Nelson, but it still seemed like an incredible waste of space and resources.

"It's huge," Vic observed.

Erin was glad to hear it from someone else. Willie hadn't grown up in a house like that, but he'd been there before, so he had known what to expect. Vic had grown up as part of the Jackson clan, but she hadn't lived in a mansion like that. She'd lived on a farm. Erin didn't know anything about it, but she pictured a quaint little traditional farmhouse when she thought about Vic growing up there as a child.

"It's insane. I can't imagine anyone living in a place like that."

Willie shrugged. "People live in all kinds of places. It blew me away when I first saw it too. But when it comes right down to it, it's just like animals living in different cages at the zoo. You can have a little barred cage, or a huge fenced environment they can roam around in. But either way, it's still a cage."

Was that what it was? Erin didn't consider her home a cage, and she didn't think Willie saw his that way either. But the people who lived in that huge mansion—he saw them as caged animals. That was how he had felt when he had lived there, or whatever place they'd put him in while he'd been an apprentice to the clan. He'd felt trapped and penned in—Willie, who could crawl through the narrowest caves and tunnels without feeling a flicker of claustrophobia.

They drove up to the house and Willie pulled into a small parking lot around the side, screened from sight by a row of trees.

He led the way to a side door. A servants' entrance, not the front door.

He knocked a couple of times and opened the door, leading Vic and Erin in.

It was a small anteroom, where a receptionist sat at an antique desk with an appointment book and there were a number of doors leading in different directions. The receptionist looked at Willie. She raised one eyebrow.

"Mr. Andrews. I wasn't expecting to see you today."

"I have an appointment with Mr. Nelson."

"Yes, I saw that. I meant before that… no one had told me that your services would be required."

"Something came up. I arranged it with Mr. Nelson this morning. There shouldn't be any problems."

"No, no problem." She picked up the wired phone handset on the desk and pressed a button. "Mr. William Andrews," she announced. She waited for a reply. "I'll send him up."

Her gaze slid to Erin and Vic as she hung up.

"I didn't realize you were bringing anyone with you."

"Miss Victoria Webster and Miss Erin Price."

The receptionist wrote their names down. She was obviously waiting for more information, but it was not forthcoming. "And they are here as your… assistants?"

"Yes."

The woman studied Vic for a long time, frown lines between her penciled eyebrows. Then she smoothed her face and nodded. "Take the back stair," she gestured to one of the doors leading out of the room. "You know the way."

Willie jerked his head at Vic and Erin and led the way through the door and into the warren of back halls and passages. Erin tried not to gape at the wealth on display as they moved through the halls. Paintings on the walls, antique furniture topped with priceless vases, lamps, and other ornaments. She wasn't as well-versed as a collector would be, but she knew quality when she saw it.

"This is amazing," she breathed, not daring to raise her voice above a whisper.

"If you think the back rooms are something you should see the ones intended for public viewing," Willie murmured back.

Erin didn't touch anything. She was intensely aware of the video cameras that undoubtedly recorded every move. In the locations she couldn't see any cameras, she assumed they were only better hidden. Miniaturized and placed in a crack, a button, or behind a mirror. They wouldn't leave an inch of the place unmonitored. And Erin had thought she'd be able to just walk in and get Charley out of there? She could just unlock whatever door Charley was imprisoned behind and spirit her away? Even though she'd been told repeatedly how dangerous the Dysons were, she still thought she could just walk in and walk out.

Vic gave Erin a look that eloquently expressed she was thinking the same thing.

Then they were there. Willie led them through a door into an office. The carpet on the floor was thick, big tomes lined the bookshelves along the walls, and a man sat behind the walnut desk. He didn't look up immediately when they arrived, but continued to read whatever report he was paging through on his desk. Willie stood quietly waiting, and Erin and Vic followed his example.

The man eventually put the report down and looked up at them.

He was blond, with a long face, impeccably dressed and groomed. When he looked them over, he didn't seem haughty or self-important. Curious and tentative. Not sure how to proceed. He looked at each of Erin and Vic in turn, then back at Willie, the one of them that he knew, eyebrows up in a query.

"Willie. I see you brought the whole gang."

It calmed Erin to hear him call Willie by his nickname, just like he was a friend. No Mr. Andrews for him. Just a couple of guys who had worked with each other.

"This is Victoria Webster. And Erin Price."

Nelson looked at them and nodded. His eyes went back to Vic.

"Victoria Webster?" he repeated.

Vic nodded. "Vic," she advised.

He pressed his lips together, frowning, then caught himself and looked at Erin. But she apparently didn't set off anything on his radar. He looked back at Vic.

"Willie said Charley is your sister."

Vic looked over at Erin, and Erin raised her hand tentatively. "Mine."

"Yours. Erin Price..." he seemed to be consulting his mental files. "I don't think I know your family."

"No. We weren't... involved with your family in any way. Not that I know of. My parents died years ago, around the time Charley was born. I haven't been around until just recently." She was about to offer up that she had a bakery in Bald Eagle Falls, then thought better of it. Did she really want him knowing all of her business? She was sure he could ask a few questions and find out, but there wasn't any point in just handing it to him. She bit her lip and waited for him to ask anything further.

"I never knew Charley had a sister," Nelson said.

"We didn't grow up together."

"I see." He nodded. "Even siblings that grow up together can sometimes be estranged. You and Charley aren't close, then?"

Erin could feel the chance to find out where Charley was and to make sure she was okay slipping away from her. If the man decided she wasn't close enough to Charley to make any difference to them, he might just send Erin on her way.

"We met just recently, but we've hit it off. I think I can help you, Mr. Dyson. I think I can convince her to tell what happened between her and Bobby."

"Nelson, please. There are too many Mr. Dysons around here for me to keep track of when anyone is talking to me."

"Oh. Okay. Mr. Nelson."

"Just Nelson. I could call you Erin, if that would help."

Erin nodded slightly. "This is all a little bit new to me. I don't know what I'm supposed to say."

"I'm not my father. I don't expect any kind of formality."

"Okay. I'll try."

"Why don't you have a seat. Would you like drinks? Anything I can do to make you comfortable?"

"Oh, no," Erin said. "We just ate." She looked down at her clothes, not feeling much more comfortable than she would have if she'd still had on her pajamas. "I mean… nothing for me. I don't know…?" She looked at the others for their input. Vic and Willie both shook their heads.

Nelson pressed a button on his desk. "Bring Charley in."

Just like that. Erin had been expecting to have to do some heavy negotiating, but apparently that was not required. Willie had already smoothed the way for them, and Nelson, not standing on ceremony, was ready for action.

Erin swallowed and looked at the floor, not wanting to have to meet Nelson's eyes.

There were a few minutes of silence, and then a door clicked open, and Charley was escorted in.

Her eyes were down. They were dark and deep-set, like she'd lost weight in the couple of days since Erin had seen her last. Erin couldn't decide whether they were bruised or if it was just the lighting. Charley walked in under her own power, free of any restraints, but they might as well have been holding a gun to her. She walked into the middle of the room and waited there for further instructions.

"Sit down."

Charley looked around and selected a seat. She raised her eyes for a moment to look at Nelson, glanced at the rest of them, and looked back down again.

Erin waited for Nelson to say something to Charley, but he didn't. He looked at Erin and made a motion toward Charley. *There she is. All yours.*

Erin licked her lips and wished she had at least asked for a glass of water. She had no idea what she was supposed to say. She had been the one to suggest to Willie that she might be able to get Charley to talk, but she couldn't find anything to say. She swallowed.

"Uh… hi, Charley."

Charley raised her eyes to look at Erin for a moment, as if she hadn't been expecting any sound to come out of Erin's mouth.

"Hi."

"I was really worried about you. When those guys showed up to talk to you, I was really afraid of what was going to happen."

"Bright girl."

Erin was amazed that Charley could still use sarcasm as a weapon in the situation they were in. Erin was there to help Charley, but Charley was acting like they were talking privately.

"I was hoping I could help you to get out of here."

"I don't see how. You don't know the way things work around here."

"I thought that if we could prove that you were innocent, that you didn't have anything to do with Bobby's murder…"

Charley let out a short, sharp bark of laughter. "How are *we* going to do that?"

"If you'll just tell the truth about what happened that night. I know you didn't kill Bobby. If you just explain what happened…?"

"How can I do that? I wasn't even there."

"Ward is pulling surveillance video from inside and around the apartment. If you weren't in the apartment, he'll be able to verify that."

But inside, Erin knew he wasn't going to be able to verify that Charley wasn't there. The police had already reviewed her alibi and decided it had been fabricated. Why would she need to fabricate an alibi unless she was really there?

"Erin… you shouldn't be here."

"I know. But… I was in danger too. People came looking for me last night." Erin looked at Nelson. "Dysons."

"Why would they want you?" Charley scowled "you don't have anything to do with this. There was no need to bring her into this," she told Nelson. "Erin doesn't know anything. I didn't even meet her until after Bobby was dead. You know she doesn't have anything to do with her death. You shouldn't have brought her here."

"I didn't bring her here," Nelson said mildly. "She brought herself."

"She shouldn't be here. The Dysons have no reason to interfere with her."

Nelson looked at Charley, his nostrils flaring. "You seem to be under the mistaken impression that I have something to do with Erin being here. I don't. She and her friends were the ones who called me. I don't know what might have happened last night…" He looked over at Willie.

"I don't know if it was something Dwight ordered, or just a couple of soldiers deciding they needed to take care of any threats. Whatever it was… I caught wind before they got there and got Erin and Vic out. Whether there is still any kind of planned action against them, I have no idea."

"We can sort that out later," Nelson made an uncaring motion. "They can't be any safer than they are here."

"Charley, what happened?" Erin begged. "Can't you tell me? If you didn't kill Bobby, then tell them what did happen, so that they'll let you go."

"What makes you think anyone is going to let me go if I tell the truth?" Charley demanded. "I've been trying to tell them for two days that I didn't kill Bobby. I threw myself on their mercy. What else can I do?"

"Charley. Just tell us what happened. The truth."

"I was out with the girls," Charley maintained. "I have no way of knowing what happened to Bobby."

"You were out having margaritas," Erin agreed. Ward had confirmed that.

Charley looked surprised. "How… who told you that?"

"And then what happened? After last call, when everybody went home, where did you go?"

"A few of us went out for a nightcap. Just because the restaurant closes, that doesn't mean you can't go to someone's apartment and have a few more. We were having a good time. We weren't ready to hang it up for the night."

"You didn't go to the apartment of one of the other girls. You went home to Bobby."

"You don't know anything," Charley asserted. "You don't know what you're talking about."

Nelson just rubbed his chin and watched the two of them.

"You went to Bobby's apartment," Erin repeated.

"You weren't there. You don't know anything." Charley coughed. It was a deep, croupy cough that sent a chill through Erin. What had they done to Charley? Had they tortured her? Waterboarded her? Left her in a cold, dark dungeon under the big house?

The coughing didn't stop. Nelson pressed the button on his desk, but didn't give any directions this time. A woman poked her head in the door, looked at Charley for a minute, red and gasping for oxygen between the deep, wrenching coughs, and then withdrew. She was back a couple of minutes later with a tea tray. She placed it beside Charley and picked up the cup, pressing it into Charley's hand.

"Here. Drink this down. It will help, just take a few sips…"

She helped Charley to hold the cup and to take a drink. After Charley managed to get a few swallows down, her coughing gradually eased. Erin sniffed at the air. Honey and lemon. But something else, too. Something medicinal underneath it.

Charley leaned back in her seat. She closed her eyes, resting.

"She's sick," Erin said. "You need to let her go. She should be at the hospital."

"Charley's fine," Nelson said, with great unconcern. "She's tough."

"I don't know what you've been doing to her, but she's not that tough. You want her to die from pneumonia?"

Nelson raised his brows at her and didn't say anything. Erin rubbed at the goosebumps on her arms. Nelson couldn't care less whether Charley died of pneumonia. She had, as far as he was concerned, killed Bobby. Maybe pneumonia would kill her, and maybe the Dysons would, Nelson didn't really care which.

"I'm fine," Charley whispered.

Erin looked at Vic and saw the same concern in her eyes as Erin felt. At least someone else in the room cared.

"Charley. You need to tell them," Erin encouraged yet again. How many times did she have to say it before Nelson decided that Erin didn't have any sway over her sister after all and sent her on her way? Or sent her down to whatever dungeon they had been keeping Charley in?

Charley rubbed her chest. She took another drink of the honey and lemon tea. The woman who had brought it in nodded respectfully at Nelson and left again. The door closed silently behind her.

"It won't make any difference," Charley said. "They're not going to believe me."

"They don't believe you because you're lying."

"You don't know that. You don't know anything."

"Remember how you told me I wasn't a very good liar?"

Charley nodded.

"You aren't either."

Charley opened her mouth to object. Then she closed it again, scowling.

"Did you go back to see Bobby?" Erin asked. "You're the one who was yelling and fighting with him?"

Charley didn't respond for a long time. Then she finally nodded. "But I didn't kill him," she reiterated.

"Someone did."

Charley nodded. "Someone did," she agreed. "Someone set me up."

"Who?"

"Someone who wanted me to run."

Erin thought immediately of the masked man. He had told Charley to run. Erin had thought he was trying to protect Charley for some reason, but what if that weren't true? Maybe he didn't want to help her. Maybe he was trying to push her. To frame her.

"The man with the mask?" she asked.

Charley's eyes riveted on Erin. Her mouth twitched. The moniker had an obvious effect on her.

"Who is the man with the mask?" Nelson asked.

Willie looked back and forth at Erin and Charley.

"The masked man is someone who came to the apartment right before you guys picked up Charley. He talked to Charley then, and he grabbed Erin in the parking lot and threatened her and told her to stay out of things that weren't any of her concern."

"Good advice."

"The point is… there is someone else involved here. Someone whose identity we don't know."

"Or you're bluffing."

"Do you know who he is?" Erin asked Charley. "He knew who I was and where I was from. Did you tell him? Did the police leak it? Or is he from…" Erin glanced aside at Nelson, "…where I'm from?"

Charley shook her head. "How would I know? I have no idea who the guy is. I've only seen him twice and he was wearing that stupid mask both times."

"You couldn't recognize him? His eyes? His voice? His build?"

"No. No idea."

"Is he one of the Dysons? Is he with the family?"

"I don't know," Charley insisted more vehemently, raising her voice above a whisper. She coughed a couple of times and had more of the tea.

"Tell me what happened when you went back to Bobby's," Nelson said.

Charley glared at Erin, like it was her fault that Charley had gone back there and gotten herself into such deep trouble. Erin hadn't even met Charley until after that, so she didn't know how it could be her fault.

"I just went home," Charley said. "Back to Bobby's apartment to hook up. Everything was fine when I saw him earlier that day. He knew I was going out with the girls. He didn't care. We didn't have to spend every minute together."

"And maybe he had someone else he wanted to see," Nelson suggested.

Charley looked at him. Her mouth formed a thin, straight line. "Maybe he did," she agreed. "She wouldn't be the first."

"But she'd be the last. You saw to that."

"It wasn't me. That's not what happened. I got back and he was flipping out. Accusing me of all kinds of stuff. Saying that I was out with a man, showing him up and making a laughingstock of him. But I wasn't. I was just out with the girls, just like I said I'd been."

"He came after you."

Charley swallowed hard. She took another drink of her tea. For a few minutes, she didn't answer.

"Yeah," she said finally. "He did. He was raving like a lunatic. I've never seen him so mad. He was all over me, grabbing me, throwing me around. He put his hands around my neck. We crashed through the coffee table. He was freaking out. He was seriously acting like he was going to kill me with his own hands."

Nelson nodded. His nostrils flared. He kept his thoughts and feelings hidden. Erin didn't know whether he was upset over his brother's death, or the fact that he had been murdered, or if he was upset about the way his brother had treated Charley. Maybe he'd sometimes been on the receiving end of his brother's temper himself. But he maintained the mask of indifference. He would be a good poker player.

Charley set her teacup back on the tray. She covered her sunken eyes with both hands.

"He was my boyfriend," she said brokenly. "I never gave him

reason to be jealous of me. I don't know if he was drunk or high, why he thought I was doing anything. I just went out with the girls."

"You had to protect yourself," Erin said. "It was self-defense."

Charley looked at Erin, her red-rimmed eyes wide. "No! It wasn't self-defense," she insisted.

"If he came after you—"

"He was going to kill me. He had his hands around my neck."

"So it was—"

"No, I didn't kill him! It was *him*. The man in the mask."

CHAPTER 26

The atmosphere in the room was electric.

Charley shook her head. "I was there and saw him do it, but I can't tell you who he was or why he did it."

"Wait—the masked man? *He* killed Bobby?" Erin's head whirled. The masked man wasn't protecting Charley. He was setting her up. He was the one who had killed Bobby, framing Charley for it. But he was the one who had told her to run. Both actions were so contradictory, she couldn't make them fit. Setting her up and then trying to save her. Were there two masked men? Two opposite sides? One from the Dysons and one from the Jacksons or somewhere else?

"Yeah." Charley shook her head bitterly. "I told you no one was going to believe me. Sure, Charley, it was a masked man. *I* wouldn't believe me."

"But if that's what happened… There must be something on the security cameras. He couldn't have gotten in and out of there without being recorded. Could he?"

There were surveillance cameras everywhere. Inside, outside, city cameras and private cameras. No one could escape them all.

"The police haven't turned up anyone wearing a mask on the surveillance cameras," Nelson said.

"How do you know?" Erin questioned.

He just looked at her.

Of course they had someone on the inside. Of course they had someone who was feeding them everything Ward turned up in his investigation. They had to know all of the details of who had killed Bobby. The Dysons couldn't have known anything about Erin unless it came from the police.

Just the same as the masked man had known who Erin was. Was he a cop? Had the police been the ones to set Charley up, hoping to either put her in jail or for her to run? Either way, she was out of the picture so they no longer had to worry about her committing crimes on their turf.

But why would they have set up Charley? Surely there were bigger fish to fry. They could have set up someone higher up the food chain. Not Nelson or Bobby, maybe, but someone who had more influence and was doing more damage than Charley.

They had gotten rid of Bobby too, though. Gotten rid of him and put Charley in the hot seat for it. Maybe Bobby was the primary target, and Charley was only a secondary consideration.

"I saw the masked man," Erin told Nelson. "He does exist. I saw him."

"You saw *a* masked man. Maybe. If you're telling the truth. But Charley could have set you up. She could have arranged for someone to act the part so you would corroborate her story."

"Charley wouldn't do that."

Charley chuckled. "The hell I wouldn't. That would be brilliant."

Erin looked at Charley in exasperation. How was she supposed to help her little sister if she was going to say things like that?

Nelson cracked a smile at Charley's retort. "Of course she would. Look, nothing about this story makes any sense. Like Charley said, we have no reason to believe her. Bobby gets blown away. Everyone heard them fighting. Charley's fingerprints were on the gun. So she's the one who killed him."

He leaned back in his chair and rubbed his head, concentrating deeply. Everyone waited on pins and needles to hear his decision. He obviously had no reason to believe Charley. Was he making up his mind whether to have Charley executed without any further regard to her protestations of innocence? What good would any further investigation do? If things had happened the way Charley said they had, then there was no way to prove it had been the unknown stranger rather than Charley.

And if he got rid of Charley, then there was no reason to leave Erin, Willie, and Vic alive. Why leave witnesses who could go to the police?

"Willie," Nelson finally spoke, "that firewall you set up for me, is it any good?"

Erin shook her head. Firewall? Why was he talking to Willie about computers? The situation was dire. His brother had been killed and, as far as he was concerned, the killer was sitting right there in front of him. Had he already decided that their lives weren't worth anything, and was more concerned with the minutiae of his life than what happened to them?

Willie shifted in his seat. "It's the best money can buy. You're looking at the level of security that the FBI or NASA has. It's very secure."

"The FBI and NASA have been hacked. You develop an encryption that's supposed to take billions of years to break, and a twelve-year-old does it with his Xbox. Anything is hackable."

"Then I'm not going to tell you it's not," Willie said. "Every system has flaws. There is no perfectly secure system."

"You've never steered me wrong in the past."

"But I'm not going to tell you it's perfect when it's not."

"And you," Nelson turns to Erin, "do you believe her?"

Erin floundered, not sure what to say. "Yes," she said finally. "I saw the masked man myself. I never believed Charley killed Bobby."

"Why do you care?"

"She's my sister."

"You never met her before."

Erin swallowed. "She's still my sister."

"Why would you get mixed up in something like this? Why don't you just go home and bake cookies?"

Erin stared at him. Was *he* the masked man? But his build wasn't right. His voice didn't have the right qualities. Terry had said that it wouldn't be hard to learn these basics about Erin. Of course Nelson had done his homework.

"I don't believe she did it. I don't want to lose her after I just found her."

Nelson turned to look at Vic. "James Jackson."

The color drained from Vic's face, turning her chalk white. "That's not my name anymore."

"Why would you bring a Jackson into my house?" Nelson demanded. He didn't look at Willie's face.

Willie reached out and took Vic by the hand. He held it protectively. "I brought Vic here to protect her."

They had walked into Nelson's office thinking they knew more than he did. They walked in there figuring they had their secrets intact. But he knew all along who each of them was and what each of them was. Of course. Had they thought he was some kind of patsy? The geeky son. The second in line. He wasn't the playboy, bold and brash and sure of his inheritance. He was a long-legged spider, sitting in the middle of his web, inviting them all in.

Had *he* sent the masked man? Had he been the one to kill Bobby and set Charley up to take the fall? If he had been the masked man, then surely Charley would have recognized him, but that didn't mean he couldn't send someone to act the part, just as he had accused Charley of doing. Had it all been a ploy for him to get in line to inherit the role of capo in his family?

Nelson watched Erin, his eyes quick and cunning. "No," he told her, "I have no interest in becoming the boss of this family or any other. I'd rather play with my toys. Willie knows that."

Erin took a quick glance at Willie, hoping for some reassurance. But Willie didn't look reassuring. He held Vic's hand in his, eyes darting around the room looking for an avenue of escape.

"But that doesn't mean I'm stupid. I've always been a much better boss than Bobby, even though he was the heir, the one groomed to take over the running of the family. I wouldn't have survived this long if I had just been sitting around, ignorant of the jealousies and politics of this organization. You think there are people who wouldn't take my position if they could? You think they want some nerdy upstart giving them orders and being promoted to a position he doesn't want or deserve?"

Nelson's voice hung in the air. No one dared say anything to him. Erin feared that, just like on TV, this was the monologue leading up to their deaths. The explanation as to why they had to die.

"Willie brought you here. Willie can tell you that I'm not just some kid who's acting too big for his britches. He knows I've been building my own network. My own organization within the family. Loyal to me. Firewalled from the rest of the system, just like my computers. I may look dull, but I've been planning this for years."

It was him. He was the one who had arranged to have Bobby killed, setting Charley up to take the fall. He hadn't been sitting on the sidelines in ignorance. He'd set the whole plan into motion.

Nelson shook his head. "No. I don't know who the masked man is. He comes bumbling into the middle of everything, winding Bobby up and then killing him when things get out of hand. I have no idea who the guy is or where he came from. With the mask on, there's no way to get facial recognition. He avoided the cameras like a pro; he'd obviously scouted the area ahead of time. So I've got nothing to go on. Nothing but what the two of you can tell me about what you saw."

"You knew all along?" Charley demanded, her voice hoarse. "For two days, I've been interrogated by your father and his thugs, and you knew all along that I wasn't the one who killed Bobby?"

Nelson lifted an eyebrow. "I'm sorry, but when you joined up with the Dysons, were you under the impression that everyone was going to play fair and have consideration for your feelings? Or did you think you were joining a criminal enterprise? When you chose Bobby over me or someone else in the organization, was it because you thought he was a kind and sensitive soul who would take care of you?" He snorted. "You knew exactly what you were getting into, Charley Campbell. Don't blame me for getting burned when you chose to play with fire."

"You got it all on video?" Erin asked, parsing what he had just told them. "You saw what happened and you have physical evidence that it wasn't Charley?"

"If you really want to clear your sister," Nelson paused to give Charley a look of distaste, "even after seeing what kind of a person she is, then you need to cooperate with me. Otherwise… no, there is no evidence. You'll have to rely on the evidence the cops have got, and the only person it implicates is Charley."

"Cooperate with you?" Erin exchanged glances with Willie, Charley, and Vic, trying to gauge their reactions. "What do you expect me to do? I don't have connections with any of these people. I don't have any skills that would benefit you, unless you're in need of a batch of chocolate chip cookies."

Nelson's mouth twisted into a smirk. "Don't sell yourself short. I think you've demonstrated considerable skills."

"Nelson, Erin isn't one of your employees. She doesn't want to be associated with the Dysons or any other family," Willie said.

"Unlike James," Nelson said, looking hard at Vic.

"Victoria," she corrected evenly.

"Changing your name doesn't change who and what you were born as," Nelson said. "If I'm right, this all goes back to the Jacksons, and here is little James Jackson sitting in my office."

"I didn't have anything to do with it. If you've looked into my background, you know I don't have anything to do with my immediate family, let alone the extended Jackson clan."

Nelson leaned his head back against the headrest of his chair and gazed at her.

"I think you could find out."

"Find out what?"

"Who the masked man is, or who sent or hired him."

"What makes you think it was one of the Jacksons?" Willie asked.

"It wasn't internal. It wasn't the cops. The next logical suspect is the Jacksons."

Vic leaned forward in her chair. "So you want me to go to my family and casually find out if they happen to know who killed Bobby."

Nelson shrugged. "I don't care how you do it."

Vic looked at Erin. Erin knew how much Vic hated the thought of running to her family or having to deal with them and their prejudice.

Erin shook her head. "You don't have to, Vicky. We'll find another way to sort it out. Charley didn't do it and there is video out there that proves it. The masked man is out there. People know things. We can figure it out."

"How? Mr. Dyson obviously isn't giving up the video. If the masked man is smart enough to wear a mask and avoid the cameras, he is smart enough to avoid our bungling attempts to find out who he is. We're bakers, not detectives."

"We know people with skills," Erin said stubbornly. She was thinking of Terry and Willie specifically, but she wasn't going to name names in front of Nelson, who was obviously too smart for his own good. Terry was a trained investigator, and Willie had set up that firewall and would know its weaknesses. Maybe there was a backdoor or administrative password in case Nelson forgot his. And if Nelson had captured video of the masked man killing Bobby, then there was a chance that someone else had seen it or had access to it. "Let Charley go with us," she told Nelson, "and we'll see what we can find out."

"Why would I let Charley go?"

"Why would you keep her here in the first place? You knew she wasn't the killer. Why would you let her take the punishment for something she didn't do?"

"She hasn't been punished for the murder." Nelson's eyes glittered. "There's only one punishment for killing a member of the family. She's just been incentivized to tell us what she knew. And apparently, to motivate you to act. Why would I take away that motivation?"

"We're still going to be motivated if she comes with us. I get that you've got people out there who can take us at a moment's notice. I get that you have eyes and ears all over the place, including in the police department. I'll be motivated because I don't want to come back here, and I don't want any of my friends coming back here."

Nelson raised one eyebrow. He went back to the report on his desk, ignoring them. Erin assumed he was thinking it through, clearing his mind by focusing on something else for a few minutes. She often distracted herself in order to relax and look at a problem again with fresh eyes.

After a few moments of silence, Nelson looked up at them. "Nobody is keeping you here," he pointed out. "I have other things to work on."

Erin looked at Willie. He was the one who knew Nelson and understood the dynamics of the clan, something Erin couldn't even come close to doing. Willie got to his feet. He motioned the three women to come with him. Erin felt panic rising as they left the room and wound their way back through the halls again. She felt like they were walking in slow motion, and that any minute, they would all be the target of one of Nelson's minions. They would shoot her in the head, or drag her back to the cell Charley had been imprisoned in. But he wasn't just going to let them walk out of there.

None of them said a word as they traipsed back to the car. They piled in and fastened their seatbelts with shaking hands. Vic sat shotgun beside Willie. Erin looked anxiously at Willie, trying to assess his stress level. He was the one who knew Nelson and the family. He was the one who knew how scared they should be. But his face was a mask and Erin didn't know what he was thinking or feeling. He shifted gears and pulled out into the driveway. They backtracked the curves and came up to the gate again. It swung open in front of them, and Willie drove through.

Erin let out a huge sigh of relief. She wasn't the only one.

"Oh, lordy," Vic exclaimed, fanning herself with her hand. "I was scared as a jack-rabbit that's heard the howl of a wolf. I about wet my pants!"

"I never would have guessed it," Erin said admiringly. "I couldn't tell."

"You don't need to lie to me. I was sweating buckets. Must smell to high heaven." Vic slumped back in her seat, trying to relax. She wiped her forehead.

"If you two are done," Charley said, "we should talk about what we're going to do."

"If one of the options is to run away and never come back…" Vic suggested.

"You think we could ever run far enough that they wouldn't find us?" Charley shot back.

"We've all run away before," Erin said, looking at each of them. "I don't think it solved all of our problems, though, did it? If we ran… there'd be no more Auntie Clem's, Vic. That life would be over. We'd go somewhere else, use new names, and start all over again. New friends, new jobs, new city…"

"I know," Vic admitted. "I'm just scared, and it's so tempting."

"I've done it before. More than once. And it never solves all the problems."

"Right now, we've only got one problem," Charley said. "And that's keeping alive. If we're going to keep alive, we have to figure this out. Who this guy was that killed Bobby."

"Should we go to the police?" Erin suggested. "Jack Ward? Terry? One of them could help us."

"No, Erin," Willie growled. "The police are not going to help us get out of this. You go to the cops, and the clan is going to come gunning for us. And I don't mean that in a figurative way."

"Then what? Do you know how to get into his system to get the video?"

"It's a possibility," Willie said. "But I think our first step should be to show compliance, not to hack his system."

Erin looked at Charley, then at Vic. Vic's arms were folded over her stomach and she was looking down. Despite her earlier jocularity, Vic looked ready to cry.

"Tell me you don't mean going to my family," she begged.

"I know that's the last thing you want to do," Willie said gently. "No more than I would go back to mine, if I could. But we need information. We need to get some clue of whether the Jacksons are involved in this. And I don't know how else to get it. I can't exactly go walking into one of their watering holes."

Vic held her hands over her face, giving a sob. Erin wished that Vic were sitting in the back so Erin could give her a hug. She had to settle instead for reaching up and giving Vic's shoulder a squeeze.

"I'm sorry, Vicky. I'm so sorry."

"It's not your fault." Vic's voice was muffled by her hands. "I'll be fine."

"What can I do? I want to help you."

Vic shook her head. "I don't know what to do. I swore I'd never go back there. They all thought it was a big joke, that I'd be back in a day or two, tail between my legs, having learned my lesson. I swore it wouldn't happen. I'd never go back there."

"You didn't. You came and worked with me and made a life for yourself. You made adult choices and took responsibility for yourself. This isn't crawling back to them, Vic. If we go back…" Erin scowled at Willie for saying that it was the next logical step. He had to know how that would affect Vic. "It's a fact-finding mission. Not because you made a wrong choice and regret what you did."

"But I can't go back there as myself. If I go back as Vic, no one is going to trust me or tell me anything. They'll just laugh and tease and keep things from me like I'm an outsider."

Erin didn't know what to say. She knew how important it was for Vic to be true to herself and her identity. If she couldn't go back as herself, she couldn't go back. Expecting her to was just too cruel.

"Willie… we need to come up with another plan," Erin said. "There has to be another way."

Willie shook his head. "Okay. We'll see what else we can come up with. We need a place to land for a few minutes to recoup." Willie looked in the rear-view mirror toward Charley. "You have a suggestion?"

"Let's just go back to my place. It's not like they're going to come back for me again. Nelson let me go. He knows the truth. If Dwight decides to overrule him… well, it doesn't really matter where we go, they'll find us one way or another."

"Your place it is," Willie agreed. He took a right turn at the next intersection, and Erin realized as they went back to Charley's apartment that Charley wasn't giving Willie any directions. He knew exactly where he was going. Erin glanced at Vic to see if she noticed, but Vic's thoughts were far from the occupants of the car and their destination.

"What about the man in the mask, though?" Erin asked. "What if he comes back to your apartment? He knows where you live."

"If he comes back, he'd better come guns a-blazing, because I'm not putting up with any more mystery nonsense. If he shows his face—or his mask—I'm blowing the dude away."

Erin wasn't sure that made her feel any better. Willie glanced at her and didn't say anything.

Once parked, everyone followed Charley up to her apartment. Charley and Willie entered cautiously, checked out the extent of the small apartment, and returned to the door to let Erin and Vic know it was safe to enter.

Erin looked around the front room and kitchen of the now-familiar apartment and gave a sigh. The day was slipping away. They needed to make a plan. The next day was Monday, and Erin would need to be up bright and early to run the bakery. It seemed like a long time since she had been at Auntie Clem's, and it felt farther away than ever before.

Charley had her head in the fridge. Erin suspected she probably hadn't eaten well, if anything, in the previous two days. At least the rest of them had started the day with coffee and a continental breakfast. But when Charley straightened and backed up, she didn't have leftover casserole or takeout in her hand, but one of the flat bowls Erin recognized as coming from the pet store.

Of course. Iggy hadn't eaten in two days, and Charley was more concerned about looking after the lizard than herself. Charley put the dish on the counter. She caught Erin's eyes on her.

"Have to let them warm up a bit," she commented. "They get too slow when they're cold. They'll be more active once they warm."

"What—?" Vic started to ask, and then cut herself off. She saw Erin's expression and realized what they were talking about. She gave Erin a little smile. "You're so squeamish. We need to take you fishing sometime."

Erin gagged at the thought of having to bait hooks. She couldn't imagine touching the worms or other bait that would be required, let alone impaling them on sharp hooks.

"No, thank you! I'll get my fish at the grocery store."

Though the truth was, Erin wasn't much of a fish person. The nauseating smell was enough to put Erin off her feed for the rest of the day.

"They're not that bad," Charley said, nodding to the bowl. "They don't stink and they're not slimy…"

"I don't want to hear about it," Erin insisted. "You go ahead and feed Iggy, but leave me out of it. I don't want to see or hear or smell what you're giving him."

"They need to warm up for a few minutes. Then I will. Sorry."

She turned back to the fridge. "Man, am I hungry! You know, there were roaches in the room they kept me in, and I just kept thinking how Iggy would love them. And with getting hungrier and hungrier, I was thinking… people can eat bugs. They're a delicacy in some countries. Lots of protein, a real lean meat."

"No way," Erin said. "Doesn't matter how hungry I got, I would never eat a bug. Not on purpose."

"What about cricket flour?" Vic suggested. "I've seen it online. It's gluten free."

"I don't care. I'm still not putting it in my baking. That's disgusting."

"You know there are bug eggs and larvae in the flour you use, don't you?" Charley asked. "That's why you have to put it in the freezer if you don't want it to go bad."

"No," Erin protested, covering her ears. "You guys cut it out. No more talking about bugs."

Willie was sitting on the couch, thumbing through his phone. The insect conversation was going right over his head. Erin knew that she and the others were giddy with their nervousness and anxiety over what was going on, but she sobered at Willie's grim expression, and Vic and Charley quickly became serious as well. Charley pulled a plastic box out of the fridge, along with a bottle of juice.

"Anyone else wants anything, just help yourself," she invited. "And don't worry, there's no more bugs in there. You can open anything up without fear."

She sat down with her scavenged lunch.

"So. What are we going to do?"

"Maybe you could make some phone calls," Willie suggested. "Is there anyone you can call on who might have an idea of what's going on?"

Charley pursed her lips and shook her head. "No… not really. If it's something to do with the Jacksons, I can't think of anyone I could touch."

"There are always people who have a foot in both camps."

"I've stayed as far away from those types as possible. I've got no intention of being accused of being a turncoat." She paused for a moment. "I thought staying away from those kinds of people would keep me safe, but obviously not. What about you? You're the big disappointment. The one who did his five years and then decided it wasn't for you." Charley popped the top of the can and had a swig. "Usually after five years, you're either dead or in too deep to pull out," she informed Erin and Vic. "People just don't do their tour and then bow out."

"Usually," Willie amended.

"Usually."

"I've got a couple of people to tap," Willie said, his eyes still on his phone screen. "But it's a long shot. I'm not confident they'll know anything or want to talk to me."

⸏

In another hour, Willie had exhausted his contacts. Pale but determined, Vic looked to Charley for help.

"If I'm going to go visit my family, I'm going to need to dress down," she said. "I'm going to need some clothes that look a little less…" She looked down at herself, trailing off.

"Less feminine?" Charley suggested.

Erin winced. Vic loved her clothes. She loved dressing up and looking good. While Erin was happiest in a pair of jeans and a t-shirt, Vic had a flair for making herself look pretty.

"Yeah," Vic agreed. "That."

"I have to admit, I've been wondering since Nelson called you James. I never met a transvestite in real life."

"Transgender," Erin corrected her quickly. "And it's really no one's business—"

"It's okay, Erin," Vic said. "I can deal with it. Yes, it's transgender, and I just need to know if you've got… tennis shoes and a hoodie… something that will make me a little less… different. More like I dressed before I left home."

"Sure," Charley agreed. "Come with me. We'll find you something."

Vic followed Charley into her bedroom. Erin looked at Willie, not sure what she should do. Follow them and try to run interference and make Vic feel as comfortable as possible? Or stay out of the way and not make such a big deal of it?

"Nothing we can do," Willie said. "Just be supportive. She knows you love her for who she is. She can take strength in that."

"And you too," Erin agreed.

"I'm not so sure. This is not something I should be pushing her into. I just don't know what else to do. I've done my best to stay on the good side of these guys in spite of not staying inside the organization. I never foresaw it causing Vic any pain."

"It's not your fault. I'm the one who made contact with Charley. If I hadn't done that, we wouldn't be here. We wouldn't be in this situation."

"You had no way of knowing."

"Neither did you."

They both sat there, lost in their own morose thoughts, waiting for Vic and Charley to return.

CHAPTER 28

$\mathcal{E}$rin barely recognized Vic when she came into the living room after changing and washing off her makeup. She wore a shapeless, faded hoodie with the logo of a Tennessee college on it, sneakers, and had her hair pulled back and hidden under the hood of the sweatshirt. Her face looked rougher and more angular without the softening lines of her makeup. Erin could still see the familiar face and expression of her friend, but she could also see the face of the boy she had first seen in the "missing" advertisement of the Bald Eagles weekly newspaper months before. She was still Vic, but she was much closer to James than she had ever been in the months Erin had known her.

Erin bit her lip and looked away, not meeting Vic's eye. Vic didn't need anyone telling her that she looked fine or that she was still the person she had always been. She hadn't changed as a way of exploring another side of herself, but because she had a job to do.

"Okay," Vic said. "Let's go."

Willie stood up. "Where to?"

"I'll have to put in an appearance at the farm. I never associated with the wider clan, so I'll have to start with where I'm known."

Willie nodded. After Charley fed the room-temperature bugs to Iggy, they all headed back down to the car.

"It's just a costume," Charley told Vic, trying to cheer her up. "Just like for Halloween or a play. It doesn't change the person you are. It's just clothes."

Vic nodded.

"It's going to be all right," Charley encouraged.

"Charley…" Willie said. "Just shut up, please? You're not helping."

"I'm just trying to—"

"Just drop it. You don't know what you're talking about."

Charley opened her mouth to argue. She stopped, looking at them, then shook her head.

"Okay. I admit I don't know thing one about being transvestite. Transgender. I'm just trying to be positive."

No one said anything to her.

"Got it," Charley sighed. "Shutting up."

They didn't say anything as they got into the car. When Willie and Vic were once again settled in the front, Vic gave Willie directions in a soft, husky voice. It took almost an hour to get to the farm.

In spite of Erin's concern for her, she was interested in seeing where Vic had come from. Here she had grown up climbing trees, shooting squirrels and other varmints, and doing whatever chores were expected of her. She wrestled with her brothers, went to church on Sunday, and went to school, all as James, another one of the boys.

A man walked out of the whitewashed farmhouse when they stopped. He walked with a cane, leaning heavily on it but giving the impression of great strength rather than frailty. She could only imagine how imposing he had been before the accident that had left him with what Vic had simply called 'a bum leg.'

"Can I help you folks?" he asked gruffly, confident they had just taken a wrong turn off the highway.

"Pa," Vic said.

He looked at her. He stared. His brows furrowed deeply. "James Victor Jackson," he rumbled. "As I recall, you said you were never setting foot on this property again."

"I know, Pa," Vic said. "And I wouldn't. I just... there's been some things going on, and I needed to see you and Mom again. I needed to make sure... everything is going okay with you."

"Your ma and I are still above ground. Every day is a blessing of the Lord."

"It's just... could I come in and talk for a bit? And my friends?"

Mr. Jackson looked at the four of them with a calculating look. Was he trying to divine their relationships? Deciding whether they were two couples? If Erin had been in front with Willie and Vic in back with Charley, it would have been a more likely scenario. His eyes lingered on Willie and he took a long, slow blink. Erin was used to Willie getting second looks due to his darkly-stained skin and the state of his clothes, but this didn't look like one of those looks. Erin was expecting him to say he knew Willie.

"Maybe you know each other," she said, "from Trenton Plaint's funeral?"

Mr. Jackson blinked. "Mebbe."

Vic didn't offer up that Willie was her boyfriend. Not when she was there looking for information. Not when she needed to be an insider for just a little while. For as long as it took to get the information they needed, and then they would be gone.

"Can we maybe come in?" Vic prompted again.

He gave a shrug and stepped back, using his cane deliberately to avoid losing his footing. "Your ma would hogtie me and beat the livin' tar out of me if she knew you'd been here and I turned you away. So you may as well come in. But you know what we think of this nonsense. You're not coming back here unless you give up these ideas about being something you're not. It's unnatural and it's a sin."

"Yes, Pa."

They all got out of the car. Not looking at each other, embarrassed to be caught between the opposite ideologies. They followed Mr. Jackson into the house, in through a door that led to the kitchen. It was overly warm. The stove was on, the air humid and redolent with the smells of fresh baking, roast, and potatoes. Mr. Jackson took a deep breath of the savory air as he stepped in.

"Like walkin' into paradise, Mother."

The heavy woman at the stove turned around, smile wide, to answer him. But her smile and words dropped away when she saw the three visitors entering her domain.

"Oh, my stars, it's James!" She put down her spoon and strode over to Vic, enfolding her in a big hug.

"You're home! You came home! I prayed every day you were gone. Thank the Lord for his goodness."

Vic pulled back from the hug. "I'm not home, Mom. Just for a visit. I wanted to make sure y'all were okay. Catch up on everything that's been going on." She glanced over at Willie for reassurance. It was putting a lot on her to expect her to be able to walk into her family home and somehow to extract a clue as to what had been going on in Moose River. Even if Bobby's death had been orchestrated by the Jacksons, there was no guarantee that her family knew anything about it, or that they would have any reason to tell her.

Mrs. Jackson held Vic at arm's length, looking over her critically. "I swear, I don't know what's wrong with you, child. I raised you right. We raised all of you to be strong, hard-working, faithful men. And you…" She shook her head.

Vic swallowed. She indicated the other visitors. "Mom and Dad, this is my friend and boss, Erin, and her sister Charlotte, and William, a friend of ours."

"Well, it's might nice to meet y'all. I'm grateful to you for being good friends to my boy."

They all tried to smile and nod and be pleasant, but Erin was fighting back her fury at them for treating Vic the way they did. Not accepting her identity, telling her it was a sin, refusing to call her by her chosen name. Vic had run away from home as soon as she could to escape their condemnation and recriminations. Erin couldn't understand how people who claimed to love everyone could treat her like a pariah for being true to herself.

"Should we go to the sitting room?" Mrs. Jackson suggested. "I can leave the stove for a bit now. We'll be more comfortable."

Everyone agreed and followed her into the next room. The sitting room was dim, almost too dark, due to the closed blinds and curtains shutting out the Tennessee sun. It was much cooler than the kitchen. Mr. and Mrs. Jackson took their favorite seats and Vic motioned to her friends to pick what places they wanted. She sat on the couch with Willie, but she didn't cuddle up to him like she would have if they were at Erin's house. Instead, she sat several inches away from him, her back stiff, hands in her lap.

"Erin is my boss at the bakery," Vic said. "She gave me a job and I rent an apartment over her garage. It's my own little place, and it's really nice. We drive to work together."

"Sounds like a good arrangement," Mr. Jackson said. "That's where you were working when we came out for the funeral?"

"Yes, sir."

"People told us about the bakery when we were there," Mrs. Jackson recalled. "Said it made those weird, trendy foods…"

"It's a gluten-free bakery," Erin explained. "And we cater to other special diets as well."

"Well, I suppose there are them that need it," Mr. Jackson said doubtfully. "Though it seems to me that it's more of a fad these days. When I was a young buck, there weren't any of these places around. Everybody ate bread and potatoes and meat. Now, you have gluten-free, and allergies, and those crazy vegans. Seems like everybody's got some kind of special needs all of the sudden."

"They've been around for hundreds and thousands of years," Erin said. "It's hard to say whether they are more prevalent now, or if we just understand more about them so that so many people aren't dying from celiac disease and allergic reactions. Even a hundred years ago, if someone had a severe reaction, they would just die."

Mr. Jackson gave a ponderous shrug. "God takes who he takes," he pronounced. "We can't always divine the reason."

Erin tried to work out what to say in response to that. The fatalistic attitude was one of the things that she never understood about religious people. As if man had no choice in his own life path, and there was no point in trying to stay healthy and extend his life. Because no matter what he did, one day, God would just reach down from the sky and point his finger and the man would die.

Mrs. Jackson whispered something to her husband and darted a glance at Erin, her face pink.

"An atheist?" Mr. Jackson repeated, as if the comment had been shared with the entire room. "I suppose that explains everything."

Erin blinked. She looked at Vic, trying to get a read on the situation, but Vic's face was blank and her attention was somewhere far away. Physically, she was sitting in the room, but it was obvious to Erin that she was in pain. It was all Vic could do to sit there and talk with her parents as if they were on perfectly good terms. All for Erin's sister. A half-sister who Erin had to admit she didn't even really like. And she wasn't sure Charley liked her either. It had been handy for her to have Erin around, but Erin wasn't at all sure Charley would have had anything to do with her if she hadn't needed someone to help her.

"Excuse me? Explains what?" Erin asked.

"Why you would hire someone like James, in spite of... his confusion. No Christian would ever have a—a person like that in their workplace."

"Then it's a good thing she came to me," Erin said, her jaw sore with how hard she was clenching it. "She's a good baker. You should be proud of how hard she works. I couldn't run the place without her."

Mr. Jackson glared at Erin.

Had she just thrown away any chance they had of finding out who Bobby's killer was? If she alienated Vic's father, how would they find out if something was going on with the Jacksons? But Erin couldn't bear to hear them maligning and misgendering Vic and not stand up for her.

"James was always good in the kitchen," Mrs. Jackson admitted. "Out of all of my boys, he was the only one who was ever interested in learning how to cook and bake."

She received Mr. Jackson's next glare and quavered under his gaze.

"I'm here now," Vic said, her voice cracking a little in desperation. "I, uh, heard some rumors about stuff going on down in Moose River and I was worried that there might be problems here…"

"What stuff?" Mr. Jackson demanded, pulling his eyes away from his wife.

"About Bobby Dyson getting shot," Vic said. "It's been all over the news. I was worried about relations between the families. Stuff like that always causes tensions."

Mr. Jackson nodded, frowning deeply. "You heard about that all the way to Bald Eagle Falls? Nasty business. Who would do a thing like that?"

Mrs. Jackson shook her head. "It could start a whole war," she agreed. "Things have been pretty quiet between the families lately. The usual upsets, but nothing major. And then Bobby Dyson." She closed her eyes and continued to shake her head slowly. "He was a horrible boy, but I would never suggest anyone killing him. It's a bad, bad idea."

Erin took a quick glance at Charley to see how she took the comment about Bobby being 'a horrible boy,' but Charley didn't seem to be offended by it. He had, after all, tried to kill Charley. If he was regularly violent with her and cheated on her as she'd said, Charley had probably had much worse thoughts about him than that he was a horrible boy.

"Do you know who did it?" Vic asked, eager to get the news and get out of there.

"I heard it was his girlfriend," Mrs. Jackson offered in a low voice.

"It wasn't," Vic said. "There was someone else there. It was all caught on video."

"Then you know who did it?"

"No, because the video didn't show his face. The police can't identify him. They need more evidence. Better proof."

"How do you know all that?" Mr. Jackson asked suspiciously.

"I… I know the police in Bald Eagle Falls. Erin is really good friends with one of the officers. So we see him and talk with him a lot. He knew I was from around here, so he thought I would be interested."

"And they have video of Bobby Dyson getting killed?"

Vic tried to avoid getting tangled up in the details. "It's so frustrating," she said, leaning forward confidentially, "because if they can't prove who it is, then they're going to think it was done by the Jackson clan. And I don't know if it was."

Mr. Jackson looked at his wife and shook his head. "I haven't heard anything like that. Do you think it was the family?"

"It *is* the Dysons," she said.

"I don't know." Mr. Jackson shook his head at Vic. "I don't think so. We would have heard something through the organization. Once news spread about Bobby getting killed, there would have been rumblings."

"And nothing…?" Vic asked. That wasn't good news. Not when they needed to prove Charley's innocence if they were all to stay safe. If it wasn't one of the Jacksons, then it was back to the drawing board, and Nelson was not going to like that. He was going to think they were just putting him off.

"No," Vic's father said. "Nothing at all. If it was someone in the family, they kept it quiet. Couldn't have been official business."

"Oh." Vic was trying to look reassured at this news. "I'm glad.

I was worried that it was… someone in the family. Someone that we knew."

Mrs. Jackson's eyes flashed, picking up something from Vic's words and body language that Erin hadn't. "Your own brothers, James? For shame. I can't believe you would even think such a thing."

"No… I didn't really think so, but you worry about your own family. And the boys are always so… so brash and boastful. They'd love to be able to say that they had done something like that."

"Certainly not," Mrs. Jackson said primly. But Erin caught an uneasy look exchanged between Mrs. Jackson and her husband. Not this time, maybe. But sometime soon.

"Good," Vic repeated. "I guess that's all I wanted to know. I was just worried."

"You should know better. Don't speculate. Don't judge your brothers. They're good boys."

"I know they are. Is anyone around today? I kind of thought I'd be able to say hi. To Jeremy, at least."

"They're all out working. But they'll be back for supper. Which I'd better check on…" Mrs. Jackson leaned forward, hands on knees, until she managed to raise herself up. She shuffled toward the kitchen. "We wouldn't want it getting ruined because we're having so much fun visiting."

Erin's stomach growled at the thought of food, but no one invited them to stay. Vic's eyes followed her mother out of the room, and Erin wondered if Vic wanted to talk to her alone. Mr. Jackson quickly took advantage of his wife's departure.

"Why don't you come home for good, James? We never turned you out. You could come back, if you weren't so stubborn. You can see that you've made a mistake. We accept that. Everybody makes mistakes."

Vic chewed on her lip, looking down. "It wasn't a mistake," she said softly. "And if you're waiting for me to admit that it was, you're going to end up waiting a long time. I could never move back here because you and Mom would never accept me the way I am. Besides, I'm an adult now. I have my own life, and I like it. I'm comfortable in my own apartment, with new friends..." Her eyes went to Willie, but she didn't out him as her boyfriend. "I love my job. I like helping people and nourishing them. Making sure that they can get really good food that isn't going to make them sick."

"I wouldn't think that such a place would make much of a profit," Mr. Jackson said, rubbing the space between his eyebrows like he was getting a headache. "It doesn't seem to me that there would be that many people who would want to eat there. Maybe in the big city, where there is more demand for... unusual foods... but in a little town like Bald Eagle Falls? You would be much better off working at a conventional bakery. Like your Aunt Angela had."

"Erin's bakery has been doing really well. It's the only bakery in town, so we get plenty of people who are just looking for good freshly-baked goods, whether it is gluten-free or not. And we're always looking for ways to expand and place our products in more locations. Like the local restaurants, bake sales, county fair, every-where you could think of."

"Who got Angela's bakery?" Mr. Jackson asked. "Are they going to reopen it?"

"He'd like to," Erin said, "but he's run into some legal trouble."

"Who is that?" Mr. Jackson asked.

"Davis Plaint."

"Davis?" He scowled. "How would it go to Davis? I thought Angela left everything to Trenton. Did Davis challenge the will in court? Or did she change it?"

Erin shook her head. "It's a little complicated. Angela left it to Trenton. But he died intestate—without making a will—and when that happens, then the state's intestacy laws go into effect. His estate goes first to his parents, if either of them is surviving. So that means it would go to Adam Plaint, who at that point was only missing. He hadn't been declared dead. The estate had to try to find him, so they hired Alton Summers for that. He's good at that, he's the one who tracked down Trenton and Davis." Erin looked over at Vic, worried she was monopolizing the conversation. But Vic was again staring off the other direction, apparently happy to have someone else keeping her father engaged. "I don't know how much of this you already know…"

Mr. Jackson was leaning forward, interested. "Go on," he encouraged.

"Then we found out that Adam Plaint was dead. He had been for years, long before Angela died. So her estate could never flow into his."

"Where does his estate go? If Trenton's assets go to him, then…"

"But Trenton's estate couldn't flow into his either. Same reason. Adam died years before Trenton did."

"So Trenton's estate, the bakery, goes to Davis?"

"Right." Erin nodded. "Since Trenton died intestate, and neither of his parents were living, it then goes to his siblings. Their sister also died a number of years ago. It was just Trenton and Davis. So the bakery that Angela left to Trenton actually ends up going to Davis… except he's in prison right now, so he can't actually start it up again. My guess is that he'll have to liquidate it instead…"

Vic's head suddenly went up and she looked at Erin. Erin tried to read the surprised expression on her face. Charley's head turned slowly toward Erin at the same time.

Erin's jaw dropped. "Except… it wasn't just Trenton and Davis."

Mr. Jackson snorted. "Of course it was. You're not telling me that Sophie is still alive and just faked her own death."

"No. Not Sophie. Adam Plaint fathered one more child just before he died."

"Angela never had any more children. He disappeared from the picture. Are you telling me he picked up with some other woman?"

"Yes!" Erin didn't mean to sound so delighted about something that had had such a lasting negative effect on her life. All eyes in the room were on her. Willie had caught up with what the others had realized and was looking not at Erin, but at Charley in wide-eyed shock. "He had an affair with my mother. And she became pregnant with Charley!" She quickly amended, as they had decided it was best not to use Charley's nickname with the Jacksons and give away who she actually was. "With Charlotte, I mean." Erin pointed to Charley. "My sister is also Trenton's sister. Since she and Davis both survived Trenton, they both receive equal shares in the estate. Half of the bakery!"

For a moment, the room just sat in stunned silence. Charley looked at Erin like she was crazy.

"What are you talking about?"

"I told you that you were my half-sister. My mother's child. With Adam Plaint. That means you're Trenton Plaint's sister too, and you and Davis both inherit a half share of the bakery."

"What bakery? Your bakery?"

"No, Angela Plaint's bakery. The Bake Shoppe. In Bald Eagle Falls."

"And you think I own half of it now?" She shook her head in confusion. "No one has contacted me about that."

Erin looked at Charley, blinking as the possibilities each clicked into place.

"Erin," Willie said, "maybe Bobby wasn't the target. Maybe that was just misdirection. Maybe this was all about Charlotte."

"*Charlotte,*" Erin repeated. "The masked man. He didn't say… your nickname. He said Charlotte."

"Why does that matter?"

"Because it means he didn't know you. He didn't know you personally, and he didn't know you through… your boss. He only knew your name."

"Okay. So he didn't know me. That's kind of a relief. I'd rather it wasn't someone I know. But again… what does it matter?"

"No one told you that you were an heir to Trenton's estate?"

"I think I'd remember that."

"Somebody should have come." Erin looked at Vic and Willie for their input. "Alton Summers was hired by Clementine's estate to find me. He was hired by Angela's estate to find Trenton and Davis and then to look into Adam's disappearance. It's what he does. So why didn't they hire him to find Charlotte?"

"Maybe they did… maybe Davis himself did," Willie said.

"I'm telling you, no one called me," Charley reiterated.

Willie's eyes were bright against his dark face. "Think about it. Davis doesn't want to split the estate fifty-fifty. He wants to run The Bake Shoppe. And if he can't open The Bake Shoppe, then he wants to get the money for it. All the money for it, not half. So he hires Alton to find Charlotte, but not to inform her of her rights in the estate. To get her out of the picture."

Charley swore under her breath. All eyes in the room were on her. "Nelson said that the masked man 'wound Bobby up' and then killed him when things got out of hand. *Why* would he intentionally wind Bobby up?"

"So Bobby would break up with you," Erin deduced.

"A messy breakup with Bobby Dyson would mean you would have to leave," Willie said. "There's no way you could stay here and continue to work with the Dysons if there was bad blood between you and Bobby."

"Wait a minute," Mr. Jackson was starting to clue in to what they were talking about. He pointed to Charley. "This is Bobby's girlfriend?" He turned to Vic. "You brought one of the Dyson clan into my house?"

"We had to find out who killed Bobby—" Vic started to explain.

"You're working for the Dysons? My own son?"

"I'm—no—they just… they kidnapped Charley, and she's Erin's sister, so we were trying to help her out…"

Mr. Jackson was struggling to his feet, using the cane to push himself up. "I thought when you left here that there couldn't be anything worse than my son deciding he was gay or a girl or whatever the crap you came up with. I thought I could never be more disappointed and embarrassed by your behavior." He made it to his feet and glared at Vic, his eyes blazing. "Was I ever wrong. Not only do you think you can switch sexes, you think you can switch families and start working for the Dysons as well! You are a traitor to this family. You've gone against everything we believe in."

Vic got up. The rest of them did as well, not sure how to react to Mr. Jackson's anger. Vic stood before her father, hands up, watching him warily.

"We'll go," she said. "I'm sorry. I'm going."

"You'll go, will you?" He advanced on her. "You've stopped using the family name, and that's a good thing. You are no longer a Jackson. You will never come by here again. We shoot trespassers in these parts, keep that in mind. I don't ever want to see you or hear from you again. Your mother, either. No contact *ever again*."

Vic's voice was choked. "Okay. I won't."

He took another step and swung the cane. Erin wasn't close enough to do anything about it, but she reacted instinctively, throwing her hands up as if she could block the cane. "No!"

The first blow landed on the back of Vic's upper thigh, with a resounding thwack. There was no second blow. Willie grabbed the cane and wrenched it out of Mr. Jackson's hand. He got in Mr. Jackson's face, the cane held threateningly in his hand.

"You will *never* lay your hands on her again!"

"If he comes back here, I'll do what I need to. How about you keep him away?" Mr. Jackson stared at Willie, eye-to-eye, not backing down. "Now that I know you all came from the Dysons, I know who you are. William, he called you. Willie Andrews. Outcast from your own family. A filthy, lazy, degenerate. You and James...?" He flicked a glance at Vic. "You're disgusting. I should have you charged with corrupting a minor."

"Vic is not a minor."

"He was when he left here." Mr. Jackson took in Willie's look of surprise. "Oh, he may have told you he was eighteen, but he wasn't. He just turned eighteen this Christmas."

Erin looked over at Vic. She had wondered more than once whether Vic was telling the truth about her age. There were times when she seemed so young. A few months really didn't make a difference one way or another, but it did confirm Erin's suspicions that the runaway hadn't quite been able to wait until her eighteenth birthday to strike out on her own.

Vic was rubbing the back of her leg where her father had struck her, clearly aching from the blow. Willie gave Mr. Jackson one more warning look, then stepped back from him, took Vic around the shoulders, and escorted her out of the room. Erin and Charley followed them out, staying as far from Mr. Jackson as possible.

Mrs. Jackson was in the kitchen wringing her hands. "Oh, no," she wept. "Oh, no, James. Please. Talk to your father. Make up. Don't leave like this, with everybody on bad terms. You can come home. He'll cool down again and he'll regret what he said. Please don't leave."

Vic shook her head. She didn't hug her mother again before leaving. She just walked on by, protected by Willie's embrace. Before leaving the kitchen, Willie threw Mr. Jackson's cane down on the floor with a clatter.

Erin was relieved when they got out to the car, but it wasn't over. A pickup truck was bouncing down the road approaching the house.

Erin watched it with alarm. With four of them facing Mr. Jackson, she had felt threatened, but not too afraid. Having more men from the Jackson clan closing in, she felt just as scared as she had been in the Dyson mansion. It was a different setting, but again facing the possibility of armed clan soldiers with overwhelming force, she felt almost sick with fear.

Vic stopped in her tracks. Willie stopped and encouraged her to get into the car. They could get in the car and drive away. They could probably outrun the truck if they had to. They could call the police.

There was probably no 9-1-1 service and they'd have to wait

until they got back into Moose River. Now that they knew—or strongly suspected—who had hired the masked man, they had something to take to the police. They could explain all that had happened and the police would drop the charges against Charley.

They would all be safe, because the Dysons would know that it wasn't the Jackson clan who had ordered his son killed. It had just been Davis, and he and Alton had screwed it up. Alton had planned to make Bobby mad enough to throw Charley out and make her run, but he hadn't expected Bobby to be so furious that he would try to kill Charley. After that, he'd done everything he could to get her to run.

The pickup pulled to a stop a few feet away from Willie's car, skidding in the gravel and sending clouds of dust into the air. The doors opened and the men jumped out of the truck, fanning out to look the strangers over.

"It's James!" one young man crowed. He pushed toward her, his blond hair streaming out behind him, and Erin recognized him as Jeremy. "Vic. How's it going, little sister?" He gave her a hard hug, and looked around at the rest of them, eyes sparkling. "Erin, Willie." He shook his head at Charley. "I don't know you, but welcome!"

"We're leaving," Vic said quietly. "Pa…"

"Aw, come on. Pa's bark is worse than his bite, pay him no mind."

Vic shook her head, rubbing the back of her leg. "His bite's pretty bad today too. I can't stay, Jer, and I won't be back."

He stared at her. The other young men were not as enthusiastic as Jeremy. They greeted Vic with awkward handshakes and slaps on the back, unsure what to call her or how to talk to her, too embarrassed to hug her.

"Y'all know where to find me," Vic said. "You want to visit, just come by Auntie Clem's Bakery in Bald Eagle Falls. It's not that far away. And Jeremy knows where the house is." She sniffled, her eyes glistening with tears. "I can't come back here and I can't call, so if you want to keep in touch, y'all have to reach out to me.

Otherwise… I'll assume you don't want anything to do with me either."

They made noises of protest. Jeremy gave her another hug. "Vic. I don't know what happened, but don't just leave like this. Mom misses you so bad. She cries all the time. You have to come back and visit. Don't worry about what Pa says…"

"He said he'll shoot any trespassers, Jer. He'll shoot me. You think I'm going to take the chance that he might just be full of hot air? He near 'nough broke my leg with that durn cane of his! I'm not coming back. You know where to find me."

"Okay," Jeremy finally conceded. "I'd never forgive myself if something happened to you. You take care of yourself." He looked over at Willie. "You take care of my sister."

There were murmurs from the other boys. Embarrassed laughs over Jeremy calling Vic his sister. But Jeremy showed no embarrassment. He stood and watched as they all got into Willie's car, then waved as Willie pulled out.

Once they were out of sight of the boys and the white farmhouse, Vic put her hands over her face and sobbed.

CHAPTER 29

Charley made no attempt to comfort Vic and tell her that everything was going to be fine this time. She didn't tell her that there was no reason to be so upset over some silly clothes. They were all quiet as Willie drove back to Moose River. Willie turned on the radio and managed to find a weak signal, and they listened to scratchy-sounding country on the way back, each of them lost in their own thoughts.

When they reached the city limits, Vic had stopped crying, had wiped her face with the voluminous hoodie, and was breathing more naturally.

"Why would Davis just try to scare Charley off?" Erin asked Willie. "After killing Trenton and Bernie, why would he balk at Charley?"

"Maybe he didn't," Willie said, glancing back at Erin. "Maybe that was Alton, if Alton is the masked man. Maybe he drew the line at murder. He's never had a problem with verbal threats and blackmail. Maybe just scaring Charley off was his idea."

Vic cleared her throat. "Or maybe it's because Davis has already lost one sister." She wiped her eyes.

"Sophie?"

Vic nodded. "He doesn't have any family left other than

Charley. Maybe he couldn't bring himself to do it. She is his baby sister, just like she's yours."

~

They called Terry rather than Jack Ward. Terry knew them and he would trust their deductions before a cop who barely knew anything about them. He got Tom to take the remainder of his shift and drove into Moose River to meet them at Charley's apartment.

They had talked about finding somewhere neutral where the Dysons wouldn't know to find them. But Vic desperately needed to put on her own clothes again and none of them had the mental energy to go shopping for replacements. So they went back to Charley's apartment. Willie scouted it out before they went in, looking for anyone who might be keeping surveillance.

"At least if they come, we'll have something to tell them this time," Charley said, not too worried about it.

"But anything we tell Nelson, he's likely to take action on," Erin pointed out. "We don't want to get anyone killed when all we have is speculation."

Charley shrugged. "Doesn't sound like these guys are exactly upstanding citizens. If they get themselves into the middle of an organized crime murder, they can expect to be targeted."

"Like you? You managed to get yourself into the middle of it, but you didn't do anything. Nelson or his father can act as judge, jury, and executioner, but that doesn't mean justice is served. Killing you would have been a mistake, and the same might be true of Davis or Alton Summers. We don't know the extent of their crimes and we don't want to get them killed."

Charley shrugged. "I'm not trying to get anyone killed, but if the Dysons show up… I don't feel like being the sacrificial lamb."

Vic had disappeared immediately into Charley's bedroom. It was a while before she came out, herself once again. The makeup was flawlessly applied, all signs of distress eliminated, other than her red-rimmed eyes and the slight puffiness under them.

Erin gave her a hug. "Are you okay?"

Vic nodded and forced a smile. "I'm just as fine as a home-cooked meal. How long will we have to wait for Terry?"

"He's going to get Tom to finish out his shift, so we don't have to wait that long. Just a couple of hours for him to drive here."

"Or however long it takes," Vic agreed. "I have a feeling he might just use his lights and siren and shave off a bit of time."

"Maybe. At least we don't have to wait until tonight."

"You really *do* look good," Charley said, looking Vic over. "I never would guess that you were..." she trailed off, suddenly awkward over how to finish the sentence.

"Vic always looks good," Erin said firmly. "I guess we just sit down and relax and wait now. Maybe order in something to eat? I'll cover the bill this time."

"You want pizza again? We didn't exactly finish it last time."

"Sure." Erin nodded. She looked at Vic. "You'll love it. It's the most amazing pizza ever. Willie...?"

Willie was distracted, looking out the window. Daydreaming or watching for bad guys? Willie looked around at his name.

"Sorry, what?"

"Pizza?"

"Sure. Sounds good."

Erin sat down with a sigh. Vic lowered herself carefully to the couch, wincing as she settled on it.

"Are you okay?" Erin asked. "Do you want... some ice or something for your... leg?"

Vic shifted uncomfortably. "Feels like I got hit by a car. That old man really has an arm."

"It must really hurt."

"I've been whipped worse, but not many times. If you guys weren't there and he got me down..." Vic rubbed the injured area, trying to sit in a way that didn't put pressure on it. "What makes him think he can still hit me like that? I'm an adult, I'm not a child anymore!"

Erin's anger rose again at the thought of Mr. Jackson hitting a defenseless child with his cane. How could any person treat a child like that and consider themselves a good person? Erin couldn't even call him a Christian in her mind, knowing that the myths of Jesus had him preaching kindness toward children. Mr. Jackson couldn't profess to follow such a man and then whip his own child like an animal. Erin would never even have treated an animal that way.

She swallowed and tried not to let her anger show.

"He's got no right to hurt you. You could charge him with assault." She knew Vic never would.

"I know… but I don't want any trouble. Things are bad enough already. You saw that. They can disown me, but I don't want to end up in a feud with them. Despite what they might say… I haven't joined the enemy. I'm just helping out Charley."

Charley had been talking on her phone, Erin presumed with the pizza restaurant. She hung up and looked over at Vic at the mention of her name.

"What?"

"Just saying that I wasn't going against my family by helping you out…"

Charley nodded slowly. "Hey, I didn't follow everything you were saying at your house, but…"

Vic raised her eyebrows. "Yeah…?"

"You're a Jackson."

"Right. Born one, anyway, I've changed my name."

"And your aunt is related to the guy who killed Bobby."

"Related to the guy who hired him, anyway," Erin clarified. "Davis. He's Angela's son."

"My half-brother."

Vic and Erin nodded together.

"So it *was* the Jacksons who were responsible for Bobby's death."

Vic hesitated. "Well… I suppose technically. But he was just doing it for himself, not because the family ordered it."

"And I'm a Jackson? Was my father a Jackson, or just his wife?"

Vic shrugged. "They're all clan. So I guess you are too."

Willie chuckled. Charley turned and looked at him.

"A Jackson working for the Dysons?" Willie said. "I think you're going to be out a job, if you weren't already."

Charley rubbed her head. "This is crazy."

Erin felt like she hadn't seen Terry in days. The handsome policeman in uniform was a welcome sight, and she felt much better with him there.

"Terry, thanks so much for coming!" She threw her arms around him. "You don't know how glad I am to see you!"

Terry cuddled her close and kissed the top of her hair.

"I'm glad to see you too." He scanned the room, evaluating each of his tired friends. "So… what have you gotten yourselves into now?"

"We didn't exactly have any choice," Vic defended them. "It wasn't like we asked to be mixed up in a murder.

"You never do…"

He sat down with them and snagged a slice of room-temperature pizza from the coffee table.

"Why don't you start at the beginning, and tell me how you ended up here again?" Terry looked at Erin. "I thought we had agreed that you should just stay out of this."

"I didn't think there was anything else I could do. I never said I would stay out of it."

He rolled his eyes and took a bite of pizza, gesturing for her to begin her explanation. Erin looked at the others, not sure where to start. "I told you about the Dysons taking Charley…"

"Well, we knew she had gone with them. By choice." He

cocked an eyebrow at Charley. "Right? You wanted to go talk to Dwight Dyson."

Charley shrugged. "Yeah… I figured it was the only way not to get killed. But things didn't exactly go as well as I'd hoped."

"They kidnapped her," Erin said.

"Kidnapped?" Terry repeated. "Were you held against your will?"

Charley nodded. "Well, yeah. I didn't exactly choose to stay there in a creepy basement room full of bugs and rats."

"Have you reported this to the police?"

"No."

"If you want to have them arrested, you need to report it."

"That's not what I want. I'm out now. Nelson let me go after he talked to Erin."

"So what do you need my help for?"

"We think we figured out who killed Bobby," Erin said.

"How did you do that?"

Erin didn't explain the how, which was too long and convoluted, and she didn't want to highlight Vic's dysfunctional family. "We think that Charley was the target, not Bobby. The idea was to force her to leave town. Killing Bobby was an unexpected development."

"You think."

"We're pretty sure."

"What makes you think that?"

Erin expanded on what they had learned from Nelson, from Charley's recollection, and their analysis of Trenton Plaint's estate succession. Terry sat, rubbing his jaw, thinking about it.

"Nelson has surveillance video of what happened."

"Yes… but I don't think he's going to give it to anyone," Erin admitted. "Even if we can prove who it is in the video, I think he's keeping his cards close to the vest. He's not going to share it with the police."

"So how do you expect to prove this? Davis has already

avoided charges a number of times. He's pretty savvy where the law is concerned. He's not going to confess."

"Then we go after Alton, get him to admit who hired him and the whole conspiracy."

"Because Alton has always been so open and honest before," Terry said wryly. "So easy to get along with."

"Well… no… but he knows which side his bread is buttered on. If he sees he could end up going to prison for Bobby's shooting, he's going to turn on Davis and make a deal, don't you think? He's always been in it for his own gain."

"We need some leverage. We need to start somewhere. We can't just go in and say that we know he killed Bobby, but we have no evidence that it was him or that he was working with Davis."

Charley shuffled forward in her seat. "We need a sting," she said. "Catch the two of them together. Maybe they'll say something incriminating."

"That might be an idea. But we'll have to get Jack Ward or someone else local on our side. Again, going to them without any evidence…"

"Davis is still in prison, isn't he?" Erin asked.

"Yes."

"Then if Alton has been meeting with him, he'll be on the visitor records."

Terry nodded. "Maybe right after Bobby's death. The timing of the visits might be informative."

"And if they've been seeing each other, there might be video or audio recordings of their visits…"

"If you're lucky. But I don't think any of the prisons around here are very high-tech."

CHAPTER 30

It took some convincing, but eventually, Jack Ward agreed to at least consult with the prison on Davis's visitor list and any surveillance they might have available. When he got back to Terry, his tone was cautiously optimistic. "You were right about the two of them meeting, anyway," he admitted. "Unfortunately, Plaint is only in medium security, and their visits have not been subject to audio or visual surveillance."

"So where can you go from there? Is there anything I can lend a hand with?"

"You've been helpful, but there's not a lot anyone can do until Plaint and Summers meet again. If they do. We just have to wait and see."

As luck would have it, it wasn't long before Alton returned to the prison to report to Davis on developments.

Davis had apparently already heard some whisperings of trouble through the prison grapevine. He leaned in close to Alton, his voice low, difficult to hear over the background of all of the other conversations in the medium-security visitor's room. But they had a microphone under the table that picked up most of the conversation.

"What's going on?" Davis demanded, leaning close to Alton.

"First I hear she'd been killed by the Dysons and then I hear she's fine and still hanging around Moose River!"

Alton ran a hand through his thin, stringy hair. "She's not dead," he said. "I'm not sure where that rumor came from, other than that she dropped out of sight for a few days. I think she was taken by Dwight Dyson." He looked back and forth, watching for anyone that was paying more attention to him than they should be. "Things are getting pretty hot, boss. I think we should pull out. Cut our losses."

"That's not good enough," Davis objected. "You said you could get her out of town. That's what we agreed to. We can't pull out. She needs to disappear."

"There's only one way I know of to make sure she disappears and never comes back. We've tried everything else. She's just as stubborn as her sister. I couldn't get anywhere with that one, either."

Davis's face was getting red. "You said you could do it. We've wasted all of this time. This whole thing has blown up into a huge mess. You need to fix it."

Summers sat back in his seat, folding his arms. "All right," he agreed. "I'll fix it."

Davis stared at him. "What are you going to do?"

"I'm going to make her disappear."

"How?"

"You don't want to ask me that."

"You remember what I said before. You promised."

Summers shrugged. "If you want me to act for you, you need to give me the freedom to do what I need to. If you're having second thoughts, I can pull out. If you want me to go ahead, then don't put restrictions on me."

"Fine." Davis's mouth formed a thin, straight line. "You do what you said you would."

~

"We've got police guards on Charley Campbell," Jack Ward assured Terry. "They're not visible, but they're close by and monitoring all of the approaches with video surveillance. As soon as Alton Summers makes his move, we'll be ready for him."

Erin, listening to the call on speakerphone, shook her head. "Why can't you just arrest him? As soon as you tell him you know what he's been doing, he'll confess. He'll make a deal so he doesn't have to go to prison too."

"Not likely," Ward disagreed. "If he's the one who shot Bobby, he's got blood on his hands and he won't confess to that, because it's a sure trip to prison."

"But he'll plead," Erin argued.

"Maybe he would plead if we had some evidence, but we don't. We just have a theory and a cryptic conversation at the prison. He didn't admit to killing anyone and didn't say exactly what it was that he was going to do, other than make Charley disappear permanently."

"Which means he's planning to kill her."

"That's your interpretation," Ward said. "He can argue that he meant he was going to talk to her. Persuade her, bribe her, whatever."

"But you know that wasn't what he meant."

"What I think he meant is beside the point. That doesn't hold up in court. Juries need proof, not speculation. Don't worry, Miss Price, we are guarding your sister. Nothing is going to happen to her. When Summers proves his intent, then we'll be able to arrest him. And when we have proof of wrongdoing on his part, then we have something to bargain with to put Davis away permanently."

Terry put his hand over Erin's, giving her a reassuring smile. Erin did her best to smile back.

"Okay. Just please take care of my baby sister."

CHAPTER 31

The fixer moved stealthily, his feet barely making a sound as he approached the door. His heart was pounding hard and fast in anticipation, feeling the euphoric adrenaline rush that was getting harder and harder for him to achieve.

She thought she could defy him, that she could ignore his warnings and just go ahead and do whatever she wanted to. She thought she was smarter than he was. She thought she could outwit him, when she didn't have a clue what was going on.

Now she was a sitting duck, oblivious to his presence. He took a careful look around to make sure that nobody was watching and no wireless cameras had been installed since he'd been there last. Stupid of her to think that a burglar alarm triggered by an opened door or window was going to stop him from doing what he was there to do.

He disabled the front door sensor and jimmied the lock to let himself in. The place was quiet. After all of her excitement over the last few days, she was asleep early, thinking herself beyond the reach of the clans. But he knew better. Charlotte needed to be shown that no one was out of reach. He could always find a way to fulfill a contract.

The carpet inside the door was thick enough to muffle any

noise from his movements. There was nothing to wake her up. He went down the hall to the room that he'd previously noted as being her bedroom, his arm down at his side, finger inside the trigger guard, savoring the moment.

Just as he stepped forward, there was a horrible screeching noise. Something thumped against him in the darkness, the howling filling his ears.

He was distracted from his target for only a moment, but when he brought his weapon up and pointed it at the bed, the covers were thrown back and it was empty.

Alton swore. It was only one misstep, but it was a big one. He couldn't complete his mission without a target.

"Erin," he said softly into the darkness. "Where are you, Erin?"

CHAPTER 32

Erin lay on the floor on the other side of the bed, panicked and disoriented. She could hear Alton moving into the room, his feet whispering over the carpet, his voice pitched in a low, soothing tone as he hunted her down.

Orange Blossom let out another furious scream, yowling and screeching like a cougar at the intruder. Alton stumbled and swore, obviously tripped up by the angry puffball.

Why hadn't the burglar alarm gone off? What was the point in having it if it didn't give her any warning of a break-in and didn't let the neighbors, Vic, or Terry know that something was wrong?

Her phone was on the bedside table on the other side of the bed. In order for Erin to get it, she would have to expose herself. But it wasn't going to take that long for Alton to make it across the room, around the bed, and to find her where she cowered. By then, it would be too late for Erin to go anywhere or try anything.

She tried to squirm under the bed. It was a pretty tight fit. She was skinny, but that didn't make her skull any smaller. She was glad the mattress on the antique frame was raised more than three inches, but she still wasn't sure she could crawl underneath without getting stuck. All Alton had to do was fire through the mattress or lift it up off of the bed so that he could get a clear shot at her.

It was dusty. Erin spent a lot of time at the bakery and not so much time vacuuming the house. With two furry pets, the dust balls reproduced at an alarming rate.

Alton was still advancing, speaking to her in that creepy, soothing voice. He knew she was in the room and he had only to get her in his sights. Orange Blossom was still dancing around him like a Tasmanian devil, hissing and yowling and occasionally clawing or biting Alton when he could. Alton tripped, scraped his shin on the iron bed frame, and swore.

"Why are you giving me such problems, Erin? It's time to stop playing around."

Erin squirmed the rest of the way under the bed, and took a couple of deep breaths, even though the dust tickled her nose and filling her lungs made it an even tighter fit. At first, she had only been trying to hide from Alton, but once she had the mattress over top of her, she had another thought. If she could get to the other side of the bed without exposing herself, then maybe she could get ahold of her phone and place a call to Terry. If only someone else knew she was in trouble, she had a chance of surviving.

Erin inched forward under the bed. She kept running into boxes and other items that had been stored under it, and was beginning to wonder if there was any clear route to the other side. She tried to gently move things out of her way without making any sound to give away where she was and what she was doing. Luckily, Orange Blossom kept making a racket and giving Alton trouble.

Erin felt a sudden shifting of air on her hand. It was out from under the bed. She felt for the phone's charge cord, and used it to drag the phone over to her, catching it when it fell. Just a few seconds, and she would be through to Terry. She couldn't tell him what was happening without alerting Alton, but she was sure he would go to her house if she didn't say anything. He would know that a call that late wasn't just a pocket dial. Erin tried to hide the brightly-lit screen from Alton as she turned on the display.

All of a sudden, the burglar alarm started shrilling. Erin jumped and hit her head on the iron frame of the bed, making her see stars and nearly black out.

Alton swore and turned toward the bedroom doorway. They could both hear footsteps in the kitchen.

"I'm sorry! I was half asleep and I forgot about the stupid alarm," Vic called out. "Is everything okay, Erin?"

The footsteps left the hard tile of the kitchen and Erin knew Vic was in the hall walking toward the bedroom.

"Stay back, Vic! He's got a gun!"

Alton swore irritably at Erin. He turned around to face the door, his gun raised to the level, waiting for Vic to appear in the doorway.

Erin had called Terry's number and laid her phone face-down on the floor so that the light would be covered and Alton couldn't use it as a beacon to shoot her. As Alton moved toward the door, Erin retreated farther back, putting space between them and sheltering behind the bed.

There wasn't a sound from Vic. Erin strained her ears. Did Vic understand? Was she still there or had she retreated? Erin held her breath, which was rasping in her own ears, and listened harder. She could still hear nothing but Alton moving and cursing under his breath at Orange Blossom, the cat still yowling and trying to drive the stranger from his territory.

There was a tinny voice coming from Erin's phone, muffled because the speaker was against the rug. Terry trying to figure out what was wrong.

Erin heard a creak from the hallway floor. She recognized it. She knew where every creaky floorboard in the house was, and she now knew where Vic was, just outside Erin's bedroom door.

Without thinking it through, Erin grabbed her phone and threw it across the room. Alton whirled toward it and fired. At almost the same instant, Vic moved into the doorway and leveled her gun, taking careful aim at Alton before firing. At her shot, Alton turned slowly back to look at Vic. The hand gripping his gun started to lower slowly, like a plant drooping without water.

Vic remained motionless in the doorway, gun still up, waiting for Alton to make a move. Erin wanted to shout at her to get out of the way and to take cover. She shouldn't just stand there where Alton could shoot her. He'd already fired his gun once, he wouldn't hesitate to do it again.

But Alton's hand lowered all the way to his side. Then he dropped his gun. Erin thought she should probably grab it before he could bend over and pick it up again, but she was paralyzed.

Sirens sounded outside. More than one. Terry had dispatched the sheriff and Tom as well. They were all closing in on the house.

Alton just stood there. Vic stood at the ready in the doorway, not moving, even though Alton had dropped his gun.

The cars stopped outside the house. She could hear running footsteps up the front walkway. Terry's voice sounded from the front door.

"Erin? Are you okay?"

Erin tried to answer, but her voice was so small it didn't register. She still didn't want Alton to hear her, even though he seemed to be folding into himself, slowly getting closer to the floor.

"I'm in the hall," Vic called to Terry. "Erin is in the bedroom. I think the gunman is Alton Summers."

Terry's voice got closer. Erin could hear K9 panting, and imagined he was eagerly pulling on his collar, wanting to get closer to the action.

"Where is he?" Terry asked. "Are you safe?"

"He's here. I shot him. He dropped the gun, but he hasn't been secured."

Terry's form appeared behind Vic. He stood there for a

moment, allowing his eyes to adjust to the dark and assessing the situation.

"Alton Summers, you're under arrest. Put your hands above your head."

Alton didn't move his arms. His knees continued to buckle, and it wouldn't be long before he reached the tipping point and either toppled over or collapsed. Erin tried to tell Terry that Alton was injured, but still couldn't raise her voice enough for him to hear.

"Move aside, Vic. Holster your gun, but I'm going to need to take it from you later."

Vic lowered her weapon. She drew aside to allow Terry to get into the bedroom. Terry entered as Alton hit the floor. He put a hand on Alton's back to keep him down.

"Can you turn on the light?" he asked Vic. "I can't see a thing. Where's Erin, is she okay?"

"I don't know."

The light came on, blinding at first, making Erin's eyes water. Terry saw Alton's gun and pushed it farther away. He turned Alton onto his back and they all saw the blood-soaked shirt. Terry pressed one hand over it, and clicked his radio with his other.

"Gunshot victim, need EMS. Center mass, heavy bleeding."

Terry's eyes caught on Erin, peeking out from under the bed. "Erin. Are you okay? Are you hurt?"

Erin swallowed. "I'm okay," she whispered. This time he was close enough and it was quiet enough for him to hear.

"Good. Are you sure? Come out of there and let Vic check you out. Sometimes you can get hurt and not even know it."

It seemed like a long time before Erin's limbs obeyed and she was able to crawl out. Vic moved around the perimeter of the room, giving Terry lots of space, and helped Erin to her feet. They both looked Erin over, looking for any injuries. Vic found a crease across Erin's forehead, bloody but not deep.

"Is that from his shot?" Vic asked, sitting Erin down on the bed and pulling several tissues from the box on the bedside table to wad up and hold over the cut.

"No. I hit it on the bed when the alarm went."

Tom and the sheriff had cleared the rest of the house and hovered around the door, not entering because the room was already too crowded with the four of them.

"Everything is clear, Terry," the sheriff advised. "Do you want me to take over there?"

Terry looked down at the bloody mess under his hand. "I'd better keep pressure on. I don't know if it's doing any good, but if we can keep him alive to prosecute, I'd sure like to see him rotting in jail."

"What happened?"

"Orange Blossom woke me up," Erin explained, trying to speak up loudly enough that they could all hear her. "I guess he didn't like Alton coming in. I don't know how he got in. The alarm didn't go until Vic came. He had a gun. He was trying to kill me."

Terry nodded, his expression grim and set.

"Why did he come after me?" Erin demanded. "He was supposed to be going after Charley! Charley was the one being guarded!"

"Maybe he knew that. Or maybe you were the final threat that was supposed to scare Charley into doing what she was told and disappearing for good. I don't know."

Erin blinked at Vic, still pressing the tissue to Erin's forehead. "How did you know?"

Vic shook her head. "I heard Blossom. He never makes noise like that when you're around. I just knew something was wrong."

Orange Blossom jumped up on the bed beside Erin and turned around. He puffed out his fur and hissed at K9, who was panting and watching all the excitement with interest.

*E*rin met up with Charley at her apartment. It had been a long, strange week. Strange because it had been so normal. No mysteries, no worries, no sleepless nights. Just working the usual bakery routine. So Sunday afternoon, after the ladies' tea, she headed over to Charley's.

Everything in Charley's apartment had been packed up and was in boxes, other than Iggy's reptarium.

"Where are you going?" Erin asked.

As they had expected, once word got out about Charley's familial connection with Davis, and how Davis had been implicated in Bobby's death, Charley was no longer welcomed by the Dysons.

"It's not really fair," Charley complained. "It isn't like anything has been proven in court. And I didn't choose to be related to the Jacksons. It isn't like I was even raised by them."

"I know," Erin agreed. "So… where…?"

"If I'm heir to Angela Plaint's estate, then I thought maybe… there might be a place in Bald Eagle Falls I could live."

"Half-heir."

Charley gave her a narrow look. "If Davis killed Trenton for the inheritance, then he can't profit by it, right? And that would make all of it mine."

"But we can't prove that Davis had anything to do with Trenton's death. Trenton had an allergic reaction to the cupcakes that Joelle bought. It looks like an accident."

"Yeah, that's what you said. And that might be good enough for you, but it's not good enough for me. Not when it's the difference between half of the Plaint estate or all of it. So I'm going to prove it, one way or another."

Erin shifted uneasily.

Everything they had just been through had been because Davis didn't want to split the inheritance with Charley. Now Charley was turning the tables.

Erin wasn't sure she was going to like the results any better.

**Did you enjoy this book? Reviews and recommendations are
vital to making a book successful.**

**Please leave a review at your favorite book store or review site
and share it with your friends.**

Don't miss the following bonus material:
Sign up for mailing list to get a free ebook
Read a sneak preview chapter
Other books by P.D. Workman
Learn more about the author

PREVIEW OF BREWING
DEATH

Erin was surprised to hear the back door opening. Vic, her partner at the bakery, entered the kitchen. The tall, blond girl surveyed the mess the kitchen was in, cookbooks and boxes of herbs and tea strewing the counters and tables and shook her head in mock dismay.

"I leave you alone for the day and come home to the house looking like it was hit by a tornado!" she drawled.

Erin looked at the clock on the wall. "It can't be that late already!"

"I suppose this means you didn't make supper."

Not that they usually had anything fancy for supper. Even on the rare days when one of them took the afternoon or the day off while Bella covered a shift at Auntie Clem's Bakery, there was usually so much else to do that the evening meal was a frozen dinner or something at one of Bald Eagle Falls's fine eating establishments. Erin shook her head ruefully.

"I don't think I even had lunch."

Vic walked toward the fridge. In the living room, Erin heard a thump as Orange Blossom jumped off of the couch, and by the time Vic had her hand on the handle of the fridge door, he was into the room, meowing chattily at one of his favorite people. Vic looked over at his food dish.

"It doesn't look like you forgot to feed Blossom, though."

"How could I? He'd never let me forget that!"

Vic opened the fridge. Orange Blossom wound around her legs, vocalizing loudly. "Oh, is there something in here you would like?" Vic teased him, looking over the shelves.

He would have been happy to stick his head in the opening and climb right up into the fridge, but Vic blocked him with her leg. She found the roast chicken from a couple of nights before and pulled the container out of the fridge. He followed her as she cleared a little space on the counter to set it down.

"Sorry," Erin apologized, looking around at the mess, "I've been cleaning."

"I think you've got it backward. Cleaning is when you put things away."

Vic cut a little slice of the chicken and put it in Orange Blossom's dish, and he attacked it with vigor. Erin's nostrils flared at the smell of the chicken, and her stomach rumbled loudly, reminding her that she had neglected it since breakfast. Used to bakers' hours, breakfast had been a long time before.

"I wanted to clear some space in the cupboards," Erin explained. "These things are taking up so much room, there's nowhere for me to put my own recipe books."

Vic nibbled at a piece of chicken. "You're getting rid of all of these?"

"No, not all of them. They're sorted into groups…" Erin knew that it looked like chaos, but there really was a method to all of the books strewn around. "I'm keeping most of the handwritten ones," she indicated the hardcover notebooks full of recipes; the same kind of notebooks that her Aunt Clementine had written her journals in, "and a few other classic ones that look really interesting. I thought Adele might be interested in some of the ones on herbs and remedies, and maybe take some of the teas."

Vic nodded. While Erin had spent some time helping

Clementine back when she was a little girl and the bakery was a tea room, she hadn't made a dent in the wide variety of teas and herbs that had stocked Clementine's cupboard. Adele, who lived in the cottage at the other end of Clementine's wooded property and acted as Erin's groundskeeper, would put them to better use.

"And the rest of them?" Vic inquired.

"You can take what you want. What's left over after that… I'm not sure what I'm going to do with. I don't know whether there is anyone in town who would be interested in them."

"Maybe you could put some of them on display at the bakery and see if anyone had any interest in them. Or we could hold an auction and get you a new car!"

"There's nothing wrong with my Challenger," Erin protested.

"Nothing that a complete overhaul of the engine, transmission, and exhaust system wouldn't cure," Vic agreed with a wry smile.

"Do you want to make some sandwiches?" Erin's stomach was protesting at the smell and sight of the chicken Vic was nibbling away at. "I'll clear some space…"

"All of these recipe books, and you just want to make sandwiches? Shouldn't we be making chicken á la king, or chicken fettuccine alfredo, or something more sophisticated than sandwiches?"

"I can't wait for anything fancy. Just slap some mayo and mustard on some bread and we can have a quick supper."

"Do you want them on buttermilk biscuits?" Vic suggested. "We had a few left over."

"That sounds great." Erin started to gather the books into piles, so they would take up less room, arranging them by the type of recipes they contained. "I can't believe how fast the time flew by today. I thought I could have this done in an hour, but it's stretched out to take all day."

"Did you get anything else on your list done?" Vic rummaged through the fridge to pull out the condiments and a salad. Orange Blossom had finished his chicken and was sniffing around the edges of his bowl like he might have missed some. He wandered over to Vic, making inquiries to see whether she would give him anything else. "That's enough, Blossom, or you're going to get fat!"

The cat sat back on his haunches, looking offended. He licked his paw and started to wash his face.

"I did some laundry and some other general cleaning up and tidying. Took three bags out to the garbage bin, so I must have gotten something done today." Erin stopped and surveyed the kitchen, hands on her hips. "It won't take that long to put these away, into boxes or back in the cupboard. At least I'll have gained some cupboard space." She had her own recipe books that she needed a place for, mostly printed on letter-size paper and inserted in clear plastic sleeves in binders. Running a gluten-free bakery that tried to cater to a variety of dietary restrictions, she was always on the prowl for new recipes and techniques, and she couldn't store all of them in the kitchen and tiny office at the bakery.

She and Vic worked together for a few minutes, Vic getting supper prepared and Erin sorting the books into boxes and putting a few back into the cupboard.

"You didn't find any journals mixed in with those?" Vic inquired, nodding to the hardcover notebooks.

"No. I was kind of hoping that that missing journal might be in there. But I'm afraid it must be lost or stolen for good."

"You think Uncle Davis has it?"

"I don't know. I don't see how he could have gotten his hands on it, but we didn't have an alarm system yet around the time of the funeral. So, who knows? Maybe."

"Officer Piper has already searched his house. It wasn't there."

"I don't think Terry could have missed it," Erin agreed.

Vic helped get the table cleared and put out the sandwiches and salad.

"Why don't you wash off the dust and take a break?"

Erin agreed. She was used to being on her feet all day at the bakery, but for some reason, her day of cleaning and sorting out the kitchen had left her feeling more tired and sore than usual. She was happy to get off her feet to enjoy a light supper with Vic.

~

Erin's usual routine of sitting with Vic in the living room and making lists before bed to organize the next day's activities was comforting to her. She liked to get everything down on paper and have some idea of what the shape of the day would be. Of course, she never got everything on her lists done, but she was pretty productive.

Orange Blossom was curled up on Vic's lap while she read a book, and the brown and white rabbit, Marshmallow, was lying on Erin's feet.

The next day was Sunday, which meant the ladies' tea at the bakery, an old tradition Erin had resurrected from when it was a tea room. Tea, cookies, and gossip. Even though Erin wasn't part of the church community at Bald Eagle Falls, she had come to enjoy the quiet Sunday ritual and the chance to visit with her friends in a more relaxed environment.

"You could take a few of Clementine's teas to the ladies' tea," Vic suggested. "There might be a few adventurous souls willing to try something new."

"I might do that." Erin added it to her list of things to take with her to the bakery in the morning.

"Just make sure they're labeled. None of those bags of unlabeled herbs."

"I can tell what most of them are, even if they don't have labels. I can identify any of the teas Clementine used to serve in the tea room."

"But some of those... I don't know. They just look *dubious* to me."

"I'll give them to Adele. She can use them or compost them if she doesn't know what to do with them. Her herbal knowledge is pretty good."

"As long as no one expects me to drink anything unidentified."

Erin laughed. "We're not going to poison you, Vicky! Has Adele ever given you anything that's hurt you?"

"So far, I've been able to avoid drinking anything she has made."

Erin was almost expecting her to make the sign of the cross to ward off any evil. Adele was a practicing witch, and despite Vic's acknowledgment that Wicca was just a pagan religion and Adele was not going to work any magic on them, she avoided eating or drinking anything Adele made. Erin had never suffered any ill effects from Adele's herbal teas, but Vic just couldn't bring herself to take the chance.

"I think Charley is going to come by for the ladies' tea tomorrow," Erin said, changing the subject.

"Really? I thought she said she wasn't comfortable around 'all those church ladies.'"

Erin smiled and nodded. "I know. But I think I've persuaded her just to give them a chance. If she wants to make friends in Bald Eagle Falls, she's going to have to socialize somehow."

"And if she's going to open up The Bake Shoppe, she's going to need to know her clientele," Vic agreed.

Erin's stomach clenched into a knot. She took a few deep breaths, waiting for it to subside. She knew she should be happy that her newfound half-sister was willing to consider opening up a legitimate business, putting her criminal activities with the Dyson clan behind her. It was just that Erin wasn't sure how it would impact her business at Auntie Clem's Bakery. She'd said from the start that she believed the town could sustain two bakeries but, deep down, she wasn't one hundred percent sure it was true.

"She won't be opening up The Bake Shoppe for a while. She's still fighting over whether she can open it up on her own while Davis is in prison, when they are each only fifty-percent owners once Trenton's probate goes through."

"She'll be able to open it. It's more valuable as an operating bakery than sitting there closed up. Uncle Davis really can't win that argument."

"I suppose."

Thinking about Charley and Davis made Erin uneasy. She was happy to have her sister in Bald Eagle Falls so that she could get to know her. But Charley had some pretty rough edges and wasn't the kind of person that Erin would have associated with normally. And Charley was determined to prove Davis's involvement in Trenton's death and get his half of the inheritance.

Erin added a couple more items to her list, and wiggled her toes, making Marshmallow shift and look up at her. "I think I'm going to head to bed."

Vic lifted Orange Blossom from her lap to cuddle him and kiss the top of his head. "Yeah, me too," she agreed. "Even though we can sleep in on a Sunday, my body just doesn't get the message."

Erin nodded. "See you tomorrow, then. Where's Willie these days? Working out of town again?"

Vic stood up and put Orange Blossom down. "I don't know. We decided to take a break for a while."

Erin stared at her, mouth open. "You decided to take a break? From each other? What happened?"

But even as she said it, Erin knew. Things had not been the same since they had returned to Bald Eagle Falls after rescuing Charley and solving the murder she'd been wrongly accused of.

Vic sighed. Her mouth twisted into a grimace that she tried to hide. "I told him who I was. I didn't keep that from him. But he didn't tell me who he was. He knew our families were enemies, and he didn't tell me."

Willie had initially had a hard time with Vic being a transgender woman, but had eventually been able to get past it. But he hadn't told her that he was a Dyson, the clan that had been feuding against Vic's family, the Jacksons, for generations.

"You told me once that you knew Willie had secrets, but you were willing to wait until he was ready to share them with you."

"Yeah." Vic considered. "I guess that's one that I would have liked to have known up front. Other stuff from his past I could wait for, but he should have told me that. At least given me the chance to decide if I wanted to get involved with someone who'd fought against my family."

It wasn't just that Willie had been born a Dyson. Vic probably could have handled that. But he had been a soldier for them for five years, and that wasn't so easy for her take.

"I'm sorry," Erin said softly, shaking her head. "You should have told me. I just thought he was off working. I didn't know the two of you were having trouble."

"I wasn't ready to talk about it. I'm still not ready. But you're a friend. You should at least know."

"Okay." Erin looked down at her lists instead of staring at Vic and trying to analyze her. "I won't ask about it. You just let me know when you're ready."

"Okay. Thanks."

Vic bent down to give Orange Blossom one last scratch. Marshmallow got up and hopped over to her for a share of the attention, and Vic scratched the base of his long ear.

"All right, babies, time for bed. You guys be quiet for Erin and let her sleep."

Orange Blossom followed Vic into the kitchen, yowling at her about how hungry he was, but she wasn't fooled. She went out the back door and across the yard to her apartment over the garage. Erin heard her pause on her way out to arm the burglar alarm. Erin wasn't sure she felt any more secure with the alarm set, since the last intruder had managed to disable it on entering. But it was just a precaution. There was no one after Erin. Not anymore, thanks to Orange Blossom and Vic's marksmanship skills. It was a good thing she'd had so much practice shooting gophers and other critters when she was younger.

Erin had expected that Charley would jam out at the last minute and not show up for the ladies' tea when church let out. She wasn't an atheist, like Erin. She'd been raised Christian, but had obviously left those beliefs behind when she had left home to work with the Dyson clan, whose views were distinctly opposed to any of the teachings Erin knew of the Christian faith. Even if they went to funerals and to Easter and Christmas services, they really didn't follow the teachings of Christ as Erin knew them.

But Charley showed up. She wasn't in a dress like most of the church ladies would be, but she wasn't in blue jeans either. She'd taken the time to find something appropriate, to put her hair, dark like Erin's, back in a knot behind her neck, and to keep to a natural look with her makeup, just accenting her brown eyes and small mouth.

"I made it," Charley declared. "I actually got myself out of bed early and got myself all dolled up for your friends."

Erin couldn't help looking at the clock on the wall. Early?

"Considering I'm usually going to bed when you're getting up, that's early for me," Charley asserted.

"Yes, it is," Erin agreed. "You're here just in time, the others should be arriving soon."

Mary Lou was the first to arrive. As usual, her short gray hair was perfectly coiffed and her neatly tailored skirt suit looked like it had been made just for her. She smiled and nodded at Charley. "I'm so glad you could make it, Miss Campbell."

"Oh, no! Just call me Charley. No one calls me Miss Campbell."

"Have a seat, Mary Lou," Erin invited, gesturing toward the tables, all ready for the group of women. "How were your services today?"

"Very nice," Mary Lou said. She chose her usual chair and sat down. She closed her eyes for an instant, looking tired. "Yes, it was a beautiful spring service. I always enjoy a talk that centers around renewal and new life."

"Good." Erin waited for Mary Lou to pick out her usual

English Breakfast, and then poured the water from the waiting teapot for her.

Mary Lou nodded her thanks and stared off, distant.

"What kind of tea do you like?" Erin asked Charley.

"Oh, I don't know. I'm pretty easy. Just tea. Black, green, I don't really care."

Erin considered, mentally cataloging the kinds of tea in the baskets at the middles of the tables. "How about... Earl Grey?" she suggested, pulling one of the yellow packets out.

Charley shrugged. "Sure, sounds good." She sat down, not right next to Mary Lou, but not off on her own, either. Erin put the teabag in Charley's cup and poured the water for her.

Other women started coming in the door. Melissa, with her mass of brown curls, eyes sparkling as she gossiped with Clara Jones, who she sometimes worked with at the police department's administrative office. Clara was wearing a green dress, which Erin wasn't sure looked good with Clara's brassy curls and oversize jewelry. Clara seemed to enjoy drawing attention to herself, positive or negative.

Lottie was there, along with several others of the usual crowd. They all got quieter at the sight of Charley. Though Erin was sure they knew who Charley was, she introduced her anyway, trying to make everyone feel comfortable. Vic brought out the platters of cookies and confections, and everyone chattered at once, admiring the treats and discussing which were their favorites. Erin circulated, pouring water and making sure everyone had everything they needed. Eventually, everyone had been served, and there was nothing much more for Erin to do than just enjoy her guests and listen to them talk.

"I understand you are trying to open up The Bake Shoppe again," Melissa said to Charley. "How is that coming along?"

"Slower than a herd of turtles," Charley answered, shaking her head. "I mean... I know small towns do things slow, but how long can it take to decide the place is worth more open than closed?"

Sympathetic nods from around the table. They all knew about

small-town bureaucracy and how hard it was to get people to make a decision.

"I managed to get ahold of Joelle Biggs," Charley went on. "Asked her if she'd come meet with me to go over everything."

The room fell utterly silent.

Charley looked around, her eyes wide. She looked over at Erin and raised her brows. "Uh… what?"

"Why would you ask her to come back to Bald Eagle Falls?" Erin asked, her voice coming out much more calm than she really felt.

"She holds Davis's power of attorney, so if I can get her to agree with me, she can just sign a consent on his behalf, and then the trustees don't have a leg to stand on. We're the only two bene-ficiaries of the bakery, and if we both say we want to go ahead and open it up again, why would they object? As soon as it's gone through probate, we're the ones who are going to be making all the decisions on it."

"Why would Joelle agree to come back here?" Lottie demanded. "She's the one who killed Trenton Plaint! How could she dare show her face here again?"

"We couldn't prove that it was done intentionally," Vic pointed out. "I guess she knows there's nothing we can do about it."

Erin saw Charley's eyes flash. She certainly intended to do something about it, and Erin worried that it wasn't just having a little chat with her. Yes, she wanted the bakery open, but that wasn't all she wanted.

But instead of protesting, Charley just gave a lazy shrug and raised her teacup to her lips. "I don't see how it's anyone's business but my own."

The other ladies huffed and rolled their eyes but didn't come up with a reason that Charley should have to justify herself to them. It was true, as much as they liked to know all of what was going on and to give endless advice on the right way to do things, they didn't have any control over what Charley and Joelle did and weren't in a position to be making any demands. Of course, that hadn't stopped them when Erin had moved into Bald Eagle Falls to open a second bakery. She had been the outsider then, and everyone had made it clear that she should be reopening the tea room rather than a bakery. Especially a gluten-free bakery, of all things.

"We'll just have to see how it all unfolds," Erin said, hoping to soothe the nettled tempers. She looked over in Vic's direction. Vic was the one who was best at defusing things. She always seemed to know the right thing to say.

"Can't knit a sweater before the sheep is shorn," Vic agreed, making everyone laugh.

In a few minutes, the conversation moved on to other things, and Erin gave a sigh of relief. She would have to keep an eye on Charley. Maybe inviting her to the ladies' tea hadn't been the best idea.

Surprisingly, it was Mary Lou who was the first to stand up and make motions toward leaving. She was usually one of the last ones to go, sticking around to help gather up the dishes and brush away the crumbs to help Erin and Vic out.

She caught Erin's eyes on her. "I'm sorry. Duty calls. Roger hasn't been feeling well this week. I don't want to leave him to himself for too long."

"Oh, I'm sorry," Erin sympathized. "Is there anything he'd like? I could send you home with some cookies…?"

"No, that's fine, thank you. Don't want to do business on the Sabbath. What he really needs is for me to be home."

"I meant I would give them to you, not that you had to pay," Erin tried to correct the misunderstanding.

"I'm certainly not taking anything without paying for it. You're running a business here, and you're going to need every sale you can get." Mary gave a significant look in Charley's direction. Her meaning was clear. Erin was going to be in trouble when The Bake Shoppe reopened.

"We'll manage," Erin assured her. She didn't feel quite as certain as she let on. The bakery's first year had not been an easy one, and she wasn't yet mentally prepared to face the competition of another bakery in town. There would still be people who had to come to Auntie Clem's for the gluten-free baking, but not enough of them to support the business. How many others would stay loyal to Auntie Clem's if they didn't need gluten-free or other allergen-free goods? Would they all just go back to The Bake Shoppe when it opened?

Mary Lou put her thin, well-manicured hand on Erin's arm as she walked by. "That's right, dear," she agreed. "I'm sure it will be fine."

~

Erin didn't expect Joelle to show up in town right away. In spite of what Charley had said, Erin figured Joelle would play it cool, saying that she would come but in no hurry to do so. What murder suspect in her right mind would just waltz back into town as if she didn't have a care in the world?

But the week wasn't out before Erin saw Joelle, with her chic yoga pants and long, spidery limbs, walk right by the bakery. Erin turned to Vic to point Joelle out, but Vic had already seen, and had turned toward Erin, eyes wide, mouth open to make a comment about it.

Erin grinned. "Miss Joelle Biggs is back in town," she acknowledged.

"Still can't believe Charley was able to talk her into coming."

The bakery was pretty quiet, with only the elderly Potters standing there looking at the display case and waffling over the choices. Vic slipped out from behind the counter and walked to the front window to watch Joelle's progress down the street.

"Where is she going?" Erin asked.

"They must be meeting at The Bake Shoppe."

"Should somebody go over there…?"

Vic's eyebrows went up. "And do what, exactly?"

"I don't know. Make sure they don't kill each other."

"And pray tell, how would we do that?"

Erin leaned on the counter, trying to come up with an answer. The last time she had been into The Bake Shoppe was when Trenton had died, poisoned by the muffins Joelle had purchased at Auntie Clem's Bakery. Just thinking about it made her muscles tense up and her breathing grow shallower. She and Terry Piper had spent hours keeping up CPR until an ambulance from the city could get there. Erin rubbed her biceps. What an ordeal that had been. And a hopeless one, as it turned out. Trenton had never revived.

"I don't know. But I don't think they should be left alone together."

"We've got no reason to go into their place of business. We can't stop them from having a meeting."

Erin fought the urge to bite her nails. She tried to distract herself, turning to the Potters with a pasted-on smile. "See anything you like today?"

"We were thinking of the chocolate muffins," Mrs. Potter started out, her quavery voice slow and deliberate.

"Good choice," Erin approved. She reached for the muffins. "How many would you like?"

"But then we were looking at the blueberry ones," Mr. Potter put in.

Erin wasn't fooled a second time. She waited for the next installment in the story.

"We did have muffins last week," Mrs. Potter noted.

"Yes. So, something a little different this week? Maybe cookies or some fresh rosemary bread? I know you like that…"

"Mrs. Potter likes the rosemary," Mr. Potter disagreed. "I like the poppyseed."

"I have poppyseed bagels today," Erin said desperately, pointing to them.

"Mmm…" Both of the Potters gazed into the display case, considering the poppyseed bagels and everything else in turn.

Erin raised her eyes to Vic, who was turning away from the front window with a mirthful smile. She walked back to her place behind the counter. "You can't rush the future," she advised placidly.

Erin settled back to wait. It wasn't like there was a line up behind the Potters. Things would be quiet until school let out. Assuming Charley and Joelle didn't kill each other.

~

The doorbell rang after supper, and Erin had a pretty good idea who it was going to be. She hadn't set the burglar alarm yet, and she took a careful look through the peephole before opening the door to him.

Officer Terry Piper and his faithful partner, K9, stood on the steps waiting. Erin smiled at her favorite police officer. "Come on in," she invited.

They made themselves at home, Terry sitting down in his preferred chair, and K9 lying down at his feet with a snort and a sigh.

"What can I get you?" Erin offered. "Coffee? Cinnamon rolls?"

"Oh, both of those sound great," Terry approved. "I don't know when the last time I had a cinnamon roll was."

"And you're on duty tonight, so coffee is okay?"

He nodded his agreement. K9 watched Erin intently while she went into the kitchen to warm up a roll. Orange Blossom jumped down from the couch, hissed at K9, and then stalked after Erin on stiff legs.

Erin tossed him a couple of kitty treats while she warmed up the cinnamon roll, and he skittered across the kitchen after them like a kitten, making her laugh. Erin put a doggie biscuit in her pocket to free up her hands for the coffee and roll, and took them into the living room.

"I should probably have come into the kitchen to eat this," Terry commented, taking the plate from her. "I don't want to make a mess in your parlor."

"If you drop crumbs, the animals will vacuum them up."

K9 put his head back down between his paws with a grumble. Erin pulled the biscuit out of her pocket.

"Did you think I forgot about you?"

K9 sat up eagerly and took the treat from her, then lay down with it to eat.

"They're just like kids," Terry said. "Feed them once, and you can expect to have to do the same thing every single time you see them. It's a good thing we spend plenty of time walking, or we'd both be fat."

"You don't need to worry about your weight," Erin dismissed, glancing at Terry's heavy work belt, buckled at exactly the same hole as always.

"Where's Vic tonight? Did she and Willie make up?"

"Did you know they were on the outs? I didn't realize it until Saturday."

He nodded, grunting something through the cinnamon roll.

"She went to see Adele," Erin said, in answer to his question. "We haven't seen much of her lately and I have something to give her."

"How is that working out? You don't regret letting her live in the cottage and being your groundskeeper?"

"No. She's great. She doesn't get in the way and make demands. She makes improvements and keeps rowdy teenagers to a minimum. It's worked out just great."

"Good. I wasn't sure, when you took her on, that it was the right thing to do. None of us really knew anything about her."

Erin gave a little shrug. "We all have to start somewhere. I felt good about her, and I know what it's like to be new in town and need a little bit of help. She doesn't ask much. She just… needed a friend, I guess."

"Sometimes people can mislead you… I'd hate to see someone take advantage of you. You can't trust everyone."

"I don't."

He studied her for a moment, then nodded and went back to

eating his cinnamon roll. He licked his fingers. "Oh, those are so rich. Great job, Erin."

Erin's face warmed at his words of praise. She took the empty plate from him, trying to mask her embarrassment.

There were voices in the back yard, and then Vic and Adele came in through the back door and into the kitchen.

"Hello," Vic called out, giving Erin and Terry a wave.

Adele hesitated for a moment. "You have company."

"Come in, come in. Terry's not company, and neither are you. You're family. The more the merrier."

Adele considered, then inclined her head. She walked through the kitchen into the living room. "I'm sorry I haven't been around much the last week. Nothing is wrong, I've just had… a lot to do."

"That's fine. We just wanted to make sure that you were okay. You're kind of isolated, and if something happened to you… well," Erin shrugged uncomfortably, "I'd want to know about it sooner rather than later."

The stately woman said nothing.

"Anyway," Erin realized she was still holding Terry's empty plate in her hand and walked into the kitchen to put it in the sink. "I have some things that you might like. You don't need to take anything you don't want, but…"

Erin gestured to the boxes she had filled for Adele. Adele opened one of the lids and looked at the jumble of teas and herbs.

"Sorry, it's not organized…"

"No, this is fine," Adele said, poking through the contents. "I'd be happy to take it back to the cottage and have a look through it. Thank you." She opened the other box and picked up the recipe books on top. "These look intriguing."

"I don't know if any of it is worth anything to you, or if you already know all of this…" While Erin had kept a few baking books for herself, she really didn't have any use for the old herbal remedy books Clementine had collected.

"These are lovely. There's always more wisdom to be gathered."

"Good."

Adele opened the hardcover notebook that had Clementine's own recipes in it. "Oh, are you sure? This looks special."

"They're Clementine's tea recipes and other herbal remedies. I've kept some of her other recipes, but I don't have room for everything. If you don't want it…"

"No, I'm honored. I just wanted to make sure you really wanted me to have that one. You can ask for it back if you change your mind…"

"No, really, it's for you. I don't have the time to spend on herbal remedies as well as everything else already on my plate." Erin giggled at her own pun. "Go ahead, use it as you like. I hope you can get something out of it."

"Thank you. I'll put it to good use."

Erin nodded and headed back to the living room. Orange Blossom sat in the doorway of the kitchen, staring intently at Adele, but not going in and demanding a treat like he normally would.

"Why is he looking at you like that?"

"Maybe he would like to talk to me."

Vic laughed. "Orange Blossom talks to everyone. It's when he shuts up that it's surprising."

Adele extended her fingers and called softly to the cat. "Puss, puss?"

Orange Blossom looked at Erin, then back at Adele, and entered the kitchen, approaching her cautiously. Erin glanced over at Vic and saw that her eyes were big as she watched the cat and the woman who called herself a witch.

"Did you want to tell me something?" Adele asked the cat.

Orange Blossom sniffed Adele's fingers, then bent his head and smelled her shoes, raising his head again with his mouth partly open.

"You must have stepped in something good," Vic chuckled.

"Maybe catnip," Erin suggested. "Does catnip grow around here?"

"Certainly," Adele said. She gave Orange Blossom's ears a scratch. "He probably smells Skye."

"Skye?" Erin echoed.

"The crow."

"Oh," Erin had seen the crow that was not Adele's pet a few times. She got the feeling that he wasn't often very far away, but he didn't go into Adele's house, and he only landed to perch on her shoulder or hand briefly, and then after communing with her would fly away again. "I guess I never knew his name. You never really talk about him."

"There's not much to say," Adele said with a shrug. She straightened. "He's a crow."

"You said he's not your pet; is he—"

"He's her familiar," Vic interrupted. "A spirit helper. Isn't he?"

Adele looked at Vic, her brows drawn down. "Skye is a crow. He likes the peanuts I give him. I wouldn't speculate on things I knew nothing about if I was you, Victoria."

Vic flushed. "I just thought… well, witches have animals to help them, no matter what you call them, don't you?"

"You like having animals around, don't you?" Adele said. "Orange Blossom and Marshmallow? You grew up on a farm with other animals, probably dogs and livestock, at least."

"Sure. I like animals."

"So do I. I like to be close to nature and I like to be close to non-human animals. When you've been around an animal for a while, you get to learn its body language and habits. You develop a friendship."

Vic nodded. "Yeah."

"Skye doesn't belong to me. But I miss him when he's not around."

Vic didn't pursue it any further.

"Come in for a visit," Erin invited, motioning to the living room. They all joined Terry in the living room. Erin sat down next to Terry. "I guess you know Joelle is back in town."

"Yes, I saw her."

"Joelle?" Adele repeated.

"Joelle Biggs," Erin explained, and proceeded to tell Adele the details of Trenton Plaint's death.

"But what is she doing back in town?" Adele asked. "Does she have friends around here? Other than Davis?"

"No, no one that I know of. Charley wanted her to come back. But I don't know why she came. I certainly wouldn't if it was me!"

Adele stared at the dark window. Erin suspected she had other things she would rather be doing. She had come back with Vic to be accommodating and to let them know she was fine, but she had said she had a lot of things to do. They were probably keeping her away from something else. While Erin and Vic had to retire to bed early, Adele would be up past midnight doing whatever it was she did in the woods.

Erin covered a faked yawn. "Well… I'm going to need to hit the sack. Stay and visit if you like…"

Terry looked at his watch. K9 looked up quickly, reading the signal that they were going to leave. "I'd better get back to it," Terry commented. He gave Erin a quick hug and brushed her cheek with a kiss. "See you tomorrow."

Erin nodded. "Keep an eye on Joelle while she's in town…"

"I'll keep my eyes open," he promised.

"I suppose I should get to bed too," Vic said grudgingly.

Adele looked relieved. She rose to her feet in one fluid movement. "Good to see you, Erin. I need to pop over and see Mary Lou. Thank you for the goodies. I'll have a lot of fun going through them."

In a few minutes, everyone was gone, and Erin was left by herself to think about the events of the day.

Brewing Death, Book #5 of the *Auntie Clem's Bakery* series by P.D. Workman can be purchased at pdworkman.com

ABOUT THE AUTHOR

Award-winning and USA Today bestselling author P.D. (Pamela) Workman writes riveting mystery/suspense and young adult books dealing with mental illness, addiction, abuse, and other real-life issues. For as long as she can remember, the blank page has held an incredible allure and from a very young age she was trying to write her own books.

Workman wrote her first complete novel at the age of twelve and continued to write as a hobby for many years. She started publishing in 2013. She has won several literary awards from Library Services for Youth in Custody for her young adult fiction. She currently has over 50 published titles and can be found at pdworkman.com.

Born and raised in Alberta, Workman has been married for over 25 years and has one son.

~

Please visit P.D. Workman at pdworkman.com to see what else she is working on, to join her mailing list, and to link to her social networks.

~

If you enjoyed this book, please take the time to recommend it to other purchasers with a review or star rating and share it with your friends!

facebook.com/pdworkmanauthor
twitter.com/pdworkmanauthor
instagram.com/pdworkmanauthor
amazon.com/author/pdworkman
bookbub.com/authors/p-d-workman
goodreads.com/pdworkman
linkedin.com/in/pdworkman
pinterest.com/pdworkmanauthor
youtube.com/pdworkman